I0564222

EAGLES
in
FLIGHT

RAMCY DIEK

FROM THE TINY ACORN …
GROWS THE MIGHTY OAK

FBI Anti-Piracy Warning: The unauthorized reproduction or distribution of a copyrighted work is illegal. Criminal copyright infringement, including infringement without monetary gain, is investigated by the FBI and is punishable by up to five years in federal prison and a fine of $250,000.

Advertencia Antipirateria del FBI: La reproducción o distribución no autorizada de una obra protegida por derechos de autor es ilegal. La infracción criminal de los derechos de autor, incluyendo la infracción sin lucro monetario, es investigada por el FBI y es castigable con pena de hasta cinco años en prisión federal y una multa de $250,000.

Eagles in Flight
First Edition
Copyright © 2020 Ramcy Diek

All rights reserved. No part of this book may be used or reproduced in any manner whatsoever, including Internet usage, without written permission from the author.

This story is a work of fiction. References to real people, events, establishments, organizations, or locales are intended only to provide a sense of authenticity and are used fictitiously. All other characters, and all incidents and dialogue are drawn from the author's imagination and are not to be construed as real.

Book cover by Damonza.

Book interior design and formatting by Debra Cranfield Kennedy.

www.acornpublishingllc.com

ISBN—Hardcover 978-1-952112-01-0
ISBN—Paperback 978-1-952112-00-3
Library of Congress Control Number: 2020908925

Acknowledgments

All my stories come from an experience, a person I met, or an event that affected my life. All important enough to create a lingering impression and spark my imagination.

Eagles in Flight is no exception, the main story inspired by a man I met years ago. A man with a private nature, a long unkempt beard and wild hair, who used to wander around our small town, always accompanied by his dog. He lived off the grid, without identification, cell phone, or car, and made a living by doing odd jobs for the locals around town. An unlikely man to form a friendship with until you look into his kind brown eyes and notice the friendliest smile. Then you understand why.

Over the years, he shared little about himself, his past, or his family. Until this day, I still don't even know his last name. And his story is solely based on my imagination.

Thank you, my friend, for being the inspiration for Eagles in Flight. Without you, it would not exist.

More thanks go out to my always supporting husband, only telling me to get moving after an entire morning behind my computer. To our two sons, who always believe in me.

To Acorn Publishing LLC, Jessica Therrien and Holly Kammier, for your much-appreciated advice and support, and not to forget your expertise and patience. We shared many emails, and I always received an immediate reply. You made the publishing process easy.

To my beta readers, Catherine Van B., Lori S., Karen A, Lori O-T, Luci O, Theresa R, and Margaret A. I appreciate your feedback, suggestions, friendship, and encouragement.

Thank you, Damonza, for creating my beautiful cover.

And big hugs and admiration for my editor, Laura Taylor. You took such meticulous care of the story; I feel confident it's the best it could be.

Jonathan, thanks for giving me confidence.

And last but not least, I'm grateful for every reader. Without you, a book is only a stack of pages.

Thank you, thank you.

EAGLES
IN
FLIGHT

CHAPTER

1

A TALL HANDSOME MAN, dressed elegantly in a gray silk suit, white shirt, silver tie, and black leather oxford shoes, made his way around the Heemstead University library. He seemed out of place among the college students, the ladies from the senior book club, and the locals who used the computers, or came in to read the daily newspaper.

Emma watched him from behind her desk. She'd recognized him immediately and felt safe partly hidden behind her computer screen and the stacks of returned books that needed to be scanned in. That was until his eyes roamed around in search of assistance. She pushed her reading glasses a bit farther up her nose and lowered her head. Her long brown hair fell halfway across her face. Sinking deeper into her chair, she wished Sue Stremler were close by. Surely someone as important as him would wish to speak to the head librarian.

Her chair squeaked its familiar protest. She held her breath, afraid he'd heard it.

To her relief, he picked up a newspaper from one of the tables. His mouth curved into a slow smile as he read the front page. He seemed pleased with whatever had caught his attention.

As if he could feel her stare on the back of his neck, he dropped the paper onto the table and headed straight in her direction. Pretending not to notice him, she shrank even deeper into her office chair.

"Miss, do you have information on the upcoming fund-raiser for the library?"

A pair of dark eyes looked down on her, and an involuntary gasp rose in her throat. Hoping she'd caught it in time, she forced her focus back to the keyboard of her computer, the letters blurry, the numbers jumping around.

"A friend of mine, Mr. Jesse Kimball, is invited to give a speech. I was in the neighborhood and offered to stop in for more information on his behalf."

Emma told herself there was no reason to be nervous. She looked up and smiled. "I could print the flyer for you if you'd like."

"Thank you," he replied, giving no sign he recognized her.

Emma recalled the mobile home park in the town of Dune-dam, where her father maintained the grounds and performed necessary repairs to the homes. When she was fifteen, he found a position as a janitor for an apartment complex in Heemstead, the neighboring city. The position came with a rent-free spacious two-bedroom apartment. Her parents celebrated the prospect of a bigger paycheck and fewer expenses, but she'd been heart-broken to move away and leave her childhood friends behind.

The kids from the park always hung out together. In the sandbox, on the playground, and later—as teenagers—under the gazebo, secretly smoking cigarettes and complaining about their parents and the teachers at school. Ruben had been one of them, and the coolest of them all.

She shook off her memories, the keyboard coming back into focus. With fast fingers, she clicked on the document to open it and print.

"Mr. Kimball is scheduled to speak next Tuesday at five, Ruben." Horrified at saying his name out loud, she got up to grab it from the printer, keeping her eyes focused on everything around her but him.

Instead of taking the printout, he furrowed his brow and stared at her. "Do I know you?"

When their eyes met, he reached out and lifted her chin with his index finger, studying her face for an uncomfortably long time.

Shocked by his inappropriate behavior, she struggled to keep her professional composure. The flyer slipped from her trembling fingers, and it floated back and forth until it reached the shiny wood floor.

"Oops," she muttered, picking it up.

Back behind the relative safety of her desk, she forced herself to return his stare, her cheeks flushed with warmth. Feeling like an awkward teenager, she straightened her spine.

"We used to live in the same trailer park, but I don't blame you for not remembering. It was ages ago." With a casual move of her hand, she tried to lighten the strained situation.

He continued to examine her face until a spark of recognition flashed in his eyes. "Now I remember. You're Emma, the brown-haired girl with the old-fashioned clothes, pigtails and braces."

Emma dropped her gaze at his hurtful remark. The inside of her cheek became the victim of her irritation as she chewed on it to process her feelings. If that were all he remembered about her, screw him. Instead of voicing her opinion, she stayed silent.

"You haven't changed much at all," he continued, fueling her anger even more.

She pushed the flyer into his hand and took off her reading glasses. "Is that all you need?"

Instead of leaving, he narrowed his eyes and studied her, his thumb and index finger rubbing his chin.

With each agonizing second that passed, her self-esteem dwindled more and more. If only she'd chosen a more flattering outfit this morning, instead of her usual cream-colored cardigan, blue pleated skirt and sensible brown flats.

"Thanks for stopping by. Please tell Mr. Kimball we look forward to welcoming him," she said, using her most professional voice in the hope of moving him along.

Ruben ignored her dismissal. "You shouldn't hide your best asset behind glasses, Emma," he said, flashing a radiant smile. "You still have the most amazing blue eyes I've ever seen. How are you?"

As a teenager, Ruben Templeton had been popular and attractive, his rebellious bent making him even more alluring. His lanky, boyish manner was gone now, replaced with an easy confidence and an air of independence that only came with unbridled success. He overloaded her senses with his immediate presence, indisputable charisma, and devastating smile.

"I'm fine, thanks," she replied, afraid of falling under his spell.

"You might be perfect, Emma," he commented. "Please, would you do me the honor of joining me for dinner this evening?"

His invitation shocked her. And what did he mean by perfect? Too stunned to speak, she fiddled with her glasses.

He arched his brow. "How about seven o'clock at Joe's Grill Bar? It's one of my favorite restaurants, and their filet mignon is the best in town."

Ruben looked striking, his thick hair dark and wavy, his eyes like midnight, his features sharp. But that didn't mean she should go out with him.

"Running into you can't be a coincidence. I would love to catch up with you." His lips curved again into a charming smile, and her resistance started to crumble.

"For old time's sake. It would mean a lot to me," he continued, his eyes pleading

Instead of listening to her intuition, telling her not to set herself up for disappointment, and warning her to keep her distance, she nodded. "That sounds great."

With a slight bow, he lifted her hand to his lips and kissed it. "I look forward to it." He released her hand with another million-dollar smile, turned on his heel, and walked away.

She watched him stroll toward the exit, broad shouldered and narrow hipped, catching the attention of more than a few women. That's how it had always been, she reflected, regretting she'd caved under his charm. What had come over her to agree? Ruben had always been out of her league, all the girls competing for his attention, gawking at him, envious of the one at his side. Many predicted he would become a famous model, his face on the cover of magazines, or an actor, revered for his talent and magnetism.

She hadn't seen him since moving away. But over the last twelve years, she'd secretly kept track of him through mutual acquaintances and social media. Pictures from football games, homecoming, prom, and graduation had scrolled across her computer screen. Ruben had been valedictorian, graduating with honors and receiving all the important scholarships. Despite the predictions, he chose a stringent education at Yale, the first student from Dunedam to enter such a prestigious school. Ruben was the golden boy.

After he exited the library, Ruben Templeton pulled his cell phone from his pocket and pressed a contact in his favorites. "Hey, it's me," he said, a calculating expression on his face.

"Hey, you. What's up?" the voice on the other end of the line asked.

"You know what we talked about, right? I think I may have found the exact woman I have in mind for you. She's about twenty-seven, painfully shy, average and modest looking, nice skin, no make-up, and dull brown hair. But she's attractive in a studious, respectable, and bespectacled way. Basically, the image of our old school librarian. With a bit of work, she could be spruced up and precisely what we're looking for."

He listened for a few moments, his disgruntled frown deepening as he stepped into his Ferrari and merged into traffic. "I know you're not crazy about the idea, but I thought I explained my reasons. And yes, I know a little about her background, but intend to find out more tonight. I'm taking her to dinner at Joe's Grill Bar. I'll keep you posted."

CHAPTER

2

THE SOFT CLAPPING of two hands woke Emma from her reverie. Sue Stremler, the librarian, stood next to her desk. "Are you daydreaming, my dear?" she asked.

Embarrassed to be caught with idle hands, Emma quickly reached for a stack of books to scan them in.

Sue smiled and gave Emma's shoulder a pat. "It's already past five. Time to go home."

"Really?" Emma gasped. The clock on the wall above the printer showed it was ten minutes after. She signed out of the computer and hurried to organize the desk.

"Are you all right?" Sue asked. "You seem a little flustered."

Emma hardly ever dated and if Sue found out, she wouldn't be able to leave without sharing the details. "I'm fine. Just surprised it's so late already," she said, not revealing anything else. To avoid Sue's inquisitive stare, she reached under the desk for her purse and headed toward the exit.

Emma hurried down the sidewalk and pulled out her cell phone. "I'm going out for dinner tonight, Mom. Do you want me to pick something up for you at the deli?"

"You are? With whom?"

She heard the excitement in her mother's voice. One of her biggest worries was that her twenty-seven-year-old daughter would stay single forever after breaking off her relationship with James.

"Can we please talk about this when I'm home?" Emma asked, trying to dodge other pedestrians.

"You sound out of breath? Are you okay?"

"Yes, I'm fine," she huffed. "But he wants to meet at seven and I need to shower and change first."

"Don't worry about me, sweetheart. I'll take care of myself tonight."

Grateful, Emma ended the call and slid her phone back into her purse. Within five minutes, she turned off Main Street into her neighborhood. Closed and boarded-up storefronts, shady businesses, and empty warehouses lined the narrow street. The littered sidewalk, a homeless man sleeping in a doorway, and piles of trash, no different than any other day. She reached the apartment complex where she lived with her mother. An empty stroller stood in front of the entry. She pushed it aside and stepped into the damp air of the hallway. Bright fluorescent lamps accented the multitude of cracks in the worn plaster. At the mailboxes next to the entrance, one of their neighbors riffled through a stack of letters. It was James, who always lurked around just after five in the afternoon, hoping to see her, to get back into her good graces, and rekindle their four months courtship. That would never happen. The fact he couldn't accept it was becoming a real pain.

He looked up with a bright smile. "Hi, Emma, how are you?"

"Great, thanks, James," she replied, opening her own box with the key.

From behind his horn-rimmed glasses he looked at her with his hazel puppy dog eyes. As always, his hair was a mess and his button-up shirt only partly tucked in.

"I came home early from work this afternoon and visited your mother," he said.

She pulled out a small stack of mail. Without checking if there was anything of importance, she closed the small door and locked it. "That's so nice of you. Thanks."

Before she could rush off down the hall, James placed his hand on her arm. "I'd hoped to run into you, but I guess you had to work late?"

Nothing new there. She turned around to face him. "Sorry, I can't talk. I have a date at seven and am in a bit of a hurry." Although the flash of hurt in his eyes made her soften toward him, she continued, "As a teenager, I was madly in love with him. Running into him this afternoon was so exciting." She exaggerated the madly in love, but it was better to be blunt. James was a sweet, honorable, and helpful guy, as her mother often said, but his continuous infatuation with her needed to stop. "Good seeing you, James."

Feeling his gaze on her back, she passed the elevator and ran up the stairs to the fourth floor. The heels of her brown flats sounded hollow against the concrete steps and bare whitewashed walls.

Pushing James from her mind, she contemplated what to wear. Besides a variety of plain skirts, pearl buttoned blouses, and faded pink, light blue, and cream-colored cardigans, she owned nothing suitable for a date with a man like Ruben. She might as well save herself the trouble and not change at all. Deflated, she slid the key into the door and entered the apartment.

Her mother sat in her wheelchair in front of the window, an unopened book and the picture of her father in her lap. He'd passed away five years earlier in a head-on collision that had badly injured her mother in the passenger seat.

"Hi Mom." She bent over to kiss her on the head. "How was your day?"

"Great," she answered with a weary smile, rubbing the muscles of her right leg.

It pained Emma to see her mother suffer. After the accident, she'd spent weeks in the I.C.U. with a crushed pelvis, hip, and leg. Emma had to sideline her college education to take care of her. Two years later, her mother finally succeeded to get in and out of the wheelchair without help. That milestone gave Emma the opportunity to find a job and start making modest payments on the student loans and stacks of other bills that had piled up over the years. Her job at the library proved to be a blessing, and her dream of resuming her studies was within reach again.

Emma pulled up a chair and sat down next to her. "Did you finish your book?"

"No, I didn't. James stopped by unexpectedly. He brought us a bag of navel oranges and a loaf of the pumpernickel bread you like so much. He's a lovely young man."

Breaking up with James hadn't agreed with her mother. She thought he would be the perfect son-in-law. What she didn't want to see was that he had no opinions of his own, forcing Emma to make all the decisions—from where to eat, what movie to watch, and what time he should go home, to his stands on abortion, marijuana, climate change, and other political issues. Yes, he was kind, hardworking, and intelligent, and he deserved the title 'Ideal Boyfriend', but she needed someone with whom she could enjoy deep discussions, who had ambitions for himself, and didn't approve of everything she said. She wanted a husband who didn't bore her to death.

"I'm going on a date with Ruben Templeton," Emma said. "Do you remember him from the mobile home park in Dunedam?"

"Yes, I remember the Templetons," her mother replied. "What a sad situation when Sheila Templeton passed away. I can't remember exactly how old those two boys were but believe they were only two and five. And their poor father. I've never seen a man hit rock bottom as fast as he did. Every night he nearly drank himself to death for as long as I can remember. The good man was heartbroken."

In Emma's memory, Ruben had walked through life carefree and untroubled, never letting on he'd lost his mother or that his father was an alcoholic. "How awful. Do you know what happened to her?"

Her mother thought for a moment. "I believe there were complications with her third pregnancy, but we weren't close friends and I don't know much of the details."

Bert, their short-haired tabby, opened an eye and yawned before jumping off the couch. Purring loudly, he rubbed against her legs, begging for attention. Emma picked him up and settled him into her lap, feeling a little more optimistic about her date. She and Ruben had both lost a parent. They had more in common than she'd assumed.

CHAPTER

3

EMMA WALKED TO JOE'S GRILL BAR, taking deep breaths to steel her nerves. Despite her natural reserve, it wasn't the first time she'd made a rash decision. Would she ever learn to think twice before only trying to make someone else happy? Some called it spineless. She called it being agreeable to a fault.

The bar, located a block from the university, was a hot spot for its students, faculty, and staff, many of the same people Emma often encountered in the library where she worked.

It was a glorious spring afternoon. The bar's outside terrace was packed and people stood waiting in line for an empty table. Ruben didn't appear to be among them. From beneath her lashes, she looked around and fiddled with the zipper of her purse, uncertain about stepping inside. When she caught the unwanted attention of a loud group of male students, drinking heavily based on the amount of empty glasses on their table, she suppressed the urge to bolt. She was far out of her comfort zone.

A quiet uneventful evening at home seemed much more appealing.

A light tap on her shoulder made her wince. Ruben had appeared out of nowhere and stood next to her, an amber-filled glass with ice cubes in his hand.

"Sorry, I didn't want to scare you," he said close to her ear.

She detected the smell of alcohol on his breath and hoped he wasn't drunk.

With natural ease, he guided her inside to an empty table next to the window, pulled out a chair and waited until she was seated.

In less than a minute, a waitress appeared with menus and two glasses of ice water. "Can I get you anything else to drink while you decide?" she asked.

"Actually, I'm famished," Ruben replied and then looked at Emma. "It's been a long day and I skipped lunch. Do you mind if we order right away?"

"Oh, that's fine," Emma agreed with a casual sweep of her hand. She hoped he would believe that having dinner in a fancy bistro was as normal for her as it was for him, while in reality, she couldn't even remember ever eating in a restaurant other than a deli or at Mondo's Pizza.

Ruben didn't even open the menu. "I'm in the mood for the poached salmon with béarnaise and cucumber yogurt. A bottle of your oak-aged Chardonnay will pair very well with that," he said. "How does that sound, Emma?"

Relieved he had taken the decision out of her hands, she smiled. "That sounds wonderful."

The waitress collected their menus and disappeared. In the silence that followed, Emma fidgeted in her chair, wishing she weren't so nervous. "It looks like a popular restaurant," she commented, not knowing what else to say.

He nodded.

"Is it always so busy here?"

"It usually is, even on weekdays," Ruben said.

From across the table, he stared at her over the rim of his glass, unsmiling and deep in thought.

Her shoulders tensed and not for the first time, she regretted meeting him. He made her uneasy, as if she were a lab rat and he the professor deciding her fate. She took a sip of water and let her eyes wander around the restaurant. People laughed and drank at the bar, couples whispered in each other's ear, holding hands under the table. A group celebrated a birthday. Everyone seemed to have a wonderful time, the new age music coming from the speakers barely audible over the cacophony of voices.

For the third time, she tried to engage him in conversation. "Do you come here often?"

"Yes, it's one of my favorite restaurants, but lately we prefer to go to the new brewpub on the heights. Are you familiar with it?"

Of course, she wasn't. She didn't even like beer. "Who is we?" she asked.

His fingers tightened around his glass, and she caught a quick uneasy flicker in his eyes.

"I'm not married, if that's what you're thinking." He emptied his glass in one gulp and wiped his mouth with a napkin.

"Neither am I," she volunteered.

"But a delightful girl like you must have many suitors."

"I do. I did. A few," she stammered, wanting to make sure he wouldn't think she'd never been in a relationship before, or that she was an old maid without experience. Heat flushed her cheeks when she thought of James. What they'd shared had been disappointing and awkward, and too embarrassing to even think about. Especially with a pair of scrutinizing eyes analyzing her every move.

"My last boyfriend was James. We dated for a while but broke up about six months ago."

"Six months, all right, . . . but how about now?" He leaned forward as if he didn't want to miss a word she said. "Tell me everything about yourself, Emma. You're so sweet and charming. I really would like to get to know you better."

Although his attention and compliments were flattering, she had no idea what his intentions were. When they were young, Ruben had barely looked at her, only dating the cool girls, the cheerleaders, the beauty queens. Why was he so interested in her now? What could she tell him? Her life had been uneventful, even boring, except for the horrible accident that killed her father and disabled her mother. But she didn't want to talk about that. It was still too painful and sharing her sorrow with a man of his stature, in a bar over drinks, didn't appeal to her in the least.

To her relief, the waitress returned with two wine glasses and a bottle, followed by a basket of warm French bread. They toasted, then he spread butter on a slice and handed it to her. While they sampled the wine and nibbled on their bread, he listened to her talk about her years in high school and college, and about her job at the library without interrupting once.

More at ease after each sip of wine, she forgot her initial hesitance, and told him about her parents' accident and that she'd taken care of her mother instead of going to college. When her eyes filled with tears, he reached out a compassionate hand, encouraging her to continue. The warm glow of the wine, the relaxing atmosphere, and Ruben's chivalry and undivided attention calmed her. He really seemed to care, and she told him about her mother's permanent disabilities and how much she still struggled each day.

"It takes a strong woman to do what you did," Ruben said. "You're truly amazing."

Their food had come and gone, the wine bottle empty, and Emma still talked. The evening had gone better than expected. "You must think I'm a veritable chatterbox by now." She blushed. Unlike the few men she'd dated, Ruben hadn't talked about himself at all. He even turned out to be such a courteous gentleman, that she almost forgave him his snide remark about her pigtails.

"Not at all. I love listening to you. Now tell me a little more about your old boyfriend, James," Ruben said. His phone on the table vibrated. He looked at the caller id and turned it off, bringing his attention back to her. "What was he like?"

"Oh, no," she protested. "I'm not answering any more questions before you tell me something about yourself."

He twirled the last of his wine around. "I don't want to spoil the mood by talking about my childhood or challenging years at law school. It wasn't the best time of my life."

She somehow doubted that. "You could tell me what you do for a living?"

"After I graduated from Yale, I joined my Uncle Travis's law firm," he said, relaxing back in his chair. "We specialize in corporate and commercial law."

"I don't have any siblings, and to have family must be fantastic," Emma remarked. Unlike many of her friends, she never had a family member to visit. Her mother was an only child, and her father's unmarried sister lived in Australia. Not having anyone around to help them cope after the accident had made the void even greater.

Something in Ruben's eyes hardened. "You may think so," he said. "My father and his brother never got along, although Travis is smart and successful, and an upstanding human being. Whereas my father . . ." His mouth set in a straight line. "Well, I don't want to talk about him."

Although she wanted to know more, she decided not to press the issue and changed the subject. "How about your younger brother? Axel? What's he doing nowadays?"

Ruben scoffed. "Another painful subject. About ten years ago, that jerk walked out of our lives. It's been hard on the family. I don't like to talk about that either." He looked away in search of the waitress. "I noticed your glass is empty. Let's order another bottle of wine."

Like her mother had said, Ruben's life hadn't been all roses, his family dynamics turbulent. It put him in a new light.

She placed her hand over her wineglass. "None for me, thanks. I've had enough."

He reached for his glass of ice water. "You're right. We shouldn't."

To her relief, the tension in his eyes disappeared, and he turned back into her charming date. Until his cell phone on the table vibrated for the third time. He glanced at it. "I'm sorry. I ignored it too many times and better take it. Do you mind?"

"Don't apologize. It'll give me the chance to use the ladies' room."

Deep in thought over everything she'd learned, Emma headed

toward the back of the restaurant. What Ruben had told her about Axel struck her as strange. Axel had been about her age, and she remembered him as an achingly shy and sweet kid, a heavy army satchel filled with books usually hanging over his shoulder. Why had he abandoned his family? she wondered.

When she returned, Ruben was just ending his conversation. "That was Jesse Kimball. He's coming over to join us, together with Ethan Snow, another friend of ours." He handed her the dessert menu. "Do you want dessert? Or rather something stronger to finish the evening with?"

"Just coffee will be fine," she answered, a little put off at the abrupt end to their intimate dinner.

"I can tell you're upset," Ruben spoke softly and reached for her hand. "But we have to go over a few things, and they want to meet you."

"You talked to them about me?"

He gave her another one of his winning smiles. "I hope you don't mind I shared with them what a wonderful evening we're having." He released her hand and beckoned their waitress. "They can't wait to meet you."

Jesse and Ethan were both high-profile men, their names often mentioned in the financial section of the Heemstead daily newspaper. Meeting them was not on her wish list. She repeatedly folded and unfolded her napkin, her confidence washed away by uncertainty.

Ruben didn't notice her unease, his attention focused on the two men who entered the busy restaurant. Both at least six-foot tall and dressed impeccably, they oozed the type of confidence that only came from money, a formal education, trust funds, and pedigree. Each had a tall blonde woman on his arm. Emma's shoulders sagged.

With cocky grins on their faces, the two men navigated the crowded bar, slapping men on their backs and kissing women's cheeks as they inched closer to their table. Everybody seemed to want their attention, asking questions and pulling them into quick conversations. Both men looked at Ruben, raising their hands in surrender and mouthing "sorry" and "give me a minute."

"If elected, do you know that at thirty-one Jesse will be the youngest mayor the city has ever had?" Ruben commented.

Several weeks ago, Jesse Kimball, only son of a U.S. senator, had announced his candidacy for mayor of Heemstead. Since then, his name had been all over the paper and local internet news sites. They called him charismatic, smart, and promising, a politician with a bright future.

For the umpteenth time, she wondered what she was doing here. Her right leg shook as her nervousness spiked. Self-confidence had never been one of her traits, and sharing a table with three successful, handsome men made her want to flee.

"And you must be Emma," a voice spoke in her ear.

She gasped. With all the surrounding noise, she hadn't noticed Ruben's friends had reached their table. She looked up into a pair of blue eyes, sparkling good naturedly under a full head of blond, wavy hair.

"I'm Jesse. Nice to meet you. And this is Ethan Snow. I hope we're not interrupting."

Stay calm, she told herself, they're just regular guys. The only difference was that these regular guys were attractive, successful, smart, confident and rich.

"Nice to meet you, too." She smiled, her voice faint.

Jesse pulled out a chair, sat down next to her, and raked his fingers through his perfectly styled hair. Up close, he was even more handsome, his sun touched skin flawless, his lean cheeks freshly shaved. The aromatic ocean scent of his aftershave reminded her of her father.

"Is coffee all you're having?" he asked. "I need something stronger and the girls are ordering drinks at the bar. Please, join us, Emma."

All she could do was stare at him, her feelings a mixture of confusion, anxiety, and excitement. She couldn't wait to tell Sue about it.

CHAPTER

4

A SOFT KNOCK on her bedroom door woke Emma.

"Honey, are you all right?"

Emma opened her eyes and squinted at the alarm clock. Almost ten. She groaned. No wonder her mother was concerned. She never woke up this late.

"Come in, Mom." A pounding headache, with tangles shooting behind her eyes, made her flinch. She'd never cared for alcohol, and now she had the pleasure of experiencing her first hangover.

Her mother used her walker to push open the door, the small gray wheels protesting under her weight as she inched across the carpet. "I thought I heard you come home last night. I wasn't certain if I'd dreamed it or not." Her right foot dragged at an odd angle behind her, each step painstakingly slow.

Emma grimaced. "Three glasses of wine and an Irish coffee. I'll never do that again." It pained her to watch her mother struggle with each step, but she knew better than to offer help. It wouldn't be appreciated or accepted.

"Would you make coffee while I jump in the shower?" she asked as she slid out from under the covers. "I need it badly."

In the bathroom, she opened the cabinet in search of the bottle of ibuprofen, her reflection in the mirror pale, her hair a mess. She filled the plastic tumbler with water, swallowed two pills, and turned on the shower. Fifteen minutes later, her hair dripping onto the towel covering her shoulders, she joined her mother at the kitchen table. A steaming cup of coffee waited for her, along with a slice of wheat toast with strawberry jam.

"I can't wait to hear about your evening," her mother said, blowing into her own mug. "Did Ruben behave like a gentleman?"

Her mother understood people nowadays weren't keen on waiting with sex until wedding vows were exchanged. But as a devout Christian, she wouldn't accept such impropriety from her daughter. Emma never argued about it. Although they were close and able to talk just about anything, her sex life, or the lack thereof, stayed absent from the equation.

"He did, Mom. He was polite, engaging, and not self-interested at all."

Her mother nodded approvingly. "Did you ask him about his family?"

"Yes, I did. His father still lives in the trailer park in Dunedam, but he hasn't seen his younger brother in ten years. He told me Axel walked out on them, and said he was jealous, vindictive, and selfish."

"That's strange." Her mother frowned. "I remember Ruben being the troubled one of the two. He was often arrogant, bad-mannered, and sometimes mean. Do you remember the day you came home crying, telling us Ruben had stabbed a hole in the plastic ball we'd given you for your birthday?"

She remembered the incident. But the other kids had laughed, and she'd believed if they all thought it was funny, it couldn't have been so bad. Ruben was cool. Ruben was popular. He had to be a good person.

The coffee and ibuprofens started to have their effect and her headache diminished gradually. "What might surprise you is that after dinner, two other men joined us at our table."

She told her mother about Jesse Kimball and Ethan Snow. "The three of them have apparently been friends for years."

"You mean Ethan Snow, the son of Stanley Snow, who owns half of the real estate in Heemstead? And Jesse Kimball, the senator's son who's running for mayor? That's very surprising. They both come from well-respected families and old money, while Ruben's background is quite the opposite."

Emma finished her toast and wiped her mouth. "I know. You can imagine how their company overwhelmed me."

Her mother stared at her over the rim of her coffee mug, both hands wrapped around it to hold it steady. "You are too modest and shy, and you shouldn't feel that way, sweetheart. They may come from money, but you come from *me*. Remember that."

Her mother said that every time she felt insecure, afraid, or nervous. "I can't argue with that," Emma laughed. "You're an amazing mother, and I'm so proud of you."

After cleaning up, they sat down at the table to make a shopping list before heading to the Saturday Market.

While waiting for her mother to wriggle into her coat,

Emma's mind wandered back to the previous evening. To the noise, the chattering people, the delicious food, the alcohol induced buzz in her head, and the three imposing men. It had been difficult to think, her dating experience limited to evenings on the couch with James. Curiosity demanded an internet search on Ruben and his friends later in the day.

"Can you hand me my scarf and hat?" her mother asked. When she was all bundled up, a blanket covering her legs, Emma pushed the wheelchair down the hallway and into the elevator.

An hour later they returned to their apartment. Her mother emptied one of the grocery bags on the kitchen counter. She seemed exhausted from the short outing. Worried, Emma wondered if she should mention that her energy level had been noticeably decreasing over the last several months. For the second time that morning, she forced herself to turn away. It was too difficult to see her mother struggle with tasks that would only take her a second.

Emma watched her mother snooze in the oversized recliner. Instead of being relaxed in sleep, her face appeared strained. Deep lines etched her forehead, between her brows, and around her mouth. Her skin color looked grayish, and there were circles of fatigue under her eyes. *Maybe it was time to talk with the doctor.* It seemed her mother was in more pain than she'd ever been before, her health lately declining instead of improving. Something wasn't right.

She sat down behind the computer and turned it on. The old tower whirred and screeched while starting. When it finally did, she opened a web browser and typed in Jesse Kimball. Hundreds of results popped up on her screen. She clicked on the first one. An article opened, the picture next to it creeping into sight. In it a man stood waving at someone outside the camera's view. Bright sunlight struck his blond locks, his smile captivating.

Jesse Kimball III greets municipal employees outside Heemstead City Hall on Thursday afternoon, seeking support for September's mayoral election. His father, Republican Senator Jesse Kimball II, joined him. It's not a secret that he hopes his son will follow his footsteps into a Senate seat.

Considering Jesse Kimball Junior's popularity, the proud father's wish might come true.

Her cell phone vibrated on the desk, the caller ID showing an unfamiliar number. To keep her mother from waking up, Emma hurried into the bedroom and closed the door.

"Hello?"

"Hi, Emma. It's Jesse."

At his voice, she drew a sharp breath.

He laughed. "Ruben gave me your number. I hope you don't mind."

His call, and the warmth in his voice, took her by surprise. She lowered herself onto the bed next to Bert. Distracted, she petted him. "Not at all. What can I do for you?"

"I want to invite you to my birthday party tomorrow."

She gulped in disbelief. "You want me to come to your birthday? Why?"

He chuckled. "I enjoyed meeting you yesterday and would like to get to know you better."

Was she dreaming? This was so surreal.

"You're different from any other woman I've met," he continued in a smooth voice. "You're smart, and a little shy. I love that combination."

"I don't know, Jesse," she replied.

"Why not? My parents, Ruben, Ethan and a lot of other people will be there, too, if that makes you feel more comfortable."

It didn't. She would feel completely out of place, and she shuddered at the thought. "I don't think this is a good idea."

He ignored her attempts to decline. "Please, accept my invitation, Emma. There's a buffet, champagne, live music. I promise you'll enjoy yourself."

She felt her resolve cave as he pressed her to accept, teasing and joking. "I look forward to seeing you again and will send a car to pick you up."

"I'm really honored, Jesse, but I don't think I should accept," she said and disconnected.

Bert crawled onto her lap, purring for attention. "Even if he sent ten cars, I still wouldn't go," she told him, hugging him. She didn't belong in a world with lawyers, senators, and real estate moguls. Last night had proved that, and she wouldn't make the same mistake twice.

With Jesse's voice still in her ears, she sat back down behind the computer and intensified her internet search. Jesse's call had heightened her curiosity, what she read validating that she'd made the right decision to decline.

Only son of a senator, raised in a mansion with nannies and servants, where they often entertained judges, lawyers and politicians. A second home on the beach, an apartment in New York, and exotic vacations to the Caribbean and Africa. A passion for fast cars, in their garage a Ferrari, a Porsche and a Mercedes. And in each photo, he had another beauty on his arm. He didn't need her in his life when women were obviously vying for his attention.

Ethan Snow's background was even more impressive, his family owning real estate holdings all over the state.

How Ruben Templeton fit in with the two of them was a mystery. His father, August Templeton, had been a clerk at the local bank, cashing paychecks, helping with car loans, and checking deposits. Their home had been modest, just like every other mobile home in the park, with no room to park your car except on the street, and a rickety fence separating one yard from the other. Her thoughts shifted to Axel. She remembered how sorry she'd been for him, having to grow up in the shadow of his popular older brother. Was that why he'd left?

Her cell phone chimed. A text message came in. "Drinks at four, buffet at five, followed by live music."

She smiled, shaking her head. *What was up with this guy? Was he for real?*

-Pling.- "It'll be fun. Please, come."

A few minutes later, her phone chimed again. "The car will be there at three to pick you up."

With each message her resolve weakened, her interest peaked. It would be her only chance to be invited to such a prestigious event. Didn't she deserve something fun in her life? Even it was just for one afternoon?

Feeling dizzy with the attention and enjoying their cat-and-mouse game, she texted another message, "Don't send a car. If I attend, I want it to be on my terms."

CHAPTER

5

THE UBER took Emma several miles out of town, to an exclusive community for only the wealthy. The driver entered the code and the tall gate opened. A paved road, lined with mind-boggling, overdone country mansions, and surrounded by lush green lawns and flower beds, meandered gradually up the hillside. Intermittent views down the valley took her breath away. In awe, she shifted in her seat, to take it all in until the Uber slowed down. They had reached their destination. From the backseat, Emma stared wide-eyed down a long driveway at the three-stories-high Kimball mansion. Ivy wove its way up the heavy bricks until it reached the maroon-colored roof tiles. The surrounding gardens resembled a park with immaculate lawns, spacious enough to play golf on.

She pulled on her bottom lip, imagining what the luxurious interior of the house would look like. Surely it would have all the things she'd only seen in magazines: shiny hardwood floors decorated with hand knotted plush rugs, robust pieces of furniture, tall ceilings, antiques, colorful oil paintings on the walls, and a double staircase with railings made of intricate woodwork.

Of course, all the male guests would be dressed in designer suits, wearing them with ease. Their backs straight, shoulders wide, casual and confident as they strolled around, making small talk with the other party guests, and sipping from goblets filled with dark red wine.

And all the women would be young, attractive, and skinny. Most probably college graduates, accustomed to a world of sophistication, wealth, and money, clad in the latest fashion, their hair intricately coiffed by stylists, their make-up perfect. All of them confident about themselves and what they wanted, competing for Jesse's attention as he would be the center of attention, an attractive bachelor, his political and professional future bright.

"You look lovely," the gray-haired Uber driver said, looking her over with a friendly gaze.

The long black sleeveless dress, she'd purchased yesterday, had a classy and subtle cut. The saleswoman had assured her she looked stunning, like a femme fatale, and that it emphasized her body's features and added to her natural allure. She hadn't believed a word of it, knowing it was the saleswoman's job to hand out compliments, even if a client looked like a sack of potatoes. Would she match up with her brown hair hanging loosely down her back, her make-up only a little eyeshadow and a natural-colored lipstick?

"You must wonder how it's possible that a woman from the public housing district is invited to a party at the exclusive estate of a senator," she remarked, mocking herself. Her right leg bounced in a nervous rhythm. "Well, I wonder about that myself."

"Don't you dare think about yourself as less worthy than anybody else," the driver said. His smile disappeared, and he studied her. "All you need is a little more confidence and you will outshine everyone else."

Hearing the words, but not acknowledging them, she bit her fingernail. Her nails were short and unpolished. Another shortcoming.

"I'm driving you down there. I'll open the door with a bow, and will assist you out of the car," the driver said. He stepped on the gas pedal and drove through the gate. In front of the house, he stopped, got out, and guided her up the four steps onto the terrace.

"This is Miss Emma Bowen," he told the man working the door. "I'm leaving her in your capable hands. Please, let me know when she's ready to leave the party. No matter how late it is, I'll be waiting for her call." The driver handed him a business card.

"Of course," the man replied before turning toward Emma. "My name is Carlton." He touched his forehead and gave her a slight bow. "At your service." He pointed down the hall to two doors that stood wide open, leading onto the back terrace. "It's unusually warm for April, so we set up outside."

"Thank you." Clutching the purse she'd found in one of her mother's closets, she crossed the marble tile floor. Her high heels pinched her toes together in the front, and the back rim of the right shoe cut in her Achilles tendon. How would she make it through the rest of the afternoon, let alone the evening?

She wanted to kick them off now.

The doors opened onto a huge stone terrace. Tables were set up, shaded by overhanging tree branches that had to be at least a hundred years old. Each table held a small vase with spring flowers in its center, most chairs occupied. The men, dressed in evening clothes, and the women, wearing spectacular gowns in every color possible, jewelry sparkling at their necks and wrists, talked animatedly. In response to all the wealth, her hand went to the silver necklace circling her neck. It was a gift from her mother. She'd always treasured it, but it was nothing compared to the elaborate selection of jewels, rings, and brooches the other guests were wearing. Shying away, she hovered at the edge of the terrace. She couldn't imagine ever being comfortable enough to enjoy herself in such a prestigious setting, conversing effortlessly, sipping from champagne glasses a server in livery handed out from a tray.

To her right, buffet tables stood underneath a row of canopies. People lined up with white porcelain plates in hand.

"You're in time for the buffet," said a woman next to her.

Emma turned in her direction.

"I just returned from the powder room and noticed you come in by yourself." The woman extended her hand. "I'm Sondra Newell. What's your name?"

The woman's hand felt like a bundle of straw. "Emma Bowen. Nice to meet you."

"I'm here with my husband and daughter," Sondra continued. "Are you meeting up with someone, or do you want to join us at our table, dear?"

"I would love to join you. Thank you," she said, relieved not to be alone anymore.

Sondra greeted several acquaintances as she crossed the terrace, until they arrived at a table surrounded by a group of young adults and an older gentleman. "My husband, Keith," Sondra said. "Everyone, this is Emma. She seemed a little lost, so I invited her to join us."

One of the young men pulled an extra chair from another table and poured her a glass of water from an elaborately shaped pitcher.

"Mom, you missed Jesse's welcoming speech," a youthful woman at the table said. She was beautiful, her canary yellow sleeveless chiffon dress with beaded spaghetti straps exquisite.

"That beauty with the long auburn hair and pouting red lips is Angela Newell," the polite young man next to her said. "We're very good friends." He handed her a glass of champagne from the waiter's tray. "I'm Eric Elrich, from Elrich Electronics. I don't think I've ever seen you before, Emma, because if I had, I'm sure I would have remembered."

Emma grinned, taking the compliment at face value. She took off her black shawl and draped it over the back of her chair.

"Gorgeous dress," he complimented. "Do you want to join me at the buffet?" He held out his arm with exaggerated ceremony, his eyes darting constantly back to Angela. It was obvious he had feelings for her.

Emma stood and took his arm. "Thank you."

They joined the end of the line. "I hope you're not here for Jesse," Eric said, noticing she looked around in search of someone. "All the girls swoon over him, including Angela, and I might as well give up." He sighed. "That guy! No one can compete with him, and I'm surprised he's still single."

Jealousy laced his words, and Emma couldn't help but

smile. Even though Eric could buy anything his heart desired, some things just weren't for sale. "I wouldn't give up, Eric. You look like a great guy, and I'm sure you have a lot to offer."

"You must be a lawyer, a psychiatrist, or a diplomat." He grinned, handing her a plate. "They always know exactly what to say to make someone feel better."

"How about a library-aide," she grinned, the buffet catching her attention, the decorated tables loaded with a variety of hot and cold options. She'd never seen so many delicacies in one place.

"What can I serve you," the caterer asked, taking orders for various choices of sliced meats. The second caterer helped with seafood. Salmon, lobster, oysters, shrimp, you name it.

Overwhelmed by the options, Emma started with a small crisp salad, a piece of fresh pink salmon, and a wafer-cut turkey sandwich.

"Is that all you're having?" Eric commented, his plate loaded with thick slices of prime rib, meatballs, a chicken breast, and lots of gravy. He had to be a meat loving kind of guy.

"I might go for seconds," she replied as they gathered silverware and napkins at the end of the table.

Before they made it back to their seats, a hand touched her shoulder.

Jesse stood next to her, dynamically handsome and confident in a sharp one-button tuxedo and black bowtie. Next to him, Eric paled into insignificance.

"I kept an eye out for you, but didn't see you until now," he said. A grin spread across his face, and the corners of his bright blue eyes crinkled attractively. "I'm so glad you made it."

"She's sitting at my table," Eric said, taking a step forward.

"Not anymore," Jesse replied and signaled a waiter to gather her belongings.

Uncomfortably aware of all the curious eyes cast in their direction, heat flushed her cheeks. "Are you sure?"

"Absolutely. You're my special invitee today," Jesse replied.

His arm slipped around her waist, and he kept it there while he maneuvered her through the guests. When they reached his table, an older gentleman she immediately recognized as Jesse's father, Senator Kimball, got up from his chair.

He took her hand and brought it up to his lips. "Welcome to my house and my table, Emma." Gray eyebrows bobbed over a pair of intelligent blue eyes, his tailored suit in a dark charcoal a perfect fit.

Taken aback that he knew her name, her blush deepened from light pink to scarlet. "It's wonderful to meet you, sir."

"Please, let me introduce you to my wife, Sarah," the senator continued, waving his hand in his wife's direction. "Our neighbors Stanley and Isabelle Snow, their son Ethan and his girlfriend Janet. Next to them my dear sister, her husband, and their oldest daughter Carly. And our other long-time neighbors and friends, Travis Templeton and his nephew Ruben."

Ruben sat beside Carly, holding her hand in his. "We know each other," he remarked.

"Everyone," Jesse's father continued, "This is Emma Bowen, a very smart young lady, as Jesse keeps telling me."

Jesse pulled out a chair for her between himself and his father, her plate and champagne on the table, her black shawl and purse already there. She reached out for her glass to quench her parched throat and loosen the knot in her stomach. The champagne was bubbly and cool. She liked it and took another sip.

From across the table, Ruben raised his glass. "Glad you made it, Emma," he said.

Carly laughed and whispered something in his ear. He smiled in answer and kissed her cheek. It seemed they were more than friends. So why had Ruben asked her out? Had it been to hand her over to his best friend? But Jesse didn't need help to find a date. There were plenty of girls interested in him, including Angela in the canary yellow dress.

Over dinner, the conversation turned to the mayoral election at the end of the summer. The current mayor, who held three consecutive four-year terms, was retiring.

Grateful the focus of attention had shifted away from her, Emma glanced around the table from beneath her lashes.

With Carly's hand still in his, Ruben talked to his uncle. Both men had the same dark, penetrating eyes, their black hair swept back from prominent foreheads in the same well-trimmed style. So, Ruben had found his way into the upper class through his uncle, the Kimballs' long-time neighbor. Now, it all made sense.

At the end of the terrace, on a small stage, a band tuned their instruments. The occasional ruffle of drums got people on their feet. Several strong men cleared tables and chairs out of the way to create a dancefloor.

Next to the stage stood a table overloaded with creatively wrapped gifts. It had completely skipped Emma's mind to bring Jesse anything. Could she be more inconsiderate? Under the table, her leg began its nervous bounce. She emptied her champagne in one big gulp.

"Can I get you anything else to drink before the music starts?" Jesse offered.

Tempting as it was, she declined. It wouldn't be smart to get drunk and repeat what had happened the other night.

"In that case..." Jesse took her hand and pulled her with him toward the stage. A microphone stood on a stand, and Jesse grabbed it.

"Hello, everybody," he said to get the people's attention. "Again, thank you for being here today, to celebrate my birthday, and for all the gifts and well wishes. I'm a lucky man to have you in my life." The crowd cheered. "As you all know, I'm taking my first steps into politics. Add that to my hectic work schedule, and I'll have a busy summer ahead of me. But with the support from my father, I'm confident I'll be able to welcome all of you here again after the mayoral election later this year, to celebrate my victory!"

The guests applauded in agreement.

"Let's drink to that." Jesse emptied his glass and handed the microphone to the waiting singer of the band who immediately started to sing Happy Birthday.

With his arm around Emma's shoulders, Jesse grinned from ear to ear and guided her onto the dance floor. Emma froze. She'd never learned how to dance, and now wasn't the time for a public first. She would only make a fool of herself, and him.

The band launched into a crowd-pleasing song.

"You can't deny me a birthday dance," Jesse laughed. His fingertips slid down her back, leaving a warm, tingling trail.

He took her in his arms, and began to sway back and forth, following the rhythm. She quickly caught on, and with his left hand cradling the small of her back, he increased the tempo until the song ended.

"You're a natural," he whispered in her ear, drawing her closer for another song. This time the melody was slow, the lyrics about love and growing old together. "You better be careful with those gorgeous blue eyes of yours. When I gaze into them, it's like I'm drowning," he smiled.

Several girls stood next to the dancefloor, waiting for their turn to dance with Jesse, but he ignored them and kept Emma in his arms. He was an excellent dancer and she fit perfectly in his embrace, the top of her head just below his chin. It was as if she'd landed in the Cinderella fairytale, the only thing to worry about leaving the party before the stroke of midnight.

Until she caught sight of Ruben, standing by himself underneath one of the vintage garden lights, his frame rigid and his face drawn. Something about the intensity of his stare made her feel off-balance. By the time they danced around, and she could look at him again, she noticed Ruben gave Jesse a thumbs-up. But instead of a smile, he seemed to smirk, his expression calculated and contrived.

What was that all about? she wondered, goosebumps prickling her arms. When they swirled around for the third time, Ruben had disappeared.

CHAPTER

6

THE PHONE ON HER DESK rang. Emma picked up. "Heemstead University Library. This is Emma Bowen. How may I help you?"

"Would you be so kind as to tell me if there's a copy available of the autobiography by the current president?"

She held her breath for a moment. "Jesse?"

He laughed, his long low rumble already familiar. Barely able to hide her excitement, she glanced around to make sure no one could listen in on their conversation.

"You want to go out for dinner tomorrow evening?"

Her heart somersaulted in her chest. "I would love that."

"Great. Do you want me to pick you up?"

That wasn't an option. He would find out where she lived, take one look, turn around, and run away. "You could pick me up at the library after work? Around 5:30?"

"Perfect. I'm looking forward to seeing you again."

They said goodbye, and she leaned against the back of her chair, too excited to go back to work. The evening of the party had been incredible. From the exquisite food, the bubbly champagne, the gorgeous people, the impressive house, and the live music, to the twinkling stars in the spring sky. And then there had been Jesse, the perfect host and gentleman.

He had introduced her to his friends, keeping her by his side the entire evening. It had been magical. She still had to pinch herself over having shared a dinner table with Heemstead's crème de la crème. It had been the most intoxicating evening of her entire life.

The next morning, she stood in front of her closet, biting at her bottom lip as she stared at her sweater sets, plain skirts, and flat dress shoes. It all screamed "cliché librarian", the clothes she preferred wearing helping her blend in and go unnoticed. But it also meant she owned nothing remotely similar to the clothes worn by the women Jesse normally dated. With a sigh, she settled on a creamy yellow sweater set, a black pencil skirt, and black flats. As she was about to walk out the door for work, she returned to her bedroom to grab the high heels she'd worn to the birthday party. At the last second, she also shoved a multicolored scarf into her bag.

Right before the library closed, Emma pulled the pins from the bun at her nape and took out her brush, compact and lipstick. Her hands trembled slightly as she applied her make-up.

"I don't believe I've ever seen you so distracted before," Sue, the librarian, commented with a warm smile.

Emma fanned her cheeks with both hands. "Jesse is picking me up. I hope I don't seem too excited."

"Maybe a little, but it only adds to your charm," Sue winked. "Enjoy yourself. I'm glad you're going out. It's been too long."

At 5:30 sharp, Jesse entered the hallway. He could have easily walked out of one of the men's fashion magazines they stocked on the library shelves. Just like those male models, Jesse was the picture of wealth and sophistication, his perfectly cut blond hair wind-blown, the top buttons of his yellow polo shirt open.

He looked Emma over with an appreciative smile. "You look gorgeous," he commented, holding out his arm.

Nerves flittered in her stomach as she linked her arm through his and they headed out. She worried she made a monumental mistake. The party at his house had been dreamlike, but that didn't mean their relationship stood a chance in the harshness of reality.

Jesse's gleaming black Mercedes sat in the no-parking zone in front of the building, the top down. She'd never seen anyone park there before.

"Special treatment for a special lady," he said with a cocky grin and opened the door.

Emma slid into the passenger seat, the smell of luxurious leather surrounding her. The car seemed brand new.

Jesse stepped in and started the powerful engine. He pulled a pair of sunglasses from his breast pocket and merged into traffic.

Emma shivered nervously and pulled her scarf closer around her neck.

"If it's too cold or too windy, let me know, and I'll bring the top up and turn on the heated seats," he said.

"No, I'm fine," she replied, enjoying the wind in her hair and the smooth ride.

They cruised through the familiar streets and it didn't take long before they left the suburbs behind them.

"I'm taking you to Northwood Country Club," he said.

Of course, he was a member of the exclusive private club, she thought.

"That sounds wonderful."

"Have you ever played golf?"

When she shook her head, he told her it was one of his favorite pastimes and offered to teach her someday soon.

Five minutes later, he turned the car into the entrance and continued down the road flanked by decorative rocks and flower beds. Men and women in collared shirts and light-tinted slacks walked on the immaculately kept greens, some carrying their own bags of clubs, others using caddies or electric golf carts. Jesse took her hand to help her out of the car and guided her to the restaurant where the headwaiter welcomed them, bowing and smiling. "A table for two, Mr. Kimball?"

"We prefer a little privacy and to eat dinner on the back patio," Jesse replied.

"Certainly," the headwaiter said. "If you want to follow me?"

With Jesse's hand on the small of her back, they made their way through the dining room. Guests nodded in greeting when they passed, others casting curious glances in her direction. Emma's eyes darted around, taking everything in. There was so much to see and admire. The indoor fountain, the intricate pattern of the floor, and the forty-foot wooden bar with a floor-to-ceiling back bar, loaded with colorful bottles.

Jesse stopped several times to shake hands and chat for a moment with acquaintances or friends.

"They're all wondering who you are," he whispered in her ear.

His words increased her apprehension.

The back patio overlooked the Heemstead River, with several tables beside the balustrade, most of them empty.

"Which table do you prefer?" the waiter asked.

They picked the one at the far end and sat down, menus and glasses with water appearing out of nowhere.

Jesse glanced over the wine list. "Do you prefer red or white, Emma?"

"Why don't you decide," she replied, taking in the beauty surrounding her, the sounds of nature and soft classical music playing in the background. It was so different from the continuous noise of the city.

In awe, she leaned over the railing to look down into the deep, lush canyon of the river, and at the towering pines, red oaks, and maple trees. She soaked in the splendor of Mother Nature, breathing in the scent of fresh-cut grass and the dampness of the earth.

"It's so gorgeous. Look at the amount of water rushing by." She smiled and relaxed her shoulders.

The waiter arrived at their table and uncorked the bottle Jesse had requested. First, he poured a splash of white wine in Jesse's glass for his approval. After he sampled a taste and nodded, the waiter filled both their glasses. "Are you ready to order?"

"We'll have the seafood platter for two," Jesse said, looking to her for approval. There were no prices on the menu, but she assumed it was the restaurant's most expensive meal. She agreed with his choice. They were still in the getting-acquainted phase, and she would have agreed with anything he suggested.

"To a new friendship," Jesse declared, raising his glass after the waiter left.

Over dinner, they exchanged casual information. Jesse told her about his day and asked about hers. With each bite, she felt more comfortable in his company. He charmed her with funny stories about the people in his life and the mayoral election coming up in the fall.

"Ruben told me the two of you were practically neighbors growing up?" Jesse said, dipping his lobster in the clarified butter. "What kind of teenager were you?"

Heat rose into her neck and cheeks. Had Ruben told him about her pigtails and braces? In a gesture of protection, she crossed her arms under her breasts. "We weren't exactly friends."

Jesse raised his eyebrows. "He mentioned he really liked you and even stole a kiss from you in a gazebo?"

She recalled the moment of mockery as if it happened yesterday, the kiss part of a dare. It had been humiliating. Her right leg trembled. She crossed her legs to force it still. "I don't understand why Ruben would talk to you about that," she snapped.

Immediately regretting her tone, she bit her tongue. She should have known the two friends talked about her. That's what people did.

The unexpected flash of a camera made them look up.

A photographer stood next to their table, snapping pictures. Emma flinched at the invasion of their privacy; her cheeks already red from embarrassment.

"Hi, Jesse," the grinning photographer said, shaking Jesse's hand. "I need a picture to fill up some space. Are you in?"

Jesse's gaze shifted to Emma. "Do you mind?"

Unlike her, he didn't seem to mind the intrusion.

"As a mayoral candidate, I need all the publicity I can get," he explained. She nodded her consent. It was the least she could do.

They posed for several shots, but when the photographer scrolled through them, he gave a disapproving glance. "Looking good, but I don't like the lighting, and we need a smile from you, lovely lady." He nodded at Emma. "Could you move to the other side of the table? . . . Now sit down next to Jesse . . . A bit closer . . . Jesse, a bit more against the balustrade? . . . Relax those shoulders if you can . . ."

With Jesse's arm around her shoulders, they posed for at least ten more shots until the photographer seemed satisfied and left.

"That was Anthony Polson," Jesse said, not noticing the beads of nervous sweat on her brow. "He's a conservative political columnist and promised an article in the Heemstead Chronicle tomorrow."

The grin on his face couldn't have been bigger.

CHAPTER

7

OVER THE NEXT SEVERAL WEEKS, their budding relationship started to blossom. They hiked together, played mini-golf, and met for lunch or dinner, sometimes for a casual burger, the next time in one of Heemstead's many upscale restaurants. On every date, Jesse was gracious, sociable, and considerate, making her feel more at ease and cherished with each passing day.

They also went out with Ruben and Carly, and Ethan and Janet. Each time, they met at a different brewpub, restaurant, or wine bar. Ruben suggested it was a smart strategy for Jesse to socialize among voters outside his typical circles. It seemed to Emma that Ruben had taken up the role of Jesse's campaign manager. He always called with suggestions and ideas that could benefit him.

Ruben's girlfriend had welcomed Emma into their small circle of friends with open arms. Carly was kind and smart, and unexpectedly insecure. It seemed everything frightened her, spiders, motorcycles, men with long hair, and camping.

"I grew up too protected," she said, openly admiring Emma for going everywhere by herself. "Aren't you afraid?"

"I'm an introvert and nobody ever notices me," Emma smiled.

"But that's changing now," Carly said. "I've seen several pictures of you and Jesse in the paper. It looks like you two are hitting it off, and you're becoming quite the celebrity."

Emma blushed, hoping no one would notice in the crowded bar. "He needs the publicity. Especially after Andrew Voss, one of Heemstead's city council members, announced he's also running for mayor."

"If you want, we could go clothes shopping together," Carly offered. "You know how important looks can be."

The words stung, hurting her tenuous self-esteem, but Emma knew Carly meant well, and she could use the help, her entire wardrobe not suitable for the girlfriend of an aspiring politician. "That sounds wonderful, Carly. Thank you for offering."

Carly led her to a dark corner of the bar. "Can I ask you something in private?" she said, looking over her shoulder to make sure they wouldn't get overheard. "It's about Ruben."

Puzzled, Emma tilted her head. What could she possibly know about Ruben?

"You see, I've known Ruben for years, but we only recently started dating. Since you and Jesse are becoming so close, does he ever talk about us? About Ruben and me?"

The insecurity in her friend's eyes surprised her. "No, not really. Why? Are you two having relationship troubles?"

Carly hesitated. "I'm not sure, but I can tell something is troubling him. When I ask him about it, he shuts me out, and that bothers me." She released a sad sounding sigh. "Ruben and Jesse are such close friends. They always confide in each other. I thought maybe Jesse had mentioned something."

"Do I hear my name?" Ruben asked, wrapping his arm around Carly's waist and pulling her in to drop a kiss on her forehead.

Carly quickly made a zip-it motion in front of her mouth before she turned toward Ruben with a smile. "I was telling Emma that we met for the first time about nine years ago. Can you believe it's been that long?"

Ruben grinned from ear to ear. "I remember the day we met as if it were yesterday." With his arm still wrapped around Carly's waist, he turned toward Emma. "I'd just moved in with my Uncle Travis and explored the grounds when I heard laughter coming from the neighbor's yard. I peeked over the fence and saw Jesse in the pool, chasing his cousin Carly around in the water. I'm still happy I asked if I could join them. It was the start of a remarkable friendship."

"You moved in with your uncle around the same time your brother Axel disappeared?" Emma asked, placing a caring hand on his arm. "That must have been hard on your father."

Ruben stared at her. "Don't be sorry for my father. He didn't care." He took Carly by the hand and Emma watched them disappear into the crowd. Jesse waved at her from the bar. Happy with the distraction, she joined him.

"Your sparkling water is getting warm," he teased her.

She took a sip and stuck out her tongue. It had gone flat. By magic, a new glass appeared, and they toasted.

"Jesse, would you like to come over for dinner at my apartment this coming Sunday? I think it's time for you to meet my mother. She keeps asking about you."

Jesse drew a big gulp from his I.P.A. before he pulled her into his arms and kissed her on her mouth. He tasted like beer and a hint of peppermint. "I would love to."

On Sunday, she added a sprinkle of parmesan cheese to her lasagna, carefully monitoring the temperature. Last time, the top had burned, and she needed it to be perfect.

"It smells fantastic," her mother commented.

Emma closed the oven, pushing her tangled hair behind her ear. "Jesse could be here any minute. I'll be right back."

Her mother's laughter followed her into the bathroom, where she wetted her flushed face and brushed her hair until it shone. Nerves stirred in the pit of her stomach. Until today, she'd let Jesse drop her off at the library, ashamed of where she lived. What would he think of their ordinary apartment? His opinion had become very important to her.

After taking a few calming breaths, she inspected her new outfit. Carly had taken her shopping yesterday. She now owned slacks, an animal-print top, a silk blouse, and cute ankle boots.

The buzzer announced somebody was at the door. She heard her mother welcoming Jesse in.

"It's so wonderful to meet you, Mrs. Bowen," he said, his voice deep and warm. Its resonance sent a tingling sensation through her spine.

After a last inspection, she rushed into his arms.

"Emma, you look lovely in slacks, and your top is gorgeous," he complimented her. He took her in his arms in the cramped entryway and kissed her cheek. "You're becoming more and more the perfect candidate's girlfriend."

He sounded more polite than sincere. She hoped it was because her mother eyed them curiously, her face flushed with excitement to finally meet Jesse.

"Make yourself comfortable," her mother said, rolling her wheelchair out of the way so he could enter.

Jesse looked around in the small space. "This is a beautiful apartment, Mrs. Bowen. It's so cheerful and comfortable. You've done an amazing job decorating."

Grateful he tried to make them feel at ease, Emma invited him to sit down at the kitchen table. "This is our dining room," she said, hating the apologetic tone in her voice.

"You both know how to get the most use out of a small space," he said, pulling out a chair.

Bert slept on the pillow and woke up. When he noticed the stranger, he narrowed his eyes and hissed, lashing his tail.

"Bert! Don't do that!" Emma hurried to pick him up, noticing the pillow was covered in cat hair. *Could it be more embarrassing?*

Jesse looked at Bert with suspicion. "I'm sorry," he apologized. "I'm not used to pets."

"Oh, no, we have to apologize, Jesse," Emma's mom said quickly. "Bert isn't used to strangers, and we should have put him away before you arrived."

Emma locked the anxious cat in the bedroom, appreciating her mother's lie for diffusing the tense moment.

Jesse pulled out another chair and sat down. "Don't worry

about it." He looked at the bottle of wine on the table. "A Cabernet from Cathedral Cellars. You have excellent taste, Emma. Do you want me to open it?"

Emma had ordered the bottle online, knowing it was Jesse's favorite winery. It was a great distraction. She handed him an opener and busied herself in the kitchen. The lasagna was perfect, the French bread toasty, and the salad crisp.

"I hear you're a busy man, Jesse," her mother said over dinner.

Jesse nodded. "People only know me as the son of Senator Kimball, with a degree in accounting and political science. Or they know me for starting my own company, the Kimball Financial Group Ltd. But what the citizens of Heemstead don't know is what kind of man I am. So, I try to make many public appearances to change that and boost my image."

Emma knew Jesse volunteered at the homeless shelter, attended city hall meetings, and sat on the board of the Heemstead Running Club. Each year, the club organized a fundraiser for cancer research with a five- and a ten-kilometer run. Jesse was an avid runner himself, often getting up at the crack of dawn to run a few miles before breakfast.

"One of my favorite outings are events organized by the Chamber of Commerce," he continued. "Small businesses improve innovation and productivity. They add to the growth of the city, the vitality of the community, and create jobs. The Chamber supports and promotes them, to encourage development and contribute to a healthy economic community. I appreciate the small business' entrepreneurial spirits. As one of the Chamber's board members, I want to assure them of my full support once elected."

"Emma told me about the few times she joined you, but I

understand you're gone at least three or four evenings a week? That seems demanding," Emma's mother commented.

"Yes, but I don't mind. With the election only four months away, I have to take every opportunity at hand to let the voters know I'm a stellar citizen, who looks out for everyone's interest." He winked and gave them one of his winning smiles. It made Emma's heart beat faster.

"With a father as senator, and my grandfather a senator before him, I've been groomed my entire life to follow in their footsteps. They give me their full support and the needed connections. That helps tremendously."

From what Emma had learned, money was no object either. All those factors combined made him the perfect candidate to become mayor and launch his own political career. She was proud of him. He was a gentleman, attentive and witty, and had a quick and discerning intellect. Nothing went by him. If they only could spend more time together, she thought, watching him enjoy his food, his tongue sliding down his upper lip occasionally to remove some of the tomato sauce.

"I'm glad Emma joined me several times. The people appreciate it, too, most of them loving her right away."

The few times Emma had joined him at different events were informative, but listening to a business plan from a local merchant seeking financial aid, or helping to set up beds at the homeless shelter, as noble as it was, was not her idea of dating. All they'd done was talk to strangers and give each other chaste kisses on the lips for the photographers, wanting to post an article in the paper or online. Although it was nice to take things slow, they weren't children, and she fantasized about how it would feel to be in his arms, with his mouth on hers, his bare skin under her fingertips, and his weight on top of her.

Seeing each other alone had also become increasingly difficult because of her mother's declining health. She suffered from night sweats, stabbing pains in her back and side, and was always tired. It looked like she lost weight, too. Clothes that once fit perfectly now hung on her shrinking frame.

"You're not eating, mother," she said, looking at her barely touched plate. Even her wine glass was still untouched.

"It's delicious, Emma," she replied. "I just don't seem to have much of an appetite today."

Jesse wiped his mouth and placed his napkin on his empty plate. "You can make lasagna every day of the week, Emma," he said. "That was a real treat."

After clearing the table, Jesse helped with the dishes while her mother dozed in her recliner.

"I'm so concerned about my mother's health, Jesse," she whispered as she let him out half an hour later, closing the door behind them so her mother couldn't overhear them talk. "She continues to refuse to visit a doctor."

"Why doesn't she want to go?" he asked.

Emma's throat constricted. "After the accident, she'd been treated by too many of them and hates to see the inside of a clinic. But she needs more and more care each day. She's weak, sometimes confused, and struggles to make it to the bathroom on time."

"I'll help you convince her, if you want me to," he offered.

"I appreciate that," she said, touching his cheek with her fingertips.

After a rough night with her mother, Emma barely made it in time to work. An hour later, the phone rang. Her heart jumped in her throat when she saw her mother's number on the display. She never called her at work.

"I made an appointment with Doctor Miller, Emma," her mother said. "She can see me this afternoon. I called an Uber."

"Take the afternoon off," Sue said without hesitation. "You should be there for your mother."

"Why didn't you come in sooner, Mrs. Bowen?" Doctor Miller asked while examining her. The doctor appeared shocked at her mom's condition and ordered a urinalysis and blood tests.

Two days later, Emma's mother called her at work. "They found blood in my urine and want me to see a urologist and set up a CT scan as soon as possible, Emma. I hate to be a bother, but do you think you can ask for the day off? I don't want to go alone."

They sat in the urologist's office ten days later and waited to hear the results. The doctor typed on his keyboard, avoiding eye contact.

"The results are worrisome," he said, with a grave expression on his face. "We'll be joined by the hospital's top urologic oncologist in a few minutes. He's on his way."

The urologist's words shredded Emma's hope at good news.

Stage 4 renal cancer. A two-inch tumor has formed in your right kidney. The cancer has spread to your liver and lungs. There's nothing we can do.

At the devastating news, Emma gripped her mother's hand, tears running down her cheeks. "No, no," she cried as the diagnosis sunk in. "This can't be true."

"I'm very sorry, Mrs. Bowen," the oncologist said. "Given the aggressive and pervasive spread of the cancer, there are no suitable treatment options. The cancer is just too advanced. Anything we could try might give you a few extra months, but the side effects would be incapacitating, robbing you of any quality of life. The best option is to make you as comfortable as possible during the time you have left."

Sobs racked Emma's body, leaving her gasping for air. Unable to face this devastating news by herself, she called Jesse.

"I'll come right away," he said.

He rushed into the waiting room fifteen minutes later to find Emma and her mother weeping in each other's arms. He leaned down, wrapped his arms around them, and held them in a tight embrace.

"I'm glad I was close by," he whispered.

She looked up, her eyes puffy, her face tear streaked. The bun in her hair had come undone and strands stuck out in every direction. "I must look horrible," she whimpered.

He gave her a loving, encouraging smile before he kissed her wet cheeks and slowly moved his mouth lower. "Don't worry, sweetie. I'll take care of the both of you." His warm lips searched tentatively until they found the soft curves of hers. Exploring with gentleness, he sighed her name.

She made no conscious decision to open her mouth to the tender, careful probing of his tongue, but she did, molding her lips with his in a kiss that touched her deeply. How long they stood like that, she didn't recall later. It could have been seconds or several minutes. All she realized was that the kiss connected them on a higher level. It assured her he would be there for her, to help her through the difficult time to come.

That kiss would change her life forever.

CHAPTER

8

THEIR KISS in the impersonal waiting room had been inappropriate. Emma knew she should have been embarrassed, with several strangers looking on and the receptionist raising her eyebrows in disapproval. Instead, she didn't care and couldn't help but glow at the memory. Jesse's kiss had touched her deeply and made her heart warm and fuzzy when she relived the moment; filled with dread, misery, and emptiness, mixed in with passion, warmth, and tenderness. Contradicting emotions that shouldn't coincide, tumbling through her, engulfing her, leaving her in an emotional mess. If not for Jesse, she would have completely fallen apart. He became her safe harbor in the storm, her rock.

With her life in turmoil, Emma roamed around the tiny apartment after a fitful night of sleep, tentacles of panic squeezing her heart and stomach. How was she going to cope with the loss of her mother, her best friend? They were so close, their lives intertwined. Everything she did, she weighed first against her mother's needs.

Breakfast time loomed and her mother remained in bed. Emma didn't want to wake her. From the disquieting moans and continuous squeaking of her old box spring throughout the night, she knew she'd barely been able to sleep. Silent tears trickled down her cheeks. Losing her father had been devastating, and now she had to face the rest of her life without her mother, too. It wasn't fair.

When Jesse showed up at nine, as promised, he brought banana bread and whole-wheat muffins with egg whites and avocado from the deli. Normally this was her favorite breakfast, but the thought of eating made her queasy. Instead of food, she needed caring words and support. Waiting for him to wrap his arms around her and assure it had all been a nightmare, that everything would be okay, she reached for his hand. He took hers in his grasp and gave it a quick kiss before disappearing into the kitchen.

She bit on her lip to fight off her tears and followed him.

"Were you able to sleep at all?" he asked as she sunk into a chair at the table.

When she shook her head, a warm hand squeezed her shoulder. "I talked to my parents last night. I want you to move into our guesthouse with your mother so we can help take care of her."

Emma breathed in disbelief. "You want what?" She turned around in her chair and stared at him.

He opened a cabinet, pulled out three plates, and placed them on the table before he sat down next to her. "I can tell the idea shocks you, but what you're facing is too much for you to bear on your own." A loving smile softened his mouth. "Do you realize how difficult it is for me to see you white-faced and anguished?" He stroked her arm with the palm of his hand, the rhythmic movement mesmerizing her. "I want to be there for you, to help you."

His kindness and concern for her well-being fanned the simmering glow deep within her. She longed to crawl into his lap and disappear in his arms. She needed to be held, to find refuge in his loving embrace. He was right. She couldn't do this alone. Hot tears threatened to spill down her cheeks as she inched closer, willing him to reach out and enfold her.

He took both her hands in his. "Our guest house is comfortable and will suit all your needs. You and your mother will love it. There's only one concern and I want to get that out of the way before you talk to your mother."

Still holding on to her hands, he lowered himself on his right knee. "Emma, I realize it's only been four months, but I love you and want us to marry. Please, say you will?"

Less than a week later, a medical transport van pulled up in front of their apartment building. Out stepped Rick, the middle-aged nurse Jesse had hired.

"They're here to pick us up, Mom," Emma said from the window, her voice echoing in the emptiness.

Jesse had arranged for movers to pack most of their belongings in a matter of days. With a heavy heart she looked around, the last moving boxes stacked up in the middle of the living room. The walls showed darker spots where family photos had told the story of their lives and warmed the room, the carpet threadbare and faded.

Time to say goodbye.

Noise in the hallway and a knock on the door came just in time before her tears flowed again. The nurse walked in with a warm smile on his face.

"Hi, Mrs. Bowen. Are you ready for an adventure?" he asked, expertly helping her frail mother from her recliner into the wheelchair. He was in his mid-fifties, but still in excellent shape and capable of easily carrying her mother down the eight flights of stairs if he had to. He was lighthearted, joked and teased, his eyes warm and filled with mirth. Exactly what they needed to keep them from wallowing in melancholy and self-pity.

"You should ask my daughter that question," her mother replied, winking at him.

Even though Rick was careful, she winced as she settled herself into the chair.

"Did she tell you she's getting married in a few weeks? They rush the occasion because of my declining health. I'm so grateful I can attend and to know Emma won't be alone after I'm gone. I couldn't be happier for her."

Emma had done a lot of soul searching, the decision to move into the Kimball's guesthouse difficult. To give up her independence had been the first hurdle. The fear they might take advantage of Jesse and his parents, the second. Especially since they insisted that Emma and her mother would stay rent-free, and that hiring a nurse was the normal thing to do for the mother of their son's fiancée.

"We're overjoyed with the prospect of the wedding," Jesse's mother assured her. "You're part of the family now, and I can't wait to start planning the ceremony, the reception, the party."

Jesse brushed aside her apprehension. "This is exactly what I want to do for the woman I love."

Although he spoke the right words, was attentive, and caring, his words didn't resonate. He seemed withdrawn and often distracted, a brooding sadness hanging over him.

"I know I've asked this before," she said. "Are you sure there's nothing bothering you?"

"Of course not," he said. "Listen, as difficult as it is, I have to keep myself at a distance until we're married. They scrutinize every step I take. Even the hint of a scandal might destroy my career and ruin my reputation.

"And you know how conservative my parents are. If we did anything outside of what they consider appropriate, I'll hear about it for the rest of my life. I love you. For now, that needs to be enough."

But was it?

The tears that burned her eyes spilled over as Rick wheeled the chair out of the apartment and into the waiting elevator. With Bert in his cat carrier in her right hand, Emma followed them, brushing her tears away before her mother could notice. Her mother was even more excited about the upcoming wedding than Jesse's parents, and her eyes lit up at the mere mention of his name. She only had six months left to live. To know her daughter wouldn't have to face life alone, gave her peace and something joyful to focus upon.

"I know your marriage is rushed because of my illness," she said, "but Jesse assured me that after the election, the stressful times will be over, and he'll give you all the attention you deserve. You'll see."

~~⋅~⋅~~

When they pulled up at the Kimballs' mansion, only Carlton waited at the front door to welcome them. Her heart dropped.

"Jesse couldn't be here. They called him away last minute," Carlton said, an apologetic look on his face. "But he assured everything is ready, including your mother's hospital bed, which arrived this morning."

Emma hadn't expected Jesse's parents to be there. They'd returned to their penthouse in Washington D.C. where they spend most of their time. But she was disappointed that Jesse wasn't there to welcome them.

"Oh, you're bringing a cat?" Carlton continued. "I love cats." He knelt next to Bert's carrier and let him play with his finger.

Emma smiled. It was wonderful to have Carlton around.

Rick pushed the wheelchair down the flagstone walkway through the garden. The guest house stood behind the mansion, next to the swimming pool. It had two bedrooms with walk-in closets and a huge shared bathroom with a shower and a separate Jacuzzi tub. The living room and open kitchen were sunny, the wicker furniture with colorful pillows enhancing it. French doors gave a wide view to the veranda. They would be comfortable there, if it wasn't for the heavy weight on their shoulders, knowing this would be her mother's last address.

"At least I'll spend my last months in luxury," her mother said with a wry smile. She seemed to have aged, her skin translucent, and her voice frail.

Fearful their time together could be shorter than the doctors had predicted, Emma put on her best face. "Let's make that years."

CHAPTER

9

"WHAT ARE YOU WRITING, sweetheart?" Her mother's voice, coming from the adjacent bedroom, was barely audible.

Emma jumped up from behind the computer Jesse had set up in the living room. They'd been here six weeks, and she found it increasingly difficult to go to work. Although Rick was more than capable of taking care of her mother, he couldn't be there every day. Sue expressed her understanding of the situation. She'd hired temporary help to fill in whenever Emma needed to stay with her mother, guaranteeing her job remained hers until she was ready to return to work full time.

She walked into her mother's bedroom, opening the curtains to let sunlight stream in. "Just working on one of Jesse's speeches."

"I thought you were working on that article about the renovation of the library?" her mother replied as she petted

Bert. Her frail hand trembled. Lately, the cat seemed unwilling to leave her side. "Didn't you promise Sue it would be ready before the end of the week?"

Emma sat down next to her mother on the hospital bed. "Don't you remember? I submitted that several days ago."

Her mother's eyes glazed over. "You did?"

"How are you feeling, Mom? Can I get you anything from the kitchen? I heard Carlton talk about a strawberry-rhubarb cobbler."

It took a few seconds before her mother answered. Her health in rapid decline, she'd slept during most of the last three days. Rick had been reluctant to take his day off and talked about bringing in hospice. Emma found it too soon. The doctors had promised them six months. They still had three left.

"Cobbler? That sounds delicious."

"How about a cup of chamomile tea with that?"

The guest house had become a refuge, where they reminisced about the past and recalled long forgotten memories. They made the most out of every day. Gratitude for Jesse filled her heart, because he'd given them the opportunity to live there.

Her mother gave her a warm smile. "Thank you for taking such excellent care of me, sweetheart. I love you so much."

"I love you too, Mom," Emma replied, her heart breaking. She knew their days of exchanging these precious words were dwindling away. After blowing her a kiss, Emma left the guest house and headed through the backyard to the kitchen in the main house. The grass and flower beds were damp from the sprinklers, giving the garden a fresh and rich smell. Two butterflies flitted from flower to flower, and birds chirped in the trees. The longest day of the year was behind them. Summer had definitely made its entry.

Balancing the tray with two pieces of pie, Emma opened the door.

"I'm back," she called out, placing the tray on the kitchen counter before heading into her mother's bedroom. She pressed the UP arrow on the electric hospital bed remote to raise the bed under her mother's head.

"Maybe we should go outside for a little while this afternoon. The garden is so beautiful, bright with colors and birds chirping in the trees." She let go of the button. "Are you comfortable like this? Mom? Are you okay? Mom?"

With her heart jumping up in her throat, she touched her shoulder. "Mom!"

Her mother's face appeared peaceful, her hands resting comfortably on the pristine white sheets. Emma clutched one of them. An overwhelming emptiness engulfed her when she touched her mother's cold skin. Whimpering, she sagged down onto the bed, took her into her arms and held on tight, unwilling to let go and face life without her.

Jesse found her an hour later. He gently touched her shoulder. "I'm so sorry, Emma. So sorry."

Emma stared into nothingness. Her mom's body had gotten cold, only still warm where she'd rested against it. "They said six months. It has barely been two." Pain and anger laced her words.

Coaxing her up in a sitting position, he pulled her up against him. "You're in shock and freezing." His strong hands stroked her back. "Let's go to the house and get you warmed up."

"No, I can't leave my mom," she protested and tried to free herself as he led her outside. "Please, let me stay with her. She needs me . . ."

Jesse did what he could to soothe her. "I understand what you're going through, honey. I'm so sorry. I know how difficult this is." He closed the door behind them, the click of the hardware emphasizing the finality of the situation. "There's nothing you can do for her anymore. Your mother is gone, and arrangements need to be made." With his arm around her shoulders, he guided her to the house and into his study, easing her down onto the soft leather couch. After squeezing her shoulder, he walked to the liquor cabinet and poured her a stiff drink.

"I was only gone for a few minutes . . ."

Jesse sat down next to her and pushed the glass into her trembling hands, encouraging her to take a sip.

The unfamiliar vodka was strong and burned its way down into her stomach.

"You have to believe she's in heaven and reunited with her loving husband."

With unseeing eyes, her back as straight as a rod, she stared blankly.

He raised the glass up to her lips for the second time. "Don't worry about anything, Emma. I'm here for you."

After the third sip, the warmth of the alcohol spread through her veins and she felt its calming effect. With a deep sigh, she dropped her head and her shoulders sagged forward.

Jesse stood. "I'll call our family doctor and make the necessary phone calls. But first, I'll call my mother and ask her to come, to keep you company. In the meantime, just try to relax."

Left alone, she remained still, deflated, listless, and empty, her hands folded in her lap. A single tear rolled down her cheek. "Please God, take care of my mother. She deserves it."

CHAPTER

10

LOUD PURRING IN HER EAR awakened Emma the next morning. She opened her eyes and found Bert on the other pillow of the king-size bed. "Who let you into the house?"

Jesse's parents had rushed home from Washington D.C. after hearing the news. They'd insisted she spend the night in their son's bedroom, telling her she wouldn't want to stay by herself in the guest house where her mother had just passed away. Too distraught to argue, she'd let Jesse's mother usher her upstairs.

With her head pounding and her brain in a fog, she vaguely remembered the slice of pizza Jesse had forced her to eat. Followed by a second and a third stiff drink. The alcohol had kept her in a daze most of the night. Now that the effect had worn off, she recalled how she'd embarrassed herself last night.

Jesse had come in to check on her. He'd kissed her forehead, as if she was a child. "Everything will be fine, sweetheart. If you need me, I'll be on the couch in my office."

Her heart had cried out. Yes, she needed him, but not downstairs. Clinging to his shoulders, she'd begged him to take her in his arms and stay, but he'd pried himself loose with a grave smile, telling her it wouldn't be appropriate. From the threshold, he'd blown her a kiss before closing the door. While she listened to his receding footsteps, a flicker of resentment nestled in her heart. What kind of man was he to refuse her comfort and love while she mourned in his bed?

Deeply disappointed, she stared at the empty pillow next to her. For weeks, she had fantasized about spending the night in his bed. Now she had. Alone. It had been the most horrible and lonely night of her life, her heart filled with grief, her brain intoxicated from too much alcohol.

Bert licked her cheek, then curled up in the crook of her neck. She wrapped her arm around the purring cat and pulled him down, closer to her body.

Aware that they expected her downstairs, Emma dragged herself out of bed and into the bathroom. The mirror reflected a pale face with deep shadows under the eyes. She pinched her cheeks to bring a little color to them. It didn't help. In the hope a shower would clear her mind, she turned on the water. The jetting spray of the hot water stung her skin. It felt good to feel physical discomfort; it brought her back to life.

Bert poked a curious head around the door and walked in. At his leisure, he sniffed around until he settled on top of the soft bath rug to groom himself. He seemed so out of place in the stunning porcelain and bronze bathroom, she couldn't help but crack a smile.

"We'll get through this," she told him. "Jesse is loving and considerate, and his parents are sweet and welcoming. I'll get married soon, and they'll be our new family."

⁓⁓

Emma stood at her mother's gravesite four days later, clutching Jesse's hand in her right and his mother's hand in her left. Through her pain, she felt gratitude for Jesse. He'd taken care of all the arrangements, making sure everything coincided with her mom's life as a devout Catholic. Emma knew she would have appreciated the entire service, especially with some rites in Latin.

A black limousine drove them from the cemetery to the funeral hall for the reception. Jesse sat next to her, handsome as always in his black suit, patting her hand and handing her a tissue whenever her tears began to flow.

Broken spirited, she moved through the motions of the day, thankful for Jesse's supporting presence. His quiet strength comforted her as she shook hands with hundreds of people. A few of her mother's friends, her old boyfriend James, Sue, and several friends and colleagues from the library came to pay their respects. Besides them, the only two other familiar faces in the crowd were Travis and Ruben Templeton.

Who are all these people? she wondered. *Jesse didn't have much family, and surely he couldn't have that many friends.*

"Despite your overwhelming grief, you look composed and beautiful," Ruben assured her after giving his condolences.

The effort of suppressing her tears had been exhausting, and she appreciated his kind words. "Thank you, Ruben," she replied and looked around for Carly.

"We broke up," Ruben said.

When she reached out to touch his shoulder, he avoided her eyes, shrugged and turned toward Jesse. The men hugged before Ruben disappeared into the crowd.

"Looks like breaking up with Carly hurt Ruben a lot. Did you see the haunted expression in his eyes?" Emma commented.

For a moment Jesse closed his eyes. When he opened them, she detected his sadness, the two lines between his brows more pronounced. "You're not the only one who has to deal with tragedy, Emma," he said.

The tone of his voice sounded accusatory, instead of comforting and understanding. She immediately wanted to withdraw into her shell. Her life had been uprooted, and she couldn't handle criticism right now. Especially not from him.

"I know that," she replied. Her exhaustion was apparent. Each night she'd spent in Jesse's bed, alone, had been fidgety and lonely. They would be husband and wife in ten days. Why couldn't he stay with her? No one would ever find out. Besides, it was the twenty-first century, where people were tolerant and modern in their thinking, not the middle ages.

"What are those photographers doing here?" she demanded. "It's such an invasion of privacy. I want them gone."

Jesse gave her a long stare, his expression absent of emotion. "You know you're involved with a man from a well-known family—a man who's running for mayor. People want to read about what's happening in our lives."

She shuddered at the thought of her grief openly displayed in the newspaper, her tears seen by everyone watching the news. They weren't the Kardashians or royalty. Why couldn't he just send them away if that's what she wanted?

"I can tell you're upset," Jesse continued, drawing her into his arms to calm her. "Be strong, sweetheart. We'll get through this."

Choking on her emotions, she rested her cheek against the lapel of his black suit jacket, grateful at least not to have to face the future alone.

CHAPTER

11

THEIR WEDDING DAY fast approached. Each day Emma became more anxious. Instead of feeling closer to Jesse since her mother's passing, they'd only grown further apart. He seemed distracted, his mind elsewhere, closing himself off from her.

What disturbed her most was the glint of sadness in his eyes she detected on the rare occasion when he let his guard down. Something bothered him, and it had bothered him for quite a while. But he kept it to himself and shrugged off her concern with a winning smile. He wasn't fooling her. Even with her grief and their rushed wedding arrangements, she knew with certainty that something was wrong. She hated that he shut her out and wondered if his distance and preoccupation had something to do with the campaign heating up. Andrew Voss, his contender, turned out to be a strong candidate. People flocked to him, drawn by his charisma and powerful words. Fortunately, public opinion had gone up dramatically in favor of Jesse after the news of her mother's passing. A few days later, their wedding plans appeared on the front page of the newspaper, with a picture of the two of them, holding hands. Jesse expressed his pleasure, cutting the article out. Relieved to see him happier than he'd been in weeks, she hoped that whatever had bothered him was resolved.

When their wedding day arrived, Emma opened the curtains after a restless night filled with doubts and uncertainty. She felt alone and unprepared for what was to come, and still struggled to comprehend why Jesse had chosen her over many other attractive, intelligent women. He assured her it was because he'd fallen head over heels for her, and that feelings like love, affection, and desire couldn't be rationalized or explained. He sounded truthful, but why didn't his words resonate? Why didn't he act on those feelings? Since she'd agreed to marry him, he'd barely touched her. Instead, he'd been distant and kept to himself, shutting her out.

"Don't worry about the details of the wedding. My mother is taking care of everything," he answered every time she asked him about it.

He also didn't want to talk about their future home.

"We'll decide on that another day. I'm too busy to make such an important decision right now."

Her in-laws were gone most of the time and the family residence was huge, but she longed for a house of their own. A place where she could be herself instead of feeling like a visitor. Especially since her in-laws started to share their sometimes unbridled negative comments about minorities and the LGBT-community in her presence. *How could such upstanding, highly-educated people talk that way behind closed doors*, she wondered.

"Stop pushing me around," Jesse said when she showed him the homes she'd found online.

The wall he'd built around himself seemed impenetrable, and she felt like a nuisance instead of his future wife.

Her throat constricted with doubt and fear. Was she making a huge mistake? Could she go on with this marriage?

Shivering in her cotton nightgown, she gazed out over the backyard. From the second-floor bedroom window she could easily look over the green shrubs that bordered the property, and into Travis Templeton's backyard. A terrace door opened. Ruben stepped out, wearing a long black bathrobe that resembled a Japanese kimono.

She took a step back, afraid he might see her, but he didn't glance in her direction. Instead, he sank down into one of the Adirondack deck chairs, rested his elbows on his knees, and hung his head. His demeanor spoke of despair and defeat. She hadn't seen him since her mother's funeral, but even from this distance she could tell he had lost weight. Jesse had told her Carly was staying with relatives in Europe. If he was so miserable, Emma wondered why he'd broken up with her.

You're not the only one who's missing Carly, she thought, wishing her friend could be here today.

Carly had boxed up all Emma's cardigans, pleated skirts, and sensible shoes for donation, and helped her to purchase a completely new wardrobe. Emma had undergone a metamorphosis. At a salon, the stylist had cut and layered her hair. With just enough length to still arrange it in a ponytail, it didn't weigh down her naturally wavy locks, and perfectly framed her face. After a mani-pedi, they'd given her a class in applying flawless makeup. She would test her new skill today.

Not wanting to spy on Ruben any longer, she turned away from the window and looked at her wedding dress.

With the recent death of her mother, Mrs. Kimball had advised that people would frown upon an extravagant wedding display. Instead of choosing the long soft lace gown swathed in ivory floral embroidery she fell in love with, Emma agreed with the recommended skirt suit. The fitted jacket framed her body gracefully. The skirt flowed into a charming flounce hem around her legs, the lace fabric soft and feminine.

Emma's throat constricted, having to get ready for the big day by herself. She missed her mother terribly. She needed her help to chase away the misgivings, and to remind her that Jesse was an attractive, well-respected man with a glorious future ahead of him. His reputation was immaculate, without scandals, former wives, children, or estranged lovers so many other newlyweds had to worry about. She should count herself lucky, she reminded herself.

Determined not to let anything ruin her day, she straightened her shoulders and prepared to become Mrs. Jesse Kimball.

CHAPTER

12

ARTICLE FROM THE HEEMSTEAD CHRONICLE:

Jesse Kimball III, one of Heemstead's most eligible bachelors, married today.

The weather forecast had called for occasional July showers, but the rain didn't let up, forcing the couple at the last minute to move their garden wedding at the groom's parents' estate to the courthouse.

The groom, strikingly handsome in a classic double-breasted tuxedo and white dress-shirt, a bowtie adding to his style and elegance, had to rush to escape the downpour. His bride, Emma Bowen, dressed in a beautifully tailored ivory skirt suit, joined him, protecting her lovely floral bouquet of rich reds, fiery oranges, and beautiful yellows from the wicked wind. Helpful friends straightened out their clothes and hair, making them ready for the official ceremony inside.

In respect of the recent loss of the bride's mother, they

exchanged traditional vows, the ceremony kept simple and short.

Corporate attorney Ruben Templeton, a lifelong friend, stood as a witness for Jesse Kimball III, and Sue Stremler, a librarian at the Heemstead University, witnessed for the lovely bride, Emma Bowen. Jesse's parents, Senator and Mrs. Kimball, looked on with pride.

Showered with colorful confetti, the newlyweds left the courthouse and drove to the Northwood Country Club for the reception, attended by several hundred people.

Afterwards followed a six-course dinner for family and close friends, preceding a party with live music from the Big River Blues Band.

Because of the upcoming mayoral election and Mr. Kimball's busy schedule, the couple decided to enjoy their honeymoon later this year, their first night as husband and wife in the bridal suite of the luxurious Elsevier Suites Hotel.

CHAPTER

13

UNSTEADY ON HIS FEET, Jesse collected the keycard for the bridal suite at reception in Heemstead's most prestigious hotel, The Elsevier Suites. Since the moment they'd exchanged their wedding vows, Emma hadn't seen him without a glass of wine in his hand. He was wasted. With her arm around his waist, she guided him into the elevator and up to the top floor.

"Wasn't it a magnificent party?" he slurred.

At the door of the bridal suite, he struggled to get the keycard in the slide to unlock it.

"Let me take that from you," she said.

"Getting bossy already?" Jesse grinned, swaying back and forth.

She opened the door and they entered the suite. Soft lights glowed inside. A four-poster king-sized bed dominated the space, the white sheets invitingly smooth and crisp. Longing to slip between them and forget about her intoxicated husband and the entire world washed over her as the long day played through her head. From the minute she woke up, it had rained constantly. Jesse's mother had been distraught, having to move the wedding to the courthouse at the last minute. Emma had been disappointed, too. The lovely garden looked like a tornado had ripped through it, and all the changes that needed to be made had added stress she didn't need. But then she remembered reading once that rain on your wedding day meant good luck. She'd told everyone exactly that, and other than trying to keep her spirit up, let it all come over her. Jesse's mother didn't tolerate interference and stayed in charge, adjusting Emma's dress and hair constantly, ordering people around, calling for transportation, and arranging for the flowers to be moved.

"My mother is completely in her element. She excels under stress," Jesse had smiled with pride.

Emma had been too weary to object to anything Sarah Kimball decided on. To argue over the kind of wedding cake, the choice of music, or the color of the flowers had only seemed trivial. Besides, she had no experience with any of it, and she'd gone with the flow, playing her part. The Kimballs didn't expect anything else.

She rubbed her jaw, still aching from the continuous smile plastered on her face, and then swallowed with difficulty. Her vocal cords were raw from overuse, and tension knotted the muscles of her neck and shoulders. She needed sleep more than anything.

Whistling one of the band's tunes, Jesse stumbled his way to the table. On top was a basket overflowing with fresh fruit, a bottle of champagne in a bucket of ice, two glasses, and a crystal bowl filled with chocolates. He opened one of the chocolate wrappers and stuck the bonbon in his mouth, seemingly not plagued by doubts or unease.

She fumbled with the gorgeous rose gold wedding ring on her third finger, her shoulders hunched and her face tense.

Had she really married Jesse?

"Just as sweet as you." He grinned around his mouthful and reached for the champagne bottle. If his intent was the theatrical effect of a champagne shower, he succeeded. The cork gave a loud pop and flew away, followed by a spray of foam and sparkling liquid. He ignored the mess and filled two glasses. With a big gulp, he emptied his.

"Oops, I forgot to toast."

He filled his glass back up and handed her the other one. "You were a beautiful bride, Emma. I think I made the right choice."

He attempted to give her a half-kiss on the mouth and downed his second glass. "Didn't you love the music tonight?" He made a few seductive dance moves with his hips while taking off his suit jacket. With a sway of his arm, he threw it toward a chair. It landed on the floor. Next, he loosened his tie and unbuttoned his shirt. "I stink and need a shower, honey. Don't go anywhere. I'll be right back."

With her champagne still untouched, she watched the bathroom door close behind him, her stomach tight in a knot. What was she supposed to do now? The hotel staff had delivered their luggage to their room. Inside her suitcase was a sexy black flowered negligee, purchased especially for her wedding night. Should she put it on, or should she follow him into the shower? Or should she forget about the shower and the negligee, strip, and lie down in bed, naked, waiting for him to join her?

The click of the bathroom door made her jump. Jesse appeared in a cloud of steam, his wet hair sticking in every direction, as if he'd rubbed it vigorously. Only dressed in a towel with an embroidered hotel logo loosely tied around his waist, she took a good look at his broad shoulders and bare chest.

Noticing her stare, he gave her a lazy smile. "If you want to use the bathroom, go right ahead."

Forcing a calm she didn't feel, she smiled back at him. "Thanks, I will." She rummaged through her suitcase in search of her toilet bag when the lights dimmed.

"This is more romantic. What do you think, darling?"

"I'll only be a minute," she replied, feeling awkward. In the bathroom, she looked at herself in the fogged-up mirror.

"Emma?" she asked her reflection. "What are you doing here?"

She turned her back on her own image and stepped into the shower, hoping to unwind and relax underneath the strong spray of hot water. It would be okay. It was normal for a bride to be nervous and have second thoughts. People didn't make a lifelong commitment every day.

Prolonging the inevitable, she lingered in the bathroom until she'd combed her hair three times, had dried each toe several times, and couldn't avoid the moment of truth any longer. Her stomach flip-flopped as she entered the bedroom. All the lights were out, the furniture outlined by the pale, luminous shimmer of moonlight.

In the deep silence, she waited for her eyes to adjust before she approached the bed. A faint, even breathing came from Jesse. His mouth stood slightly open, his features relaxed. He didn't stir when she touched his shoulder. "Jesse?" she whispered, but no answer came.

Not knowing what to do, she roamed around the suite in total silence, her bare feet sinking into the thick carpet. Clouds drifted in front of the moon, giving the room an eerie glow. As if she floated in midair, her existence surreal, her life a fantasy, and Jesse and their wedding day the products of her overactive imagination. Barely able to keep it together, she shivered in her negligee, wanting to scream or cry or die. With her last bit of energy spent, she slipped into bed beside her sleeping husband. The sheets smelled like summer flowers, the mattress soft and welcoming. With her head on the pillow, she warily placed her hand on his hip, torn between wanting him to awaken and praying he wouldn't.

"Room service."

Emma stretched and yawned, then opened her eyes at the smell of fresh coffee, bacon and eggs.

Dressed in a casual suit, Jesse tipped the waiter and dismissed him with a flip of his hand. After the door closed, he looked at Emma as she sat up, raking her fingers through her tangled hair.

"Finally, you're awake." He opened the curtains all the way, allowing sunlight to flood the room. "I didn't know what you like for breakfast, so I ordered sausage, bacon, eggs, pancakes and fruit." He filled two glasses with orange juice and then poured coffee.

"How long have you been up?" she asked, surprised to see how well he looked considering the amount of alcohol he'd consumed.

"At least an hour, Sleeping Beauty." He smiled, avoiding

her inquisitive stare. It was obvious he didn't want to talk about last night. Probably embarrassed, she thought.

In her sexy black flowered negligee, she stepped over his discarded wedding clothes still scattered on the floor. He didn't even look in her direction. Instead, he focused on his laptop and scrolled through a website.

Rejected at his lack of attention, she disappeared into the bathroom, splashed cold water on her face and pulled a comb through her hair. Behind the door on a hanger, she found a luxurious white bathrobe and swathed herself in it before she joined him at the breakfast table.

"You must try these eggs," he said in between bites. "And this is the crispiest, most delicious bacon I've ever eaten."

Breakfast looked inviting, but she felt tense, and her hungry stomach now protested. Instead of the eggs and bacon, she buttered an English muffin and sipped her orange juice.

"You looked lovely yesterday, Emma," he complimented her. "The wedding suit my mom picked out for you is precisely what I had in mind."

For months, her body and soul had cried out to experience closeness with Jesse. To feel his hands on her naked skin, to touch him intimately, and get to know every nuance of his personality.

In the harsh morning light, while he complimented his mother on the choice of her wedding dress, Emma felt dejected. All she could figure out was that her sex-appeal was so insignificant that not even her husband was interested enough to make love to her on their wedding night.

Desperate for the smallest praise, a kind word, a tiny inclination that he cared for her, her gaze was glued to his lips. Lips she wanted to feel on her breasts while he caressed her.

While she sunk her fingers in the strong muscles of his back.

"Thank you, Jesse," she replied, fighting to keep her voice steady. "You looked very handsome yourself."

"Of course." He averted his eyes back to his laptop.

Her heart sank. God, she sounded pathetic, begging for his attention, fishing for compliments. Wasn't she better than that? Her gloomy thoughts nearly made her burst into tears. She swallowed the lump in her throat.

He looked up and reached across the table to touch her hand. "Are you thinking about your mother?" His voice held a wealth of empathy, the expression on his face filled with concern. "You have to believe she was there in spirit, Emma. Just like she always will be."

His compassion and thoughtful words lifted her spirit. This was the tender, caring man she'd come to adore. Maybe not everything was lost? Perhaps he only wanted to give her more time to grieve.

With his warm gaze on her face, he raised her hand and kissed her palm. "I know these last few months have been difficult, but from now on it'll all be better."

She touched the side of his face with her fingertips, his skin warm and soft against her palm. Her breathing quickened, and a gentle throbbing of excitement stirred between her legs. It was still early; they could remain in their room for at least a few more hours. She lowered her right shoulder just enough for the bathrobe to slip down and expose the curve of her neck.

Pulling back, Jesse reached for a napkin and wiped his mouth. "I hate to rush you, but we need to leave as soon as possible. Channel 41 has invited us to the studio for an interview at eleven."

CHAPTER

14

THE INTERVIEW LASTED the entire afternoon. They were both tired by the time they came home.

Carlton was busy in the kitchen, preparing dinner. Tomorrow, Jesse's parents would return to their home in Washington D.C., taking him with them.

"Does Carlton always leave together with your parents?" Emma asked.

Jesse nodded. "He splits his time between here and there. Besides a cleaning lady, who comes in every morning, I take care of myself when my parents are gone. It would be nice if you'll take care of the cooking from now on. I'm tired of microwaved meals."

Emma enjoyed cooking. "I would be happy to."

They spent the entire evening with Jesse's parents. By the time they retired, Emma couldn't keep her eyes open and fell asleep right away, exhausted.

The next morning, voices and the slamming of car doors outside awakened her. A car drove off and she heard the front door close. Eight o'clock already? She had wanted to be there, to say goodbye to her in-laws.

She dressed in a hurry and headed downstairs. Jesse sat at the breakfast table, drinking a cup of coffee, the newspaper in front of him.

He looked up. "My parents just left."

"Why didn't you wake me?"

The day was off to a bad start, the three dirty breakfast plates like accusing fingers.

He folded the paper and stood. "There's plenty of food. Help yourself. I'll be in my office, preparing for tonight's fundraiser. Tomorrow, I'll go back to work and life will return to normal."

After he left, she sat down, poured herself a cup of lukewarm coffee from the thermos, and nibbled on a piece of toast. The house was quiet with everyone gone. Not a sound penetrated through the walls, the newspaper her only distraction. Man killed in early morning crash. Grandson plotted to murder grandparents. More rain in the forecast for today. The news didn't cheer her up.

Ten minutes crawled by, the silence becoming oppressive, until a car pulled into the driveway. It was Tonya, one of the cleaning ladies. She entered the house through the backdoor. Emma met her in the kitchen.

"Good morning, Ms. Bowen," Tonya said. "How are you?"

"I'm fine, Tonya. Mr. and Mrs. Kimball went back to D.C. I assume it's best you take care of their quarters."

"Of course," Tonya replied. Before she left, she turned on her heel. "I'm sorry, Ma'am. I forgot about your wedding yesterday. Congratulations. I hope the two of you will be very happy together."

The smirk on the young woman's face startled Emma. *What was that about?* She didn't dare to ask.

By herself again, she heated water for a fresh cup of tea. It seemed with her in-law's departure, the house had become an empty shell. It dismayed her she felt that way, instead of excitement at the prospect of being alone with her husband.

Half an hour later, she headed up to their bedroom, made the bed, folded some clothes, and cleaned the bathroom. With everything tidy, she went downstairs to talk to Jesse. If this indicated how her days would transpire from now on, she needed to find something to do. Sue had promised her job would be available by the time she was ready. She felt ready now.

The door to his office stood ajar. Without hesitation, she walked inside.

He looked up from his computer screen. "I'm glad you're here. I want you to improve upon my speech. I can't get it right."

"Of course. I'm happy to help. You know that," she said. "Do you want me to use your computer?"

He shook his head. "No, with my parents gone, use their office. I'll make the document shareable."

Before she left, she lingered by the door. "I was thinking about going back to work in the library."

He folded his hands in front of him on his desktop. "That's not happening. I told Sue you won't return to work and to look for your replacement."

Her jaw dropped. "You did what?"

A blank stare appeared on his face. "Sit down, Emma. I want to set some ground rules."

Taken by surprise, she sunk into the chair in front of his desk.

"First, I want you to be available for me at all times. Second, there will be no whining about intimacy. I'm not a passionate man and hardly ever in the mood. Third, I always need to know where you are and expect to be informed whenever you wish to leave the house. That's it for now."

The silence his statement caused seemed to stretch forever.

"I can tell you're shocked," he said in a flat voice, his eyes empty. "Get used to it."

She trembled in her seat, her emotions in disarray. "What's going on Jesse? I don't understand."

"Sorry, Emma. I'm busy and want to be left alone, please." He waved her off before returning his attention to his computer screen.

Stiff-limbed, she stood and walked out of his office.

In the hallway, she ran into Tonya. The young woman looked away, but not before Emma had seen another sneer on her face.

"I hope you're not eavesdropping," Emma snarled, close to shattering into a million pieces. With every inch of willpower, she straightened her shoulders. "Get to work!"

Immediately ashamed of her rude behavior, she said, "I'm sorry. I don't know why I said that."

This time, instead of disrespect, Emma noticed empathy in her eyes.

"No, I'm sorry, Mrs. Kimball. Please, let me know if you need anything."

Tonya rushed off, leaving Emma in the middle of the empty

hallway, the young woman's running footsteps sounding hollow against the tiles.

⚬⚬⚬

The rest of the day passed in a blur. Emma struggled to believe the distant man she shared lunch and dinner with was her husband. This wasn't how she'd imagined her marriage. She'd assumed he would relax in her company and that they would finally grow closer. The opposite was true. He stayed silent, dismissing every effort to start a conversation, his cell phone more important than her presence.

"You don't like dinner?" she asked, the carefully prepared meatloaf and potatoes only half eaten still on his plate.

"It was fine, but I prefer chicken and fish," he said, dropping his napkin on the floor as he left the dining room.

"I don't understand. Why are you behaving this way?" she asked, following him. He seemed like a different man from the one she'd fallen in love with.

Something in her voice made him stop. He turned around and stared at her, rolling his shoulders as though they ached. "Sorry I can't be the man you want me to be, Emma. Just be patient. One day it'll all make sense."

Emma's lips tilted at the corners as relief washed over her. Jesse dealt with a problem, probably so significant or secret that he couldn't talk about it. If she gave him space, and proved to him he could trust her, he would confide in her. Until then, she had to have faith, support him, and do the best she could.

"I'll be there for you whenever you need me, Jesse," she smiled. "I love you."

"That's exactly what I want to hear," he replied.

CHAPTER

15

OVER THE NEXT WEEK, Jesse left the house each morning to work at his financial group downtown. Emma stayed home to write his speeches, maintain and improve his online presence, and reply to his emails. He didn't return until dinner and left immediately afterwards. Most evenings, he slipped in bed after she already slept, or he spent the night on the couch in his office. The only activity they did together, an early morning run.

"We have another important political event tonight," Jesse said. "I like that white dress. Be ready at five."

Nothing he ever said was a request, just an order, the look in his eyes making it clear he demanded obedience, a discussion out of the question.

She wanted to protest, to tell him how she felt, but swallowed her pride. Again.

Although she was a bit of a recluse and enjoyed alone time,

it had always been by choice. Now it was forced upon her, and she looked forward to the opportunity to leave the house. To see someone else besides the housekeeper, the gardener, or the man delivering the groceries she'd ordered online.

"I was thinking, Jesse, couldn't we move into the guesthouse together? It's so cozy and it will make me feel closer to my mom."

He glanced up from his paperwork, seemingly surprised she was still there, and sighed, rubbing his forehead. "How many times do I have to tell you I have more important things on my mind?"

Emma stiffened and he heaved another sigh. "Please, just let it go for now, would you?"

Jesse seemed busier than ever, with long days at the office and events he had to attend each night, his face strained, his manner short, the lines around his eyes deepened. She was exhausted, too. From the endless tension, from waiting for him, longing for a normal relationship, and from keeping up appearances. She was so lonely. Not once had he taken her into his arms, spoken kindly, or shown affection. Not once had he displayed any gratitude for the work she did, the food she prepared, or the efforts she made to make their relationship work. It was as if he lived on autopilot, with his mind elsewhere, his face only showing genuine emotion at public appearances.

Three weeks later, on the small stage set up outside for the two mayoral candidates, Jesse flashed his confident, engaging smile.

"Thanks for all your support," he spoke into the microphone before looking down at Emma. He lowered his head. With exquisite sweetness, he pressed his lips onto hers. Cameras flashed as he pulled her closer, his mouth covering hers.

The warm, heady sensation that spread through her body made her forget the evening chill and his constant, emotional distance. She settled into his embrace, her unfulfilled longing for him erupting like a volcano.

Just as unexpectedly, he broke off the kiss, leaving her mouth burning and her knees weak. Anger flared inside her. She was done playing his games, but with hundreds of eyes focused on them, it wasn't the time to start a fight.

With her hand in his, they descended the steps and waved their goodbyes at the crowd while they walked toward his parked car. He opened the door for her, evading her accusing stare.

"You were wonderful," he said as they drove off. "I could tell the people loved you."

Emma didn't answer. She stared vacantly at the passing landscape. Raindrops slid down the window, reminding her of tears and adding to the despair that had been her companion since their wedding day.

Every time Jesse looked at her, she hoped he would finally take her in his arms and make her his. But every time he turned his back to her, his excuses vague—too tired, too late, I have a nasty cough. It wasn't normal. Something was very, very wrong.

The drive home took less than ten minutes. It couldn't go fast enough, the atmosphere frigid and laden with tension. When they arrived, there were cars parked everywhere.

"I hope you didn't forget about the party?" Jesse said. His parents had returned from Washington D.C. for a few days, the empty house filled with laughter, the meals extravagant.

"Of course not," she lied.

Jesse took her hand and pulled her with him into the crowd. They were welcomed as celebrities, jokes and well wishes coming their way.

The entire charade saddened her, the fake smile on her face hurting her jaws. She ate a few bites from the buffet and sipped from her second glass of merlot, keeping up the front of a happy newlywed, while all she wanted was to be left alone, or to confront Jesse. An honest conversation was long overdue.

From a distance, she studied him as he talked to Ruben, their heads close together. Ruben had showed up with a sexy, dark-haired beauty in a tight red dress, her heels so high it was amazing she could walk in them.

The woman in red pulled out a lipstick to fix her already perfect makeup. Is she what men wanted? Emma wondered with disdain. A gorgeous, brainless creature with fake physical attributes they could show off to their peers? Should she display her cleavage, pout her lips, and drape herself around Jesse's neck? Would he then finally pay attention to her?

Frustrated and fed up with his lack of interest, she emptied her third glass of wine and headed in his direction. "Can you pour me another glass, sweetheart?" A little unstable on her feet, she grabbed his arm for support.

"Maybe you already had one too many," he whispered, a frown of disapproval on his face. He took her arm and guided her toward a chair.

"I don't want to sit," she protested.

His grip around her arm tightened. "You're drunk. I think it's best you excuse yourself and go to bed. It's been a long day.

Everyone will understand." He took her empty glass and placed it on the table.

"Only if you join me," she replied, her bottled-up frustration spilling over.

Jesse narrowed his eyes. "Stop making a scene. You're embarrassing me."

She tried to free herself, but his fingers wrapped viselike around her arm as he pulled her from the dining room into the hall. After the door closed behind them, he forced her around to face him, his hands gripping her upper arms. "How much did you have to drink?"

"Enough to realize you must get your fill from someone other than your wife," she snarled and jerked free of his tight grip.

His face drained of color. "What are you talking about?"

"It's simple," she hissed, rubbing her arms where his fingers had left red marks. "We're married for an entire month and you haven't even tried to touch me. Either you're getting it somewhere else, or you're having a serious problem."

"Maybe we should continue this conversation in privacy," Jesse replied. He pulled her up the stairs and into their bedroom. After he let go of her arm, he locked the door behind them. "Since you're so desperate, take off your clothes, lie down on the bed and I'll give you what you want."

At the sight of the angry stranger in front of her, her confidence evaporated, her alcohol-fueled courage disappeared like a wisp of smoke. "I'm not desperate."

He scoffed. "You've been begging for it for months, and I'm ready."

Her eyes widened as he took off his suit jacket and jerked on his tie. "What are you doing?"

His features were composed when he faced her. "I'm complying with my wife's wishes and taking what's mine." He unbuttoned his shirt, his gaze focused on the generous swell of her breasts. "Come on, sweetheart. Let's see what you're made of."

She backed away until she bumped into the bed. "But this is not how I want it."

With an impatient gesture, he threw his arms up in the air. "Then what do you want?"

She looked down at her feet, avoiding his icy blue stare. "I . . . I want it to be romantic."

"Romantic?" His terse laugh made her cringe. "We have guests. I don't have time for this." With one swift movement he flung her onto the bed where she landed on the soft, colorful comforter.

"Please, Jesse, you don't want to do this," she cried out. "I'm sorry I pressured you."

He followed her onto the bed, reaching out. "You wanted it, and now you're getting it, so stop your whining."

She quickly crawled out of his reach, but he came after her, grabbing her hips between his powerful hands. In search of something to hold onto, her fingers clawed at the bedspread. "No, no," she cried, too panicked to coordinate her movements.

His arm went around her body as he climbed on top of her, his strong fingers pushing up her skirt. She was no match for his brutal strength, and she heard the lace of her panties give way.

"Don't do this. Please, stop it!" she screamed.

His hand closed over her mouth. "You want everyone to hear I'm finally having some fun," he hissed in her ear, his body weight crushing her. "Shut your fucking mouth." He thrusted his crotch several times against her buttocks, his breathing noticeably heavy. "You've ever done it from behind?"

For a second, he shifted his weight off her to fumble with his zipper. Overcome with terror, she took advantage of his momentary distraction, and rolled onto her back, kicking at him with both feet. "How dare you? Let me go!"

He cursed when she hit his shoulder with her heel. "Bitch!" With a swift movement he lifted himself up and backhanded her.

Stars exploded in her brain. "You bastard," she whimpered, reaching for her burning cheek.

"What's gotten into you?" Jesse roared. "That's not the way to treat your husband when he finally gives you what you want?" He stared at her with resentment, his fists clenched. "Who the hell do you think you are?"

His powerful body exuded masculinity, resentment and anger. He was so strong. He could snap her in two like a twig.

She cowered against the headboard, pushing down her skirt to cover her half-naked body. "I'm sorry," she whispered, her voice constricted with fear. "I shouldn't have challenged you."

"You're pathetic," he snorted, a look of disgust hardening his mouth. "You should see yourself. You're drunk and a blubbering mess. Why do you assume a man would ever want to touch you?"

His words hurt like daggers, crushing her self-esteem, destroying her. With tears streaming down her face, her heart racing, she watched him move away and straighten his shirt.

Why did he treat her like this? Filled with loathing and disdain, hurting her, assaulting her?

"I'll tell our guests you weren't feeling well and went to

bed," Jesse said as he walked out of their bedroom, leaving his tie and suit jacket on the floor.

After the door closed behind him and the sound of his footsteps disappeared, she rushed into the bathroom. The contents of her stomach wound up in the toilet.

CHAPTER

16

EMMA SPENT THE NIGHT in a state of despair, humiliated and afraid, wondering how to deal with Jesse when he returned. He never did. She realized he'd probably slept in his office, as had become the norm.

After checking her appearance in the mirror, she applied makeup to cover the bruise that had formed on her jaw and added a little color to her cheeks. She still looked haggard.

Hoping her in-laws wouldn't notice, she joined them for breakfast before they departed again for Washington D.C.

"You should eat a little more, Emma," her mother-in-law said with genuine concern in her eyes. "It looks like you're losing weight, and you don't have an ounce to spare."

Emma wished she could confide in her but knew it would infuriate Jesse if she complained to his mother. Instead, she only nodded. "I promise to take better care of myself."

She hugged her in-laws and waved them goodbye from the

front door. As the car pulled out of the driveway, a profound sense of loneliness enveloped her. Her shoulders sagged as she walked back inside. Her trust in Jesse was destroyed, the chance for a happy future together ruined. The charade had to end.

Why had she been so stupid not to see that all he wanted was a wife he could manipulate? An innocent library aid without a scandalous past, honored by his attention, who would never speak a cross word or voice her own opinion. A woman he could use as a doormat and show off to the public as the acceptable politician's wife. And that was exactly how it had transpired. She'd been such a fool to fall for his scheme.

That evening, she waited for hours in Jesses's office. At some point he would come home, and her first question would be why he'd married her. He didn't love her. That was clear. After that she would demand they enter therapy with a marriage counselor. Although she feared they'd already reached the point in their relationship where only an annulment of the marriage or a divorce was the option. She didn't want to stay married to a man who didn't want, need, or respect her. A man who more than likely cheated behind her back with a woman he really wanted. A gorgeous female, like the one from last night in the sexy, red dress. A gal with a scandalous past, multiple marriages, maybe even children, who was open to all kinds of games between the sheets. A woman who would never be accepted by his conservative parents.

She'd never experienced physical violence of any sort and now considered him a cold-hearted animal, her self-respect destroyed by his humiliating disregard. She rubbed her jaw, the throbbing pain a constant reminder of his brutal strength. The caring man he'd portrayed to be had only been an act to accomplish a selfish goal, in complete disregard of her feelings and the consequences for her future.

The hands on the clock announced the passage of time. As she waited, she tried to read, the book still on the same page. She glanced at the clock again. Almost ten. The soft comfort of the leather couch beckoned her. Exhausted, she fluffed up the pillow and pulled a blanket around her body. With Bert nestled at her feet, she curled up. She received more love and attention from her cat than from her husband. Was she that tedious and undesirable?

The click of the door handle awakened her from a restless slumber. Jesse walked in, talking on his phone and clearly unaware of her presence.

"I'm sorry we couldn't get together tonight," he said. "I realize I promised, but the meeting lasted much longer than expected." He listened for a few seconds before continuing. "There's nothing more that I want than take you in my arms and fuck you for hours. I love you. You know that. But with this damn marriage you forced upon me, my business dealings, and the upcoming election, it's gotten a lot harder to find any free time for us."

She had no idea who Jesse talked to, but it didn't matter. She'd been right. He had an affair and loved someone else. Why in God's name had he even married her? she wondered for the umpteenth time. Was it forced upon him, as he'd just said? Was that even possible in this day and age? Most certainly not.

"Now listen," Jesse continued. "I understand how hard this is. It's darn difficult for me, too. But save your strength, go to bed, and try to relax. I'll call you tomorrow morning. I promise." Jesse ended the conversation, tossed his phone on his desk with a deep sigh, and yawned.

Wide eyed, she pushed herself into a sitting position. The blanket rustled and the leather of the couch creaked. Jesse whirled around. An accusatory glare came into his eyes at the sight of her. "What the hell are you doing here? Eavesdropping?" He stepped closer to the couch, raising his arm as if he was preparing to hit her.

Frightened, Emma shivered and held her hands up in self-protection. She knew now he didn't care for her one bit, his angry demeanor sufficient proof of the violent temper he'd kept hidden for months.

"I was asleep, so I didn't hear anything," she managed to say. Her teeth chattered so hard that it hurt.

"Get out!" he ordered in a threatening voice. Towering over her, he planted his hands on his hips and glared at her.

Panicked and frozen in place, she stared at him.

"I said, get out." He grabbed her arms and jerked her to her feet.

She trembled violently, her thoughts a muddle of fear and shock.

He waited to give her a few seconds to compose herself. When she didn't move fast enough to the door, he gave her a powerful push.

"No," Emma cried as she tripped over her own feet and fell. Her forehead split open when it banged against the floor. As fast as she could, she scrambled back up, fled the office and ran up the stairs. After she reached the bedroom, she flung the door shut and leaned against it, choking back sobs. Warm blood trickled down her eyebrow, dripping onto her cheek, and her right hip throbbed from crashing onto the floor. Her life had spiraled completely out of control.

She locked the door and walked into the bathroom. At the sight of the blood streaking her face, the haunted look in her eyes, and her ashen complexion, she quickly turned the light off. She'd seen enough.

With a towel pressed against her forehead, she warily made her way to the bed and lay down. Her emotions had never been in such chaotic disarray, the only sound in the darkness her racing heartbeat.

At first light, she removed her wedding ring and placed it on the nightstand next to the bed. It would send a clear message. In front of the walk-in closet, she stood on her toes to pull down one of Jesse's suitcases from the top shelf. She put it on the bed and opened it to throw in a random selection of clothes, socks, underwear, and shoes. After it was almost full, she went into the bathroom to collect a few toiletries, closed the suitcase, and grabbed her purse. She quietly descended the stairs. In the hallway closet, she found her coat and one of Jesse's baseball caps. She put it on top of her head and pulled it down as far as she could.

With a last glance at the closed door of the office, she hesitated. Bert was probably still inside, but she couldn't risk fetching him. Jesse wouldn't allow her to leave. Trusting that Tonya and Carlton would take care of her beloved pet, she walked out. The wheels of the suitcase rolled smoothly down the paved driveway as she pulled it behind her. When she reached the gate, she drew her cell phone from her pocket.

"I would like a taxi to pick me up at the corner of Birch and Spirea Avenue in about fifteen minutes. Is that possible?"

CHAPTER

17

RUBEN TEMPLETON RUSHED into the law firm of his uncle and stopped at the receptionist's desk. She had called over breakfast, to tell him Emma Kimball had requested a meeting and waited for him.

"Where is she?" he asked.

"In the waiting room, Sir. Is that okay?"

He nodded. "Can you show her into my office and bring coffee?" It sounded like an order.

Without waiting for an answer, he opened the door to his office. Full windows offered an expansive view over the city, but he was too agitated to look outside.

"What in the world is she doing here?" he muttered to himself, sinking down into his ergonomic office chair.

A soft knock announced his unexpected visitor.

"Good morning, Emma," he said, recognizing the dark blue New York baseball cap. He'd bought it for Jesse himself. "What a surprise to see you." He waved her toward a chair in front of his desk, wondering why she brought in a suitcase. "Please, take a seat."

Emma's eyes shifted nervously around the room. "Thank you for seeing me, Ruben. I need your help."

He raised an eyebrow at her wrinkled clothes and disheveled appearance. "Of course. What can I do for you?"

She sat as straight as a rod, her hands clutching the handle of the suitcase.

He clicked the pen in his hand several times, suppressing the urge to check the time. In his profession, he primarily worked with males, and the few females he encountered were usually tough broads with hair on their teeth. He had no use for drama and wasn't a patient man.

"Take your time," he said, thinking about his full agenda.

Finally, she spoke up. "I want a divorce."

At her words, his jaw dropped. Had she lost her mind? He struggled to hold his temper in check. "A divorce? After one month of marriage? That's ridiculous."

A single tear rolled down her cheek. She brushed it away with the back of her hand. "He doesn't love me, Ruben. He never did."

Anger built up inside him. He lowered his gaze, so she wouldn't notice. "Of course, he does." He cleared his throat a few times before continuing. "Why else would he have married you?"

"I can come up with several reasons, one of them his desire to have a dutiful, docile wife by his side, who doesn't dare to speak up while he does whatever he pleases," she replied, her eyes bitter. She pulled off the baseball cap so he could see her forehead. "I don't want to spend another night in that house. He hurt me, Ruben. He did."

Ruben's eyes flew open in surprise. "He did that to you?" Agitated, he got up from his chair and paced the floor. "That's completely out of character for Jesse. I have a hard time believing it." He stopped in front of her. "He has too much to lose and would never risk a scandal."

At his harsh words, Emma hunched over in her chair. "I understand how important the election is for him, and I don't want to cause any trouble. That's why I'm reaching out to you instead of bringing this out in the open. You're his best friend. You're a lawyer. I'm sure you know best how to handle this."

A knock on the door distracted them. "That must be the coffee." Ruben opened the door to take the tray. "Hold my calls," he ordered. "I don't want to be disturbed." He placed the tray on the conference table and poured two cups, handing her one.

"Thank you," she said gratefully. "I've had nothing yet this morning." She'd waited for hours on the sidewalk in front of the law firm until finally someone arrived at eight to unlock the door.

"You're skin and bones and shouldn't skip breakfast," Ruben chided. He added sugar to his coffee and stirred, staring at her with narrowed eyes.

She didn't meet his gaze.

"I'm willing to stay out of the public's eye and keep my mouth shut until after the election," she whispered, "but you must understand that I have no intention of returning to Jesse."

This was a problematic situation, Ruben realized. Jesse was his best friend. He had to look after his interests. Luckily, she'd come to him, the spineless bitch. Tension tightened in his neck and he massaged the taut muscles with his right hand. "Is there anything else I need to know?"

Emma dropped her face in her hands, weeping as she spoke in spurts.

Of course, here come the waterworks, he thought. "Are you saying he's seeing someone else? That he's unfaithful?" Why were women always so bloody dramatic? He took a calming breath in the hope to release some of his own tension.

No answer came from the bundle of misery in his office. Her shoulders shook as she sobbed. His annoyance flared to anger, the headache he'd tried to stave off leaping to vicious life. He opened a bottle of ibuprofen and downed three pills with the rest of his coffee. What a disappointment she turned out to be. He'd assumed she was accustomed to setbacks in life, with the loss of her father and a sickly mother. That she would be tougher than this, having grown up in a trailer park and a low-income housing apartment, among the poor, the drunks, and the miserable. He should have known better. Women were pathetic, weak, and melodramatic. He had yet to meet one who could face life's realities with dignity and perseverance.

"I hope you realize I'm a corporate lawyer and that you should see a divorce lawyer," he growled.

He found a box of tissues and slapped it in front of her on his desk.

Emma pulled a few tissues from the box and blew her nose. "I do, but if you want to prevent everyone from finding out how Jesse treats his wife, you'd better figure something out."

He raised his eyebrows at her unexpected feisty remark. She wasn't completely beaten down. He needed to tread carefully.

"Don't worry. I'll help." He moved back behind his desk and sat down. "I just need a little time to figure this out." He picked up his phone. "Isabelle, call in to the deli for a breakfast sandwich with egg and sausage and a bottle of orange juice. When it arrives, bring it into my office." He broke off the connection and turned his attention back to Emma. "I have to attend a business meeting. In the meantime, have something to eat and try to rest a little on the couch. You look completely worn out."

He hoped his words resonated concern for her well-being. When she gave him a grateful watery smile, he knew he had succeeded. "I won't be long," he assured her, giving her shoulder an encouraging squeeze before he walked out of his office.

On his way out he informed the receptionist, "I'll be gone for an hour and a half, possibly two. Cancel all my meetings this morning."

"Any particular reason?" she asked.

"Family emergency," he barked in reply, his mind working overtime to concoct a plan.

Ten minutes later, he hopped out of his car in the parking lot of the high-rise that housed Kimball Financial Group Ltd. Shortly after Jesse had earned his B.A. degree from the University of Heemstead, where he majored in accounting and political science, he'd founded the company. They specialized in investment analysis, retirement planning, and asset protection. Initially Jesse had only rented a small office in the building, testing the waters. It didn't take long before he needed a secretary. Now, he had fifteen full-time employees, his business benefiting from the strong economy.

With a polite smile, he entered the building. The secretary behind the reception desk in the lobby looked up when he approached. Ruben was a familiar face and she waved him through. The elevator brought him up to the sixth floor. He found Jesse waiting for him in the hallway.

"I can't believe that mousy bookworm is becoming such a nuisance," Jesse said in greeting. Together they disappeared into his office. As soon as the door closed behind them, Jesse exploded, "That stupid bitch. I can't believe she came crying to you."

Ruben scowled at him. "There's only one person who's stupid," he said between clenched teeth. "And that's you. Come on, Jesse. Have you seen her? If she goes out on the street like that, you can wave the election goodbye."

"I only slapped her face, but she kicked me first and was asking for it," Jesse protested. "The next day, she fell and hit her head. That's it! So why should I worry about it?"

"Well, I'm telling you, as your lovely wife, she's become a public figure too. It only takes one person to hint at abuse and the gossip will start a life of its own, instantly raising doubt about your character and integrity."

Jesse sank into his chair, huffing with exasperation. "Since this entire thing was your idea, and you seem to have all the answers, why don't you come up with a solution for this, too."

Ruben walked toward the window and looked out over the city. The morning cloud cover had cleared, leaving behind a deep blue sky. "She wants a divorce," he said.

"What the hell, man?" Jesse swore. "That would mean I did

it all for nothing, and you know damn well how difficult it has been. I won't agree. Forget it."

"Then you should have worked a little harder at it," Ruben replied with an accusatory tone. He heard Jesse's chair squeak and footsteps moving in his direction. Shoulder to shoulder, the men stood in silence, each deep in thought.

"Maybe I can kill two birds with one stone," Ruben said pensively. The sides of his mouth crept up into a calculated smile.

With a grin, Jesse punched him on the shoulder. "I knew I could count on you. Tell me all about it."

CHAPTER

18

AFTER RUBEN LEFT, Emma asked the receptionist to point her toward the ladies' room. In the harsh light of the fluorescents, her head wound looked far worse than the previous night. An enormous bruise had formed, and blood caked into her eyebrow. She shuddered and wet a paper towel to carefully wash her face, avoiding another look in the mirror. Nothing was worse for her self-esteem than seeing herself at her lowest.

The receptionist looked at her with empathy when she came out. "I left your breakfast on the conference table in Mr. Templeton's office. It shouldn't be too long before he returns. But if there's anything you need in the meantime, let me know."

A delicious aroma wafted in her direction the moment she opened the door. The tray she found contained a full breakfast, with pancakes, toast, hash browns, and an omelet smothered with cheese. The kindness of the receptionist warmed her, and she made a mental note not to forget to thank her.

Since accepting Jesse's proposal, a touch of foreboding had simmered in the back of Emma's mind. Instead of listening to her subconscious, she'd convinced herself gloomy thoughts were normal considering all the dramatic changes in her life.

Now she realized, her instincts had tried to warn her she moved too fast. Was she making that same mistake again?

She laid down on the couch and pulled up her legs, wired and fidgety, and too exhausted to sleep.

When Ruben returned, she sat up and stretched the taut muscles in her back, her insides a tangle of nerves.

"I made a mistake and shouldn't have bothered you," she said. "Thanks for breakfast, Ruben, but I've got to go."

Ruben scoffed and closed the door. "Before you do something unwise, let's talk about your options first."

She reached for Jesse's baseball cap and her coat and got up. "All I want is a divorce. I'll figure out the rest myself."

He lifted an amused eyebrow. "Think about it for a moment, Emma. Do you have money? Transportation? A place to stay?" He walked around his desk, sat down, and gestured for her to do the same.

Instead, she grabbed the handle of her suitcase and headed toward the door. What did he know? She had saved a little and knew several people she could call who would surely offer a temporary place to stay. Her heart cried out for her mother. Why had she died? She needed her now more than ever.

"Before you go, hear me out first, Emma," Ruben continued. He booted up his computer. "I want to help. We're adults, and I'm sure we can find a solution for your dilemma."

Emma hesitated at the door. Ruben had introduced her to Jesse, the two men so much alike in many ways. But that also meant Ruben might be the only one who knew how to handle the situation, and that was the reason she'd come here in the first place.

With several impatient snaps of his fingers, Ruben tried to grab her attention. She turned around, her hand still on the door handle.

"Do you remember that you told me once your dream was to become a private investigator. I realize it was probably just a silly childhood fantasy, but it got me thinking."

That had been ages ago. "How do you even remember that?" she asked.

"A sharp memory is a skill and proof of intelligence," he said with a smug grin. He opened one of his desk drawers and pulled out a manila envelope. "Please, sit down. There's something I want to show you."

Unconvinced, she remained where she was, and Ruben released a deep sigh, rubbing his chin.

"You've been through a lot these past few months, Emma. I believe you need time to come to terms with the loss of your mother, your sudden marriage, and your falling out with Jesse. I may just have the answer to help you with that."

Still lingering at the door, Emma warily eyed him. His sudden change of attitude and the compassion in his voice struck her as insincere and forced. At his next words, her spine stiffened.

"I talked to Jesse. He's devastated, miserable, and worried about you. You have to understand that he's been under a lot of pressure lately. He has a lot of responsibilities at work. And running a campaign is exhausting and stressful, especially since

Andrew Voss decided to run. He loves you and is very sorry for what happened. Please, Emma, he begged me to talk to you, to ask for forgiveness, and to give him a second chance."

To ease the spasms in her back, she rolled her shoulders, scolding herself to assume Ruben would keep it a secret she'd shown up in his office.

"He's not coming here to see me, I hope?" she stuttered, fingering the buttons on her blouse.

"No, I told him to stay away, but I had a hard time convincing him," Ruben answered. "He truly loves you and is heartbroken. He isn't himself and made me promise I would take excellent care of you while you recover from the scare he gave you."

Since last night, she'd been telling herself she didn't care about Jesse anymore. His sexual indifference and betrayal had hurt her deeply.

"He wants a second chance and will do anything to make it up. He was almost in tears."

It was obvious Ruben tried to remind her of her love for Jesse and to make him the innocent, overworked, and brokenhearted victim in this. To her chagrin, it worked, a little.

"A woman should never have to endure unfaithfulness and physical or mental abuse," Ruben continued with a most convincingly sincere smile. "Especially not by the hands of her own husband. But Jesse assured me he didn't mean to hurt you. He said you fell and hit your head. Is that true?"

She touched the wound on her forehead, playing last night's event in her mind. "Yes, I tripped, but only because he pushed me."

"I'm so sorry, Emma. But can you blame him? He found you eavesdropping."

She caught the pity in his voice and wanted to scream. There was so much more that had happened between them, their confrontation not the only reason she was here.

"He humiliated and hurt me, Ruben," she insisted as she pulled on the door handle, ready to flee.

Before she could run from the room, Ruben rounded the desk and took hold of her arm. "Please, I only want to help," he said. He drew her against his chest until she calmed down.

With a strangled sob, she freed herself from his arms and sank into the nearest chair. "I want him out of my life, Ruben. Can you take care of that? If not, I'll just try to find another attorney and the secret will be out."

Ruben massaged the bridge of his nose with his thumb and forefinger, a weary look on his face. For the first time that morning, she actually looked at him. Besides his obvious weight loss, she noticed other subtle changes in his appearance. Like the gray hair at his temples, the thin lines running down from his nose to the corners of his mouth, and his slightly grayish skin tone.

"Are you feeling okay?" she asked.

He scoffed. "You're not the only one in the world dealing with problems, Emma. It's my father. He's diagnosed with cancer. A brain tumor. Before he dies, he wants to see Axel, whom we haven't seen or spoken to in ten years. You remember him, right?"

"Of course," she replied, remembering the adolescent boy, all legs and arms, his head full of unruly curls, his brown puppy eyes always darting around, as if he was afraid of the world.

"Cancer is not only a disease of the body," Ruben continued with a solemn expression on his face. "It also affects the mind and the soul. My father believes a proactive and positive spirit will help him fight this horrible disease. Since his biggest wish is to reconcile with Axel, I want to do everything in my power to make that happen." He moved his hand across his face, looking tired and harried.

Emma couldn't help but feel empathy at his unexpected distress. Perhaps she'd judged him too harshly. He obviously cared deeply for his father and maybe there was more to him than met the eye.

Ruben sat back down and placed his elbows on his desk, his hands folded. "Emma, you know what Axel looks like, and I thought you could help us find him. Besides, this assignment could be the distraction you need. It'll give you several weeks to deliberate your own situation, and help you decide which path to take."

He unfolded his hands, picked up the manila envelope and emptied the contents onto his desktop. Several photos and a small stack of postcards fell out.

"Every year, around Christmas time, Axel sent us a card. Wishing us happy holidays." He pulled off the rubber band and handed her the stack.

She turned the first one over and read: '*A bit of a rough year but doing well. Hope you're doing fine too. Cheers. Axel.*'

The second one read: '*Don't worry about me. Life is good. Merry Christmas and a Happy New Year. Adios. Axel.*' The other cards were similar, not revealing much more than the fact that he was alive.

"If you look at the dates, you can put them in chronological order. The first two are from Iowa, the third from South Dakota. The next cards are all mailed in the vicinity of Portland,

Oregon. It's safe to assume that's where he lives."

Ruben gave her a pensive stare, but she wasn't sure he was seeing her. He seemed far away, his eyes narrowed, his mouth curved in a soft smile. Were they both thinking about their childhood in Dunedam, and about Axel, the shy boy who always stayed in the background and never joined the other kids playing outside?

She shifted in her chair, bringing Ruben out of his reverie.

He straightened his shoulders and handed her the photos. "Two were taken on graduation day." Ruben grinned. "He hated the color of his cap and gown. Who wants to graduate in white?"

Emma looked at the first picture, Axel's white cap and gown in sharp contrast to the evergreen trees behind him. She'd worn white, too, graduating the same year. And just like herself, in her own graduation pictures, he looked the typical awkward teenager, too self-conscious for his own good.

The second photo was the same, only taken up close. Several bright red pimples on his forehead and chin stood out. It made her remember how horrible she'd felt when at fifteen she'd broken out. Her mother had bought all kinds of magic solutions, but nothing helped. Three years later, to her utmost relief, her skin cleared up on its own, with just the occasional blemish making its appearance during her period. She hoped he'd been as lucky.

In the third picture, Axel slouched in a recliner chair. He seemed to be about sixteen years old. By his relaxed posture, she could tell he didn't realize someone was taking his picture. And in the last one, he looked straight into the camera, his arm around an elderly woman. On his other side stood a man she recognized as his father, his gray hair an unruly mess, his yellowish skin sagging around his eyes.

"Who's the elderly woman?" she asked. From the way Axel hugged her and the relaxed smile on his face, it was obvious he cared about her.

"That's our old nanny, Martha Clark. She passed away last year at seventy-eight."

"How long was she your nanny?"

Ruben thought for a moment. "I was five and Axel two when Mom passed away. Several weeks later, she arrived, and she was still around after twelve years."

Emma realized Ruben had been without a mother for about twenty-five years. Much longer than her. It must have been difficult, growing up without a mom.

"Well, how about it?" Ruben asked. He rapidly tapped his fingers on his desk, trying to rush her into a decision.

"Give me a minute to think, Ruben. I haven't seen Axel in ages and I'm sure he's changed a lot over the years."

Although his proposal piqued her interest, the idea of searching for someone, who more than likely didn't want to be found, made her uncomfortable. She'd also never crossed the state line in her entire life. To imagine herself on the other side of the country, scared her more than she wanted to admit.

On the other hand, this might just be what she needed; to be away from Jesse, to see something of the country, and to distract her mind from the painful loss of her mother. She choked up and tears threatened.

Ruben opened a drawer and moved around, every ten seconds staring at her.

She recognized he tried to pressure her into a decision. "I don't know," she said, blinking her tears back. "Can I give you my answer tomorrow?"

"If you try to find Axel, I'll take care of the divorce," Ruben said. "But it's all right. I can find somebody else." He stood with the intention to scoot her out the door.

"You would?"

"Isn't that what I said?" he smirked; his voice laced with impatience. "Come on, Emma, I need your decision now. It's important."

A divorce was all she wanted. If she could get it in exchange for a trip across the country, that wasn't a bad deal.

"Great," Ruben replied, as if he'd read her mind. "I'll book a flight to Portland, Oregon, reserve a hotel room, and rent a car."

She shook her head the moment he mentioned flying. "After ten years, I don't think a few extra weeks will make a difference, right? Or is your father's condition already so serious that time is of the essence?"

Ruben raised his eyebrows in questioning. "What do you have in mind?"

"It's August. The weather is beautiful. I'd like to take my time and drive across the country. That way I can retrace Axel's journey."

Axel's postcards had spoken to her imagination. She could envision herself driving along the interstate, visiting Iowa and South Dakota, leisurely taking in the gorgeous landscapes she would cross. That idea suddenly appealed to her. In her entire life, she'd never spent a night by herself. Her dependence on others, and the fear of being alone, had contributed to her current situation.

It was time to grow up, to find herself, and gain some independence.

CHAPTER

19

EMMA GLADLY ACCEPTED Ruben's offer to pay for a room at the upscale Hildegard Hotel, a block away from his office. She'd reached a state of physical and mental exhaustion and needed sleep, preferably a good twenty-four hours of it.

The room he'd reserved on the second floor was old-fashioned, with lots of tassels, lace, and ruffles, the king-size bed heaped with velvet pillows. It beckoned, her bone-deep fatigue making it impossible to resist. She yawned and closed the heavy insulated curtains, plunging the room in semi-darkness. When her head hit the pillow, the satin cover pulled up to her chin, she sank into oblivion.

A wedge of light sliced across the room and awakened her several hours later. The alarm clock next to the bed told her it was five-thirty in the afternoon. Groggy, she pushed aside the covers and got up. A leisurely shower in the luxurious bathroom refreshed her, but not enough to want to venture outside. Instead, she ordered room service and binge-watched two movies in bed, propped up against a stack of pillows. The distraction kept her from picking up the phone to call off her road trip. She'd been out of her mind to agree with Ruben's crazy plan.

The next morning, Ruben joined her in the dining room of the hotel. Over breakfast, he explained the course of action.

"Yesterday, I went to the bank, opened an account in your name, and deposited five thousand dollars to cover your expenses. Here's the debit card with pin-code. I hope you have your driver's license with you. You'll need that, too."

She lowered her eyes to her half-empty plate; the blueberry waffles the best she'd ever had. "I don't know, Ruben," she mumbled, working up the courage to tell him she'd changed her mind. She wasn't adventurous. She couldn't possibly do what he had in mind. Just to look someone straight in the eye was already enough to make her cower; the trip and a search for Axel making her cringe. Surely Ruben would understand. All he had to do was notice her strained face and hunched shoulders.

"I transferred your phone number to a new cell phone loaded with apps you may find useful on your trip." He handed her the latest smartphone. A brown leather case protected it, with room for several credit cards, money, and her driver's license. It felt heavy.

"After you check out of the hotel, I'll drive you to the car rental office. I reserved a four-door SUV for a month. That should be enough time to find him."

The trip became very real. *Speak up*, she told herself, *before it's too late*. But an unexpected bubble of anticipation kept her mouth from opening. Her heart raced and her nerves tingled with excitement as she listened to him provide additional details.

She was going to do it. She was *really* going to do it.

At the car rental office, Ruben lifted her suitcase into the trunk of the shiny red SUV. It was all-wheel-drive, with remote engine starting, intelligent climate control, automatic braking, G.P.S., and only three thousand miles on the odometer. Almond-cloth lined the interior, with a heated steering wheel and heated seats, a seven-inch touch-screen display, multiple cup holders, and plenty of cargo space. Quite a contrast to the thirty-year-old clunker her parents had owned until the engine blew up several years ago. She hadn't driven since. When she slid behind the wheel, renewed apprehension took hold of her. What if she got into an accident? What if she got lost? Before she could voice her doubts, Ruben said, "Drive safely," and slammed the door closed. Without looking over his shoulder, he walked to his own car, stepped in, and drove off.

Beads of perspiration formed between her breasts as she tried to figure out how the wipers and lights worked, how to adjust the mirrors, and start the car. The man from the rental company looked at her strangely when she was still in the parking lot fifteen minutes later. She avoided his stare and didn't put the transmission in drive until she felt confident enough to merge into traffic. At twenty-five miles an hour, her knuckles white from her tight grip on the steering wheel, she drove the familiar streets out of the city that led her to Interstate 90. Once she reached the interstate going west, she stayed in the far-right lane, cruising exactly at the speed limit. She felt overwhelmed behind the wheel of the unfamiliar car, twice the size of anything she'd ever driven before.

Soon, she left the city behind. Traffic lightened and a sense of relief washed over her. She'd passed the point of no return and the road was wide open in front of her. Watch out, Axel Templeton, here I come!

She drove for several hours until neon lights beckoned her off the interstate. Although still at half full, she pulled into a gas station to top off the tank, using her new debit card for the first time. The transaction got approved, the pin-code firmly etched into her brain.

At the sandwich shop, next to the gas station, she ordered the largest veggie-club sandwich the menu offered and an iced tea. She took her food to go and sat down at one of the outside tables under the shade of a metal umbrella. It was blistering hot, the temperature in the low nineties.

While she ate, she watched cars drive in and out. People pumped gas, entered the sandwich shop, and went their own way. No one gave her a second look. The anonymity made her feel safe; the normalcy easing her anxiety. She touched her forehead, the wound already scabbing over, the bump less pronounced. In about two weeks, the evidence of her fall would be gone.

She wrapped up the uneaten half of her sandwich and stepped into her car. It was her goal to cross the state line today, the air she breathed filled with excitement, expectation.

···⤳⤶···

More than an hour later, she found herself in the state of New York, the exhilarating moment a major achievement.

"Wow, I did it," she jubilated aloud, proud of all the fear she'd overcome today. But only a few miles farther, the long hours of driving took its toll. She wasn't used to it and the muscles in her shoulders and neck were tense from gripping the steering wheel too tight.

A sign along the road indicated several motels were nearby. It was time to take a break. She turned onto an off-ramp, and it wasn't long before she drove into the parking lot of the Renaissance Inn. Before her wedding night, she'd never stayed in a hotel. Her life had changed drastically in a very short time. How it would unfold from here on was anyone's guess.

In the room, she finished her sandwich, showered, and crawled between the crisp clean sheets to watch another movie.

The next day she drove until she reached Pennsylvania where she spent another fitful night in a motel. Her mind still worked overtime, the wounds in her heart fresh, the painful memories festering in a dark corner of her brain.

On her third day, she crossed Ohio and Indiana. By now, she'd grown tired of interstate driving. She also felt confident behind the wheel. In the hope to find more interesting routes, she stopped at a visitor center.

"I'm heading to Iowa," she told the lady working the counter. "What are the best tourist attractions to visit along the way?"

The woman gave her a bright smile and pulled out a map of Illinois. "Which route do you want to take?"

"I don't care," Emma answered.

"Illinois is beautiful with lots of farmland, forests, rolling hills, and wetlands," the woman said. "I grew up in North Utica, close to Starves Rock State Park, that's definitely worth a visit."

With a stack of free maps and lots of information, Emma thanked the woman for her help.

"Don't forget to adjust your clock, Ma'am," she smiled. "You'll be entering Central Time when you cross the state line."

Emma traveled through towns, past farmlands, gorgeous lakes, and forested areas. Each passing day was glorious, filled with sunshine, making the colors seem more vivid than back home.

With each mile, tension lifted from her shoulders and a sense of freedom and accomplishment slowly manifested inside her. The woman who stared back at her in the mirror nothing like the sleep-deprived, insecure, and emotional creature she'd left behind. It felt fantastic to extend her horizons and venture into unknown territory, and no one could be more surprised about it than herself.

The destination of the first leg of her trip was Bloomsberry, a small farming town in Iowa. It was the town in which Axel had mailed his first two Christmas cards. She hoped to arrive at the end of the day.

After gassing up at the next station, she bought a box of garbage bags in the mini mart to tidy up the litter of candy wrappers, empty fast-food containers, water bottles, and soda cans in the backseat. She'd never eaten such unhealthy food in her life. She had let herself go, but that would change. From now on, she would eat healthier and search for restaurants that served home-cooked meals.

✼

Iowa's landscape opened up in front of her, the highway stretching straight ahead, endless, as if by following it, one would reach the end of the world. All around her were prairies and fields of corn, unpaved roads leading to the occasional farm, and the distant horizon hazy and sweltering in the heat of another summer day. Even though her air conditioning operated at full blast, it didn't ease the humidity and perspiration shimmered on her skin, her dress plastered to her back. The thermometer on the dashboard read ninety-nine degrees. She adjusted the vents to take advantage of the cold air flowing from both sides of the steering wheel. It didn't make much difference. As a distraction, she counted the electrical poles along the side of the road.

Born and raised in the city, Emma was used to thousands and thousands of people. She'd never realized how much unpopulated land there was in the country, the vast emptiness of the terrain astounding. It was eye-opening, and instead of obsessing over Jesse, a divorce, and everything else she'd left behind, her mind filled with new impressions. But also, with new concerns. What if she ran out of gas? Or had car trouble in the middle of nowhere. Help could be hours away. Mile after passing mile, she checked her cell phone. She had full bars. At least coverage was not an issue.

When she reached the next community, she stopped

alongside the road for a quick break, to stretch her legs and eat the warm and mushy banana that had been baking on the backseat. When she took her first bite, several high-pitched piping notes caught her attention. She looked up. High in the deep blue sky, two eagles soared in unison. They appeared to be floating, rising on the warm air. She'd seen several more of the majestic birds along the Mississippi River, where they had abundant food and open water. On her map, she'd noticed an eagle wildlife reserve next to a nearby river. It had to be close by. With distaste, she finished her banana, following the eagles with her eyes until they were mere specks in the far distance.

CHAPTER

20

AFTER ANOTHER HOUR, she stopped along the road to snap a picture of the welcome sign of Bloomsberry, population 548. She'd already taken many pictures along the way. Everything tweaked her interest and seemed worth capturing. There was so much beauty. But this was the first photo she wanted to share. Ruben would be interested to see she'd reached her first destination, and she texted it to him.

To the right, she noticed a gas station next to a business called Randy's Wreckers and Auto Service. The sign said they were open, but there was only one car in the parking lot. It would be hard to make a decent living in such a small town, she thought, but it could be an advantage in finding Axel.

At a slow speed, she followed the sleepy main drag in search of a motel or a Bed and Breakfast. Within two minutes she reached the other side of town. All she'd seen were a hardware store, an auto body shop, a fire hall, a Mexican restaurant, and a boarded up antique store. In the parking lot of a Catholic Church, she turned around and backtracked. There were plenty of spaces to park between the few cars, dust covered pickup trucks, and nondescript sedans. When she got out, she noticed her car wouldn't stand out. The once so shiny SUV was coated with a thick layer of grime, too.

Indecisive, she looked from left to right. There were only a few people on the sidewalk, two of them women, each pushing a stroller with a toddler. Both smiled and nodded as they passed by.

She smiled, too wary to initiate a conversation. *Don't be a coward*, she told herself. *It's time to step up. Otherwise you won't get anywhere and will never find Axel.*

The next person she came upon was a young man clad in blue jeans, a plaid shirt, and cowboy boots. He touched his baseball cap with two fingers in greeting. He seemed barely eighteen.

She followed him down the sidewalk, mustering enough courage to ask him a question. "Excuse me."

With a curious look on his face, he stopped and met her gaze. "Yes, ma'am?"

"I've never been here before and hoped to find a place to spend the night. Do you know if there's a hotel around?"

He gave her an inquisitive glance. "Of course. Just east of town are the Bloomsberry Country Cabins, but they're a bit rundown. I suspect you might be more comfortable at the Rancourt Inn."

She took that as a compliment.

Following his directions, she drove a short distance and parked in the gravel lot beside the small hotel. The sign warned her it was for registered guests only. She hoped they had a vacancy.

As she entered, the brightly carpeted lobby embraced her with refrigerated air. A bored-looking teenager, draped across a swivel chair behind the front desk, leafed through a magazine. "Grandpa, somebody's here!" she yelled.

"Be right there," a man answered.

Emma heard water running and the clattering of pots and pans in what might be a kitchen.

"Do you serve food here?" she asked.

The girl looked up. "What?"

An elderly man appeared behind her, drying his hands on a white towel. "Gabriella," he said with a stern voice, his brow furrowed. "Where are your manners?" The man pushed the towel into the teenager's hands. "Go make yourself useful."

Deliberately slow, the teenager got up, the sullen frown on her face mirroring the one from her grandfather.

"Teenagers," the man said with a twinkle in his eyes after the girl was out of earshot. "Welcome to the Rancourt Inn, Ma'am. My name is Bernard Rancourt. What can I do for you?" Tufts of white hair stood up behind his ears, matching his bushy eyebrows. His brown eyes radiated both warmth and genuine interest.

"I was hoping you have a room available for two nights."

Bernard nodded. "The Eleonore suite is available. It has a queen-sized bed and a bathroom with a tub. It will be perfect for you."

He spoke with a slight French accent, which she found charming. "That sounds wonderful. I'll take it."

Bernard entered her information in the computer, ran her debit card, and handed her a key. "May I help you with your luggage?"

He followed her out to her car, lifted her suitcase out of the back, and carried it inside and up the stairs, chatting along the way. "In case you're hungry, our dining room will be open until eight. Breakfast is served between seven and ten."

"I'll take you up on both," she promised, counting herself lucky when they entered the room. The carpet was soft and plush, the wallpaper and bedspread in the same bright floral print, and the bathroom sparkling clean. The air conditioning zoomed softly.

"This is lovely. Thank you," she said.

After Bernard closed the door, she freshened up and slipped on a pair of blue dress shorts and a colorful tunic with cropped sleeves. It wasn't an outfit she would have chosen. It was too flamboyant. But Carly had assured her the bright purple and yellow flowers brought out her blue eyes. The memory made her smile. She needed to call Carly, to give her an update about her falling out with Jesse and find out how she coped after breaking up with Ruben.

Guests occupied most of the tables in the dining room. Two waitresses, carrying trays with drinks and food, maneuvered between them.

"Glad you joined us, Emma," Bernard welcomed her. A white towel hung over his shoulder, in his hand a small tray with chocolates and a guest check.

She liked the way he pronounced her name, with an accent on the second syllable.

"Let me help you get seated," he continued. He briefly stopped at a table, thanked the guests for coming to the restaurant and left the small tray before he turned his attention back to her. "Is the room to your satisfaction?"

He pulled out a chair at an empty table for two at the window and left. A moment later, he returned with a menu and a glass filled with ice water. "It's been a hectic evening," he told her over the cacophony of voices. "Very unusual for a Thursday."

She assured him everything was wonderful, ordered a glass of white wine, and slid down her reading glasses from the top of her head to look at the menu.

"A salad, chicken breast with a baked potato and fresh veggies sounds great," she told Bernard when he came back with her wine.

The restaurant slowly emptied, the waitresses cleaning the tables with a few quick moves after the guests departed. At the exit, Bernard thanked them all for coming and wished them a wonderful rest of the evening. He seemed to know everyone by name, even the little ones.

It didn't take long before her dinner was served. While she ate, Bernard stopped by to check on her and refill her water glass. She complimented him on the cozy atmosphere and the delicious meal.

"My wife Eleonore and I bought the building and started this hotel and restaurant over thirty-five years ago. Just after we emigrated from France to the United States." He spoke with genuine pride. "Our son and daughter keep telling us to slow down, but we love what we do. It's what keeps us alive."

A woman sat behind the bar, folding napkins into the intricate star pattern Emma had seen on each table.

"That's my Eleonore," he said, and blew the woman a kiss. "The love of my life, my rock, my everything."

Bernard and his wife had something she would never experience with Jesse, Emma realized. Her spirit dropped. Since she'd left Jesse, she'd pushed every thought of him to the back of her mind, pretending she didn't care. Until now it had worked, but the devoted and affectionate way in which Bernard talked about his wife shattered her carefully constructed facade. The objects on the table blurred as tears filled her eyes. Faking a cough, she pressed her napkin to her lips and prayed no one would notice her distress. When she looked up, Bernard remained standing at her table. She met his inquisitive gaze. The last thing she wanted to do was discuss her failed marriage. She took another bite, hoping he would leave and allow her to pull herself together.

He gave her a heartwarming smile. "Please, let me know if there's anything else we can do for you."

Left alone, a somber mood settled over her. What had she been thinking, going on a long solitary road trip? What was she doing here, eating dinner by herself in the middle of nowhere? A desperate loneliness engulfed her. Had she lost her mind? That lying, cheating Jesse. If not for his cruelty, she would have never been so far away from everything she held dear. Her job, her friends, her parents' graves. If not for Jesse, she would never have found herself in such an impossible and isolated situation.

By the time she took her last bite, she also finished her wine, the warmth of the alcohol spreading through her veins.

Bernard placed a steaming cup of coffee in front of her after clearing away her place setting.

"I thought you might enjoy a cup before retiring to your room," he said.

"You're very kind," she managed to whisper, tears filling her eyes.

"I'm a great listener," he said. "And I never repeat anything I'm told in confidence."

Emma swiped at the tears on her cheeks and gave him a thankful smile, embarrassed at her public display. She rarely indulged in self-pitying behavior. Even at her mother's funeral, she'd remained composed, until she closed the bedroom door that evening. Only then had she completely fallen apart.

"I'm around people every day and can always tell when someone is in need of a listening ear. Please, let me know if I can help to make you feel better."

Under normal circumstances, she would never talk to a stranger about her problems, but nothing about her life was normal anymore. Sipping her coffee, she told him about her mother, Jesse, and their hasty wedding. And how she'd over-heard him talk about their fake marriage and declare his love to someone else. She didn't share how he'd kept her in isolation after the wedding, that he had forced her to stop working at the library, and their absence of sexual intimacy. Nor did she speak of begging him to make love to her. Or about the brutal way he'd tried to take her from behind, ripping her clothes from her body, only to reject her a few minutes later. That was too personal and humiliating.

"It's wonderful you could help Jesse by writing his political speeches," Bernard complimented her. "I'm a klutz in English. And in French, too." His remark made her smile.

"Thank you so much for listening, Mr. Bernard." Confiding in a virtual stranger had helped and the outpouring of emotion was cleansing. "I feel much better."

CHAPTER

21

Emma slept soundly and without dreams. Rejuvenated, she donned a sexy white dress, the spaghetti straps accenting her suntan. Before heading down for breakfast, she draped a sheer wrap around her bare shoulders and knotted it in the front.

Downstairs, there was no one behind the reception desk, the lobby empty.

"I'd hoped to talk to Mr. Bernard this morning," she told the waitress, taking her order.

"He's not expected to come in until lunchtime. Is there anything I can do for you?"

Emma thought about her smelly clothes, demanding to be washed. To take care of that would be a useful way to spend her morning.

"You probably can. Is there a laundromat in town?"

When she returned to the Inn around noontime, all her clothes clean, smelling fresh, and neatly folded in her suitcase, she found Bernard behind the front desk, sifting through paperwork.

"If it isn't our lovely Emma," he said. They exchanged a few pleasantries about the weather and charming historic Bloomsberry with its well-preserved brick Main Street. Bernard explained that only a few businesses were still open since the school closed and that most of them had relocated along Highway 163. Fortunately, the decline hadn't affected his business much since they were located close to the Highway, and the only hotel in miles.

"Since you've lived here for so long, can I ask you a question?" Emma said. "I'm sent out by a family member to look for a man who used to live in Bloomsberry about eight to ten years ago." She opened the gallery on her cell phone to show him the photos of Axel she'd uploaded. "His name is Axel Templeton. Do you recall ever seeing him around?"

Bernard's eyes lit up. "That rascal. He told everyone he didn't have any family, but I always had the feeling he wasn't quite truthful about his past. Edwina will be so excited to hear this."

"Edwina?"

Bernard opened a phonebook and leafed through it. "Let me call her." He picked up the desk phone and dialed a number. "It might take a while for her to get to the phone. She's well in her eighties, hard of hearing, and slow on her feet."

"Hello, Edwina!" he yelled in the mouthpiece. "Can you hear me? This is Bernard. Are you home? Can I stop by?" After listening for a minute, he shouted, "We'll be there within half an hour." He hung up the phone and chuckled. "After Axel rolled off the Amtrak with just a knapsack of clothes on his back, Edwina and her husband Henry gave him a place to stay. But instead of me telling the story, I'd rather let Edwina. She's lonely since Henry passed away. I'm sure she'll appreciate the company."

Bernard disappeared into the kitchen and came back with his car keys. "I told my wife where we're going. She's as delighted as I am. This is wonderful."

With the air conditioning at full blast, they left Bloomsberry and followed the highway until they reached the neighboring town.

"That's the new school," Bernard said, pointing at a modern structure with several stories, surrounded by athletic fields, playgrounds, and a huge parking lot. A sign with scrolling red letters told her summer vacation had started. A fenced-in parking area next to the bleachers was filled up with yellow school busses.

Bernard slowed down and turned into the parking lot of the Morning Glory Assisted Living Community, a contemporary complex featuring bright colors and tall windows. They both stepped out and headed toward the entrance, the doors of the lobby opening automatically as they approached. Inside, the air was cool and soft music played in the background.

The concierge at the front desk greeted them with a smile. "Welcome to Morning Glory. How can I be of service?"

"Like you don't know who I am, Dave," Bernard grinned.

"Here to see Edwina, I assume," Dave replied, not falling out of his role of the guardian of the house. "You can find her in the dining room."

"Eleonore and I visit Edwina about once a month since Henry passed away," Bernard told Emma, leading the way down a bright lighted hallway. They passed several doors, most of them wide open to reveal comfortable living quarters, the inhabitants nodding kindly. At the end of the hall, Bernard pressed a button on the wall to open the automatic door. The smell of coffee and the lemony whiff of a cleaner hung in the air.

A gray-haired lady in a floral dress perked up the moment they walked in. She raised her hand and waved.

"There she is," Bernard said, waving back.

They joined her at the table close to a window. It overlooked a paved courtyard with flowerpots. A birdfeeder with several sparrows fighting over a piece of bread attracted the attention of several residents.

Bernard kissed the top of Edwina's head and squeezed her puny shoulders. "It's so good to see you," he said, close to her ear. "This is Emma. She's one of Axel's relatives. She's looking for him."

Emma decided not to correct him. It wasn't important.

"One of Axel's relatives?" With a spark of pleasure in her rheumy light blue eyes, the frail woman looked at her. "It's so lovely to meet you." She stuck out her hand, the joints of her fingers swollen, her paper-thin skin covered in liver spots.

Careful not to hurt her, Emma took her hand, holding it for a little while, before she sat down in one of the plastic chairs.

"How's Axel?" Edwina asked. "He usually calls several times a year, but I haven't talked to him since Christmas."

Emma smiled, happy to hear Edwina was still in touch with

Axel. "His family hasn't heard from him in a long time. They're concerned about his well-being and asked me to help find him," she explained.

Edwina's face lit up. "I'm so glad to hear our Axel has a caring family. That sweet boy was so lonely and troubled when I met him, fresh off the train, with no place to go. I'll never regret bringing him home. He was a true blessing for me and my dear Henry."

"Edwina and Henry owned a small deli on Main Street for as long as I can remember," Bernard said. "They worked it together until they were well into their seventies, but it was getting harder and harder on them. When they met Axel at the train station, they offered him a job. Didn't he work for you for at least two years, Edwina?"

Edwina's soulful eyes filled with memories. "Yes, he did, until Henry fell and broke his hip. That's when we decided we'd worked long enough and would close the deli. With Henry in the hospital, Axel took care of everything, even though he knew he would be out of a job soon."

The conversation veered away from Axel as she recalled her husband's final days.

A short woman in a lilac-colored scrub top and matching pants stopped at the table with a wheelchair. "Are you getting tired, Edwina? Shall I take you to your room?"

Edwina nodded her consent, her eyelids already starting to droop.

Emma watched the caregiver help the delicate elderly lady into the wheelchair. She folded down the metal footrests and gently placed her feet onto them, just like Emma had done so many times for her mother.

"It was so wonderful to meet you," Edwina said, her voice barely detectable. "Please give my love to Axel when you find him. Tell him I miss him dearly."

What a sweet old lady, Emma thought on the way back to the Inn, recalling Edwina's fond memories of Axel, filled with praise. Then she thought about her mother, who remembered him as a shy and sweet boy, matching her own vague recollections.

It began to dawn on her that Ruben may not have been honest about his brother's character, and the events leading up to his disappearance.

What would the real Axel be like? she wondered. Would he be caring or mean-spirited, kind or vindictive, helpful or lazy, a loser or a fighter?

She stared out the window, enjoying the drive through the rolling hills. The views only extended as far as the next rise or bend. Narrow streams crisscrossed the landscape, and each turn offered a different scenery. Bernard called them the southern Iowa drift plains.

"Do you know what happened to Axel after he left Bloomsberry?" she asked.

"I'm not sure," Bernard replied. "But I believe he hitched a ride west with one of the regulars from the deli. A trucker named Hank Briggs. He hauled livestock to and from the Dakotas, even going as far as Wyoming. Hank always talked about the ranches and farms needing hands, so there's a fair chance Axel might have jumped on one of those opportunities."

The third Christmas card Axel sent home had come from

Cody, Wyoming. Would her luck hold out?

Bernard agreed it couldn't be a coincidence. "The city calls itself the rodeo capital of the world. It attracts a lot of people with an interest in the pioneers, cowboys, and the history of the west. It's named after Colonel William Frederick Cody, who's better known as Buffalo Bill, adding additional allure. The museum in town preserves his legacy and vision. You should make it a point to stop in."

Cowboys on horseback, and herds of livestock, roaming around on uninterrupted open ranges, appeared in her mind. It would be wonderful to see it in person.

Bernard drove into his private parking spot behind the hotel. "South Dakota and Wyoming have so much to offer, Emma. The Badlands and the Black Hills, Mount Rushmore, Devils Tower, the Tetons, the Missouri River, and so much more. On one of our trips, Eleonore and I visited the Jewel Cave National Monument and took a ranger-guided tour. It's a true adventure to meander through the maze of those underground chambers where spectacular crystals line the walls."

They entered through the backdoor into the kitchen. Two men in white chef jackets chopped vegetables. A cloud of steam rose from a pot on the eight-burner cooking range.

"The soup of the day is Garbure," Bernard told her. "It's a thick French soup with cabbage and other vegetables. One of my favorites."

"I won't miss dinner tonight," Emma promised. She'd skipped lunch and the delicious aroma made her stomach growl. "Is it too late to order lunch?"

CHAPTER

22

CRISSCROSSING THROUGH IOWA, Emma took her road atlas out at each major intersection, deciding what direction to take solely based on the names of the towns, streams, rivers, or lakes that seemed worth visiting. The freedom to travel by herself and make decisions on the spur of the moment proved to be an intoxicating experience.

She continued her journey along Interstate 90 into South Dakota, an expansive, sparsely populated midwestern state, with rolling prairies and sprawling ranch lands dominating the landscape. The sweltering August days were bright with sunshine. After four hours of driving, the formations from the Badlands rose abruptly from the surrounding prairie. She wanted to take the exit, to visit the National Park, but decided against it. Ruben had only rented the car for a month and she'd already been on the road for an entire week. So far, everything had gone well, but she needed to travel many more miles.

Along the interstate, billboard signs with big bold letters counted down the miles to Wall Drug. 'Free ice water', 'doughnuts', 'hot coffee', and 'to cowboy up with boots, buckles and belts' were the slogans. The brochure she'd picked up at the visitor center informed her it was a major tourist attraction in the flat prairie land, and it explained how it had become famous. Her curiosity was peaked, and the excessive number of signs pulled Emma off the road.

Wall turned out to be a small town. Its main street welcomed tourists, with the famous drugstore the driving force behind it all. Except that it was far more than a drugstore. It featured a food parlor, western shopping mall, camping store, chapel, rock shop and jewelry store, with Native American turquoise and Black Hills gold among the treasures.

With a pair of brown leather cowboy boots in a box on the passenger seat, Emma continued her trip. She'd also purchased a matching western style backpack decorated with a belt buckle and studs. The smell of leather surrounded her as she cruised farther along the interstate.

She entered Rapid City, where she spent the night. Her goal was to make it to Cody, Wyoming the following day. The GPS. told her it wouldn't give her much time to visit Mount Rushmore. But after skipping the Badlands National Park, she wouldn't miss the sculptures of four famous presidents—George Washington, Thomas Jefferson, Theodore Roosevelt, and Abraham Lincoln—carved into the granite rock face.

When her cell phone rang, her first thought was that it might be Jesse who wanted to confront her, order her to come home. To her relief, it was Ruben. She pushed the green button on her steering wheel to accept the call.

"I still don't understand why you needed to take this road trip instead of a fast flight," he growled after she informed him of her location.

She could tell he wasn't happy with her progress.

"Are you making any headway with the divorce?" she countered. When he didn't answer, she tried to suppress a satisfactory grin. In the old days—meaning the days before Jesse—she would have never dared to speak her mind. But she no longer felt like an introverted, mousy bookworm. Life had delivered one too many punches.

"What are you looking for in Wyoming anyway?" Ruben grumbled.

On the card Axel had mailed from Cody, he'd written Merry Christmas from the North Fork. Since Bernard had told her Hank Bridge hauled cattle, she'd googled North Fork Cattle Ranch and found an address. Of course, it was a long shot, but it was all she could think to do.

"You know I only asked you to find him, not to retrace his steps."

Ruben seemed to be in a foul mood.

"Just send the bill for the extra expenses to Jesse," she told him. "He'll take care of it." This time, she couldn't hide her pleasure at the thought of Jesse's angry reaction if he was asked to pay for her adventure. Until she realized part of her courage might have something to do with the hundreds of miles between them, the distance making her feel safe and out of reach. That insight toned down her pleasure. So did Ruben's next words.

"You think this is funny or about money. It's not! It's about my father."

For Emma, the sole purpose of the road trip had been to get away from Jesse. She'd conveniently forgotten about Ruben's father. Shame welled up inside her, and she sank her front teeth into her lower lip.

"His headaches are worsening, and he's experiencing fatigue and a light tremor in his left arm," Ruben continued.

"I'm so very sorry. You're right." She knew all too well how fast this horrible disease could take someone's life.

They ended their conversation; her planned visit to Mount Rushmore, the Buffalo Bill Museum in Cody, and the sights in Yellowstone National Park gone up in smoke. Her conscience wouldn't allow her to enjoy the side-trip.

After spending the night in a motel on the outskirts of Cody, she helped herself to a Danish pastry and a cup of coffee to go. She entered the address of the North Fork Ranch in her G.P.S. and drove through the city. The constant views of Heart Mountain rising from the floor of the Bighorn Basin were spectacular.

At the western edge of town, she crossed a bridge over a deep canyon formed by the Shoshone River, the wind funneling through the rift, coming from all directions. Soon she drove past a reservoir and turned onto a side street. After a few miles, the road narrowed, and the pavement ended. A dilapidated sign nailed onto a tree told her she'd reached the North Fork Cattle Ranch, the words No Trespassing underneath it sun-bleached, shot up, and barely readable.

As she crossed the cattle guard onto the property, the entire car rattled and the box with her still unworn western boots bounced off the seat. So far, she hadn't seen a single car, livestock, or any other sign of life. Except for a few Steller's Jays and a grouse on the narrow road, right in front of her. The potholes worsened the farther she drove up the mountain and forced her to slow down to five miles an hour. The car washboarded more often than not, rattling much more than just her nerves. At least her SUV was all-wheel-drive. The tires firmly gripped the loose gravel and gave her a sense of safety. When a branch scraped the side of the car, she looked for a place to turn around. This was a mistake.

After the next hill, the dirt road joined a gurgling stream, coming down a rocky hillside, and the view opened. The mixed grassland and arid mountain basin, populated by sagebrush, juniper and prickly pear cactus, was exactly how she'd imagined the Wild West would look. It was breathtaking.

A few hundred yards farther, she noticed the remnants of a burned-down structure. Only one wall still stood, held up by blackened beams that must have come crashing down in the fire. Sheets of ribbed steel, warped metal window frames, two burned-out vehicles, and the remnants of farm equipment showed the intensity of the heat. Even the surface of the road was sullied. The surrounding trees had caught fire too, several dead, others barely hanging on with burned bark and dead branches. From the enormous amount of blackened debris, she assumed the structure had been a huge barn, possibly with stables.

Farther down the road stood a ranch house. One wall showed evidence of fire damage, the windows boarded, the white paint stained and blistered. The entire property appeared abandoned, the only sign of life a white pickup truck parked in front of the house.

It was a bit too much for comfort. She should not have come out here by herself. Who knew what kind of person lived in that house? Her mind worked overtime with thoughts of what could happen to a woman alone in the middle of nowhere. After she turned the car around, she caught sight of the sweeping panoramic views all around her. With her hands on the steering wheel, she stared at the magnificent Rocky Mountains vistas, a solitary eagle soaring high above.

Maybe living so far out wouldn't be so bad if you woke up to a view like this every morning, she thought.

A loud thump against her window made her heart thud in alarm. She turned around and found herself staring down the barrel of a shotgun. Behind it stood a woman with her feet firmly planted apart, dressed in a camo tank top, shoulders and arms suntanned and brawny. Her dark hair with gray strands was pulled back in an unruly ponytail.

"Open the window," the woman yelled, making an up and down movement with the gun.

Emma pressed the buttons on the door, unlocking and locking the door by accident before she found the right one. The window rolled down and muggy, warm air streamed into the interior of the car. Drops of perspiration immediately formed on her forehead.

"I'm not leaving," the woman snarled with a grim expression on her face. "Not even if you send the cavalry. Now get off my property." She motioned again with the shotgun, this time in the direction of the road. "Vultures! That's what you all are. Get out and don't come back, or I'll shoot!"

"I believe I'm not who you think I am," Emma squeaked, working to keep her voice from shaking. "I was ... I was ..."

She removed her sunglasses and wiped the perspiration off her forehead with the back of her hand. "I'm just a tourist."

The woman scoffed, still aiming the shotgun at her. "Not a single tourist would make it several miles up a dead-end road on private property. Did they send you to spy on me?"

Alarmed at the fierceness of her expression, Emma started shaking. "No, no. I'm not here for you. Please, believe me. I'm sent here to look for Axel. Axel Templeton."

To her relief, the woman finally lowered the gun.

"Here, I can show you his picture." Still quivering, Emma reached for her cell phone, opened her gallery and displayed Axel's photo. "He lived in this area about eight years ago."

Barely glancing at the picture, the woman shook her head. "I don't recall."

"Please, can't you give it a second look?' Emma asked, regretting her words when the woman raised her shotgun again.

"What about *I'm not interested* do you not understand? You're trespassing. Leave. Right now."

Acknowledging defeat, Emma tossed her phone in the passenger seat. "Sorry to have bothered you," she mumbled and rolled up the window.

Just before it closed, the woman tapped against the window for the second time. "Eight years ago, the barn burned down. It took my husband, two men, and all the horses, pigs, and equipment with it. I lost everything and had to let every hired hand go. I believe your Axel was among them." She turned around and made her way back to the farmhouse, her shoulders sagging with obvious weariness.

Before the woman turned away, Emma caught a glimpse of deep sorrow in her eyes. Despite her hostile attitude, Emma empathized. It had to be horrible, to lose your husband and property due to circumstances beyond your control.

Emma put the transmission in drive and slowly made her way back down the mountain.

CHAPTER

23

WITHIN THREE DAYS, Emma entered Portland, Oregon. The busy city traffic overwhelmed her after experiencing vast emptiness since she'd left Heemstead.

Ruben expressed his relief when she called to give him an update. He'd become increasingly impatient with her slow progress. As if skipping Yellowstone National Park had been easy, she defended herself.

Ruben was not impressed. "You've been on the road for almost two weeks. It's time you began searching for him."

Two incredible weeks, she mused with a lighter heart than she'd had in months.

❧

In the late afternoon, she checked into an affordable hotel in the downtown area, leaving her car in a parking garage down the street. The room was tiny, but it offered free Wi-Fi, a desk, a coffee machine, and mini fridge. She dubbed it her office.

The next morning, she made a waffle at the buffet, a free continental breakfast part of her stay. Combined with a cup of coffee and a glass of orange juice, it was just what she needed to start the day.

Without a clue where to search for Axel, she aimlessly drove around for several hours to get a feel for the city. Her next goal: printed flyers she could hand out on the street and post in store windows, on bulletin boards, at metro stations, bus stops, and the library. Additional public locations like the post office, shopping malls, playgrounds, and parks also came to mind.

Dressed in a pleated summer blouse and olive-green shorts, Emma hit the city's streets, a stack of flyers in her backpack. She was pleased with the quality of the heavyweight paper, Axel's pictures, and the easy-to-read bold lettering.

MISSING
Axel Templeton, 28 years old.
Hair Color: Dark Blond
Eye Color: Brown
Axel hasn't been seen by his family in ten years, the latest communication coming from the Portland area.
Please call (998) 949-3941 if you have any information about his whereabouts.

The Central library was within walking distance of Emma's

hotel. The building, more than a century old, had red brick walls and tall windows. A drinking fountain built into the wall contained an inscription from Shakespeare. Emma read it while filling up her water bottle. "Tongues in Trees, Books in Running Brooks, Sermons in Stones, and Good in Everything".

Libraries were cathedrals for books, and the best place to read, study, or sit in contemplation, with the faint musty-book smell taking you back in time. For Emma it was a magical place, a sanctuary that never failed to give her a sense of serenity and peace. In awe, she climbed the stone steps that swept up from the sidewalk and entered through one of the three arching doors into the lobby. Marble columns loomed while a black granite staircase led up to the second floor. Beautiful lighting, large rooms, and rows of books welcomed her. She immediately felt at home and snapped several pictures to share with Sue Stremler. She hoped the images would do justice to the grandiose building and its interior.

"The use of library computers is limited to four hours per day. Can I have your photo ID?" a helpful staff member said.

Emma hoisted the western-style backpack she'd bought in South Dakota on the counter.

"Do you have a place where I can hang a missing person poster?" she asked, handing her the ID and two posters.

"Of course. I'll take care of that," she offered.

To make the most of her time, Emma sat down at one of the large tables and got to work. Four hours later, she'd visited multiple websites and left posts under lost and found, local news, and community events. She'd also paid for classifieds in several newspapers, and she'd done more research about missing persons and how to find them. The website from the Portland Police told her to call the nonemergency number, which she planned to do later, and she did an internet search under Axel Templeton. Through Facebook she found two profiles that might be him, age-wise. The first one had no activity for six years, no profile picture, and only one friend, a Goth looking girl named Raven Wintersdream. She'd left her a message, but the latest post from the girl was from more than five years ago. It probably wouldn't lead anywhere. The second one was even worse. With just a picture of a long-haired guy, his back to the camera. He didn't have a single friend or post since the profile was created over eight years ago.

Although tempted, she'd refrained from running an internet search on Jesse, afraid to read anything negative about him. Or worse, that he was losing ground in the election. He would definitely blame it on her disappearance. She didn't need the extra stress.

Hungry, she closed off all the sites and nodded her goodbye to the other computer users sitting close to her.

In the days that followed, she posted flyers in bars, restaurants, coffee shops, supermarkets, museums, and colleges. Her many miles of walking brought her all over the city. She began to know her way around. Portland, on the Columbia and Willamette Rivers, nicknamed the City of Roses, impressed her. The city was a charming blend of historic and modern architecture, and had many bridges and bicycle paths. It also offered an impressive music and arts scene, and spectacular vistas of snow-capped Mount Hood and Mount St. Helens, and the scenic Columbia River Gorge. Portland's residents seemed overall very active, with runners, bicyclists, and pedestrians everywhere. With a twinge of homesickness, she thought of Heemstead. Her hometown was just as vibrant, with its many coffee shops and restaurants, colleges, the university, and students roaming around.

All the while, her phone stayed disappointingly quiet. After an entire week had gone by, the only calls coming in were from curious people, asking questions and wanting more details.

A disgruntled Ruben had ordered her to widen the search perimeter and to include all the bordering cities and towns, like Beaverton, Gresham, Milwaukie, and Vancouver, Washington across the river. He'd also talked about creating an age-enhanced photo of Axel, hoping it could be helpful. His calls had become increasingly frequent. He demanded results. As if she didn't feel bad enough without him rubbing it in.

"Your charges keep piling up. If you don't have any results in three days, I'll cancel your debit card," he threatened.

"You're not making any progress with the divorce either, are you?" she barked back and disconnected without saying goodbye. Ruben wasn't the only one running out of patience.

During her morning run, she regretted hanging up on him. He paid for all the expenses. But it also felt good. She learned to defend and stick up for herself. Approaching strangers on the street had become much easier as well. Remarkable what a road trip and a manhunt could do for one's self-confidence, she mused with a determined grin.

Bored to death, she went to the laundromat, and bought a pair of flip-flops at a store down the road. Portland usually received an abundant amount of rainfall, but with summer in full swing there was no sign of that. The warm afternoon took her back to the waterfront park. Children splashed underneath the spray of a fountain. Their excited screams brought a smile to her face. Until she caught sight of white clouds mushrooming above the Cascade Mountains in the east. She watched them expand, progressively changing into a light gray as the sky darkened. It seemed like a rapidly developing thunderstorm was coming their way. People gathered their belongings. Most of them picked up speed, not wanting to take the risk of getting caught in the rain.

"Thunderstorms are unusual in the city," a passerby warned her, "but they can wreak havoc as they unleash their fury. Better take shelter, ma'am."

Lightning struck in the distance, followed by a second flash and deep rumbling. Mesmerized by its dangerous splendor, Emma stayed where she was while the wind picked up and the temperature dropped. When the first cold raindrops fell, she regretted her decision to linger. The park was already empty. Everyone had taken refuge against the deluge. As she headed toward her motel, the rain intensified, pelting the streets. Ill-protected against the elements in her sleeveless shirt and shorts, she got soaked in minutes. With one arm wrapped around her shivering body, the other protecting her eyes from the lashing water, she picked up her pace. Cars honked their horns in warning when she almost veered onto the road, their tires splashing up more water. She stepped over a foot-high barrier and took a shortcut down a steep embankment to the waterfront. The torrential downpour had drenched the thick lawn, her new flip-flops the wrong footwear for the uneven, soggy, and slippery terrain. The next moment, her left leg slid away from under her.

"Darn it," she cursed, followed by a loud scream as she tumbled down and landed on the sidewalk, ten feet below. Slightly dizzy, she pushed herself up to inspect her painful hands and knees. It didn't look too bad, except for her ankle. Tears of pain slid down her cheeks and mixed in with the rain when she rotated her foot. It hurt but didn't seem broken.

"Are you okay, lady?" a deep voice asked close to her ear.

She looked up at the grimy face of a homeless man, his long hair tangled beneath a navy stocking cap.

"What?" she cried out.

"I thought you might need help, sitting here in the rain after your tumble," he continued. All his teeth were missing, and he stank like rotting garbage and stale cigarette smoke.

She leaned away from him. He'd come far too close for comfort. "I don't have any money, if that's what you're thinking."

The man took a hasty step back, holding up his two hands in front of him, as if to protect himself. "I only wanted to help, ma'am." His ragged shirt was plastered to his skin. Just like her, he was completely soaked.

She reached for her backpack and scrambled to her feet. "I'm okay. Don't worry." She turned away from him, and almost fell again.

The stranger grabbed her arm.

"I don't need your help," she hissed and jerked free of his grip. With pain shooting through her entire foot, she hobbled away.

After one hundred feet, she glanced over her shoulder to make sure he didn't follow her.

The man stood in the pouring rain, watching her.

By the time she made it back to the hotel, her room was bathed in sunlight. The rain had already let up, and the sky was a brilliant blue. The sun warmed the earth and quickly evaporated the puddles the thunderstorm had left behind. She peeled off her clothes and stepped under the warm water spray of the shower. The water pooling around her feet was brown from the mud. She scrubbed the grime from her hair and body and inspected herself. The pain in her ankle had already subsided. Aside from a few scratches on her knee and the palms of her hands, she was intact.

In clean clothes and with a soothing cup of hot tea in her hand, she roamed around her comfortable room. The rain-soaked image of the homeless man remained engraved on her retinas. *What's gotten into me?* All he did was offer a helping hand, and she'd responded with rudeness.

The next morning, she still felt ashamed, regretting her behavior from the day before. Come on, Emma, she thought to herself at breakfast. To offer someone an apology isn't nearly as bold as driving across the country. You can do it!

The stirring of nerves in the pit of her stomach belied her courageous thoughts, but she refused to let them hold her back. In her room, she opened the box with her still unworn Western boots. Combined with a pair of blue jeans and a regular plain T-shirt, she hoped to give the impression she could kick ass as she went on her daring venture to find the man and apologize.

At the spot where she'd slid down the embankment, only a handful of grass and smudges of dirt on the pavers below showed evidence of her fall. Cars whizzed by while people cycled and strolled around the area. Life was back to normal, everyone going about their daily business. It all looked so different from yesterday afternoon, the bright sun and cloudless sky promising another gorgeous day.

She contemplated what to do. A few hundred feet away sat a middle-aged man on a folded up blue tarp, his back against a concrete retaining-wall. His thinning dirty blond hair looked unkempt. He stared down at the ground, his hands in his lap. Next to him lay several empty plastic bottles and a black garbage bag with dirty clothes spilling out. Hesitant to disturb him, she walked past. The man didn't move, unaware of her presence.

Like many other cities, the Portland metropolitan area had a homeless problem. Thousands of vagrants, drifters, and other unfortunate men and women slept under bridges, in parks, on sidewalks, and in doorways. Portlanders were known for their tolerance and generosity. Combined with the mild weather and many nonprofit homeless services, life on the streets was less brutal than in many other cities. Nevertheless, it unsettled her to encounter so many people holding up cardboard signs at intersections and asking for money. Emma couldn't imagine how difficult it had to be to live on the street, especially when winter hit.

She neared one of the city's many bridges. Underneath it was a miserable-looking homeless camp set up, constructed of tents, plastic tarps, and shopping carts.

Her courage dwindled, but the persistent memory of the

homeless man's sincere concern kept her from turning on her heels. The closer she got to the bridge, the more pronounced the stench of feces and garbage became. Her heart thumped nervously.

A heavyset woman leaned against one of the bridge pillars. Cigarette smoke circled around her head. Emma nodded in greeting as her stomach clenched.

The woman flicked her cigarette bud on the ground and crushed it beneath the heel of her sneaker. White flesh bulged from underneath her top, and she drew her sweatpants up to cover it. "Where you heading, ma'am? Down there's a dead end and no place for the likes of you." She took a step in Emma's direction. "Can I bum a cigarette off you, honey?"

When Emma's gaze met the woman's stealthy, calculating eyes, her fingers tightened around the straps of her backpack. "Sorry, I don't smoke," she replied and hastened away.

The woman snorted after her. "That's what they always say."

It was noticeably cooler and drafty in the shade of the bridge, the low concrete overhang creating a wind tunnel. Dark water lapped against the quayside, and two seagulls screeched while they fought over a piece of garbage.

Emma steered around a dented oil drum, blackened from campfire smoke, the pungent smell of creosote and soot hovering in the air. Extensive graffiti on the concrete walls, loose gravel, flapping tarps, stained mattresses, and overflowing bashed-in garbage cans surrounded by piles of junk added to her distress. When she heard two men scuffing around in between two tents, she lost the last bit of courage and backed away.

"You're a fucking thief, Larry! This is my loot, and you know it!" one of the men yelled. He grabbed a garbage bag and swung it over his skinny shoulder, empty aluminum cans rattling inside. To her distress, he headed in her direction, giving her an unpleasant glare in passing.

The other man grumbled to himself, raising his fist. "I'll get you for this. Always the same. Asshole. Don't come near my camp again." He kept on ranting and raving, although his skinny adversary was long gone. When he noticed Emma standing there, stiff and white-faced, he blinked hard as though to clear his vision.

"Excuse me," Emma said, ready to bolt. She wiped her damp palms on the thighs of her blue jeans. "I'm looking for someone I met here yesterday and was wondering if you could help me."

"What's it to you?" the man answered, throwing her a calculated stare. His creased face was partially hidden behind an unkempt beard, but his eyes were vigilant.

The sound of a zipper made them both look toward a sagging tent. A man crawled out and got up on his feet. Dressed in a long black pea coat and shorts, he wore sandals, and his hairy legs were filthy and discolored. The baseball cap on his head had a bullet hole in it. Emma suppressed a shudder.

The elderly vagrant made a threatening gesture with his fist to the newcomer. "Stay out of this, Pea. The lady and I are just starting to talk business."

"What kind of business could you have with a nice lady?" the other man asked witheringly.

This was the moment to walk away, Emma decided. She spun around, her nerves shooting into overdrive when the newcomer followed her. "Maybe I can help you, ma'am," he yelled after her.

Emma didn't stop to listen to what he had to say until she'd left the homeless camp behind and stepped back into the warm sunshine. Goosebumps covered her skin.

"Hey! Are you the woman Jackbone stumbled upon yesterday during that thunderstorm?" the man asked when he caught up with her. "He ain't here, Missy, but for a little change I can give him a message."

Not wanting to offend another homeless person, Emma slipped off her backpack, opened the zipper, and searched around at the bottom. She found a few dollar bills and some change.

"They call me Pea, after my coat." The man grinned, showing three rotten teeth when she handed him the cash.

"Just tell, uh, . . . Jackbone that I wanted to thank him for offering his help. He was very kind." Before closing the zipper, she pulled out three flyers. "I'm in town looking for a missing person. His name is Axel. If you want to hand these out to your friends, that would be great."

Pea glanced at Axel's picture, holding the posters between his grubby fingers. "Ha, for a moment that young chap reminded me of Sheep's old buddy," he said. "Mainly the eyes. I don't know. It could be."

"Who's Sheep?"

Pea scratched his head, his baseball cap moving back and forth when he did. "Oh, Sheep used to hang out around here all the time, but that's been years. Last I heard was him collecting garbage for the city. Hanging on the back of one of them green monsters. Some of us can better ourselves, but most can't." Pea turned around and walked away. Emma did the same.

CHAPTER

24

AT THE HOTEL, Emma prepared a sandwich and ate on the tiny balcony of her room. Her view comprised of a parking lot, a fast-food restaurant, and the backside of a warehouse. Ruben had called again, warning her she was running out of her allotted money and time. The view depressed her even more. She closed the balcony door and turned on the air-conditioning. With the afternoon stretching out in front of her, she followed up on her only lead, no matter how futile.

Pea had said Sheep worked for a garbage company. On her phone, she found a list and started calling the ones closest by. The first two gave her a simple 'no, never-heard-of-someone-called-Sheep' answer. The third one was an out-of-service number, the company probably no longer in business. Her fourth call to one of the smaller companies yielded success.

"Yes, I remember Sheep," the secretary told her. "I was

always jealous of his full head of blond curls. They gave him his nickname."

Emma held her breath, her pulse racing.

"I believe his actual name is Floyd McCall, McCoy or McCollum, or something like that," the secretary continued.

With a pen and notepad in hand, her phone under her chin, Emma wrote down the three names. "Does he still work for the company?"

"Hey, Jimmie!" the woman yelled. "You remember Sheep, right? Whatever happened to him after he left? Do you know?"

Emma heard the secretary talking to a man in the background before she came back on the phone. "Jimmy says he works for Case Coleman. He's got a landscaping business about half an hour west of here. Let me look up his phone number." A keyboard clicked. "Found it."

Thrilled with the result, Emma thanked the efficient secretary and called the number. It rang multiple times and went to voicemail. Not giving up, she called three more times, each time leaving a message. A search on her phone gave her an address. Filled with nervous anticipation, she grabbed her backpack and headed out the door. Forty minutes later, she stopped in front of a metal shop building. In front of it was a parked truck with a magnetic sign on the door that said Coleman Landscaping since 1995. Hooked up to the truck was an eight-foot trailer, loaded with lawn mowers, trimmers, and blowers, and a variety of shovels, rakes, and other hand tools. One of the overhead doors of the shop stood open.

"Hello? Anybody here?" she yelled, peeking inside.

A man in stained and wrinkled blue coveralls stood in front of a workbench. "One second," he said without looking in her direction. His right arm moved down. The instant harsh sound of grinding metal made her cover her ears. He repeated this same action several times and then turned off the machine, the long chain of a chainsaw gripped in his oil covered hand.

"Sorry for the noise. I was sharpening the teeth," the man said. "What can I do for you?" He put the chain down next to a bright orange saw and wiped his hands on a rag.

"I was told a Floyd McCoy might work here?" Emma said.

"Floyd? Most people know him as Sheep," the man replied with a grin. "I sent him up to Green Heights, a fancy gated community at the east end of town. I don't expect him back until four or five."

Emma's eyes lit up. "Do you have the address?"

With the GPS turned on, Emma drove up steep roads, lined on both sides with trees in lustrous shades of green, until she reached a gate. The community was perched at the end of the road, high atop the hill. She now understood how Green Heights got its name.

Next to the gate sat a small concrete building with cameras mounted on the roof. A security guard stepped out, dressed in long black pants with military creases and a bright yellow T-shirt, the name of the community embroidered on his pocket. With his hand on the roof of her car, he bent slightly forward.

Emma rolled down her window. "I'm looking for the landscaper. Any chance you'll let me in?"

He gave her a scrutinizing glare. "ID please."

Emma pulled her wallet from her backpack and showed

him her driver's license. He compared the picture with her face and nodded. As if by magic, the gate slowly opened.

"Take a left at the first intersection and you'll find him." The guard stepped back to let her pass.

The architecture and well-kept gardens of the homes inside the community reminded her far too much of Jesse's neighborhood back east. To distract herself, she looked at the ducks floating around on a pond surrounded by perfectly manicured lawns, shade trees, and flower beds. A man with a head full of blond curls, in brown work boots and shorts, trimmed the grass around one of the park benches. He had the gas-powered trimmer harnessed to his back. His plaid shirt was short-sleeved and unbuttoned, showing wiry muscles and a deep tan on his chest and arms.

Emma parked the car, stepped out and headed over the sidewalk in his direction with one of Axel's flyers.

The moment the man caught sight of her, he stopped working, keeping the engine running at slow speed to let her pass safely.

She raised her hand to let him know she wanted to talk to him.

He shut down the engine and took off his ear protectors and plastic safety glasses.

"Sorry to bother you," she said. "But is your name Sheep?"

He frowned and drew a handkerchief from his pocket to wipe the sweat from his forehead. "What can I help you with?"

"I know it may sound far-fetched, but I met a man with the name Pea. He mentioned you may have been friends with Axel Templeton?" She handed him the flyer.

A quick smile tugged at the corner of his mouth, immediately followed by a glare of caution. "Is he in trouble?"

"Not at all. His family is looking for him," Emma assured him.

"Eagle told me he didn't have any family. How can I believe you?"

Now it was her turn to look surprised. "Eagle? His name is Axel. Axel Templeton."

Sheep unstrapped the weed eater and stretched his back. "I met him years ago, when I was homeless." A water bottle hung from a clip on his belt. He opened the cap, splashed water over his face and took a long swig. After staring into near space for a while, he shook his head and smiled. "We became friends."

Emma moved jubilantly from one leg to the other. Finally, she had something to report to Ruben. "Does he still live around here?"

Sheep shook his head, made an upward wavy movement with both his arms, and looked up at the sky. "May your heart be like an eagle and soar above in the storm of your life," he quoted with a solemn voice.

Automatically she looked up too, in her imagination seeing eagles fly across the brilliant, blue sky, carried by the sweltering currents of the air.

"Eagle also liked to say: those who drink booze with the night owls can't soar with the eagles during the day. Sometimes it helped him to stay sober. Sometimes it didn't." A warm grin lopsided his face. "Eagle liked to come up with interesting quotes. He read a lot, to work himself through some heavy personal shit. We both did, and we both persevered."

Emma couldn't wait to find out more. "What else can you tell me about him?"

Sheep drew another swig from his bottle before answering,

"He'd just arrived in town when we met. He'd hitched a ride from some farm back east with a chick called Raven. I always believed she adopted that name because of Eagle. She was smitten with him."

During her Facebook search in the library, she'd found a page with the name Raven. Could that be a coincidence? "Raven Wintersdream?" she asked.

"That's what she called herself," Sheep nodded. "You know her?"

She told him about the Facebook page.

"Raven must have set that up for him," Sheep replied, shaking his head. "Eagle wasn't interested in computer stuff and would be dead set against it if he'd known."

While strapping his trimmer back on, he paused. "Funny. I hadn't seen Raven in years until a few weeks ago. She sold me one of them fancy coffee drinks at the drive-thru espresso stand on Bleeker Street."

After promising Sheep she would give his regards to Eagle if she found him, she thanked him and returned to her car. On one of her phone apps, she searched for nearby drive-thru espresso stands and found The Golden Grinder on Bleeker Street. It was three-thirty in the afternoon. If her luck held, Raven might be working.

Traffic into the city was heavy. It took her almost a half an hour to get to her destination. When she pulled in, all the lights of the small stand were off, the hours of operation from 6AM to 4PM. Undeterred, she stepped from the car. Her phone told her it was only one minute past four. Somebody still had to be there.

At her knocking, a blonde head appeared, the girl pointing to an imaginary watch on her wrist. From her lips Emma read, "We are closed." In answer, she made a yapping movement with her right hand, indicating she wanted to talk. The window slid open, and the girl leaned out.

"Are you familiar with a woman called Raven Wintersdream?" Emma asked.

The girl raised her eyebrows with a bewildered look. "That's me, but I dropped that name years ago." Her surprise changed into a look of understanding. "You must know Sheep."

Emma handed her one of Axel's flyers. "Sheep told me you and Axel, or Eagle, were friends. I'm trying to find him. Do you have any idea how to contact him, or where he might be?"

A flash of pain flickered in Raven's hazel eyes before she released a deep sigh. "He was so messed up for a long time," she replied. "I did what I could, but he kept pushing me away."

"Axel's brother hired me to find him. His father is seriously ill and wants to see him. Are you still in contact?"

Raven's demeanor changed, her expression hard and distant. "His asshole brother?"

Her sudden hostility came as a surprise. Emma stayed quiet, unsure of how to react.

"Eagle broke up with me because he didn't trust women. No matter what I said to convince him otherwise, it didn't make any difference. Did you know he found his brother naked? In his own room. In his own bed. Fucking his own girlfriend."

Her sentences were short, her voice clipped.

"Eagle told me a serious relationship wasn't in the stars for him. It took me years to get over him. It wasn't until I met Greg and started this coffee stand that I was able to move on."

CHAPTER

25

RAVEN CLOSED the coffee stand and joined Emma at one of the two tiny tables, Axel's flyer in her hand. She placed it on the tabletop in front of her.

"Anything you can tell me could be helpful in finding him," Emma encouraged her to speak.

Retreating into thoughts, Raven traced the contour of Axel's face with her finger. "This brings back a lot of memories," she smiled. "Some of them I'd rather forget, but you seem sincere, and family is important. So, I'll tell you what I know." She turned the flyer upside down and crossed one leg over the other.

"I used to own a rusty cargo van. Traveling back home from college, I noticed Eagle hitchhiking along the highway. I'd never picked up a hitchhiker before but decided to stop. He told me he wanted to go west."

Traffic rushed by and a disappointed customer sped off,

finding the stand closed. Raven didn't seem to notice.

"He introduced himself as Eagle and told me he'd just lost his job. From the start, I knew he battled a traumatic event. His eyes held such deep sadness. Sometimes, he would retreat into hours of silence, a profound loneliness hovering around him, but I didn't care. I'd fallen for him the moment I found out he loved the music from my favorite bands Royksopp and Lord Huron just as much as I did. After he checked the oil of my van and tied up the loose muffler, I was head over heels."

A car driving by honked its horn, distracting her. She pulled out her cell phone. "Let me text Greg real quick, to tell him I'm running late."

"Eagle must have been handy?" Emma said, watching her fingers move rapidly over the keyboard.

"Eagle is an amazing mechanic," Raven said. "He worked on a farm where he learned a lot and wasn't afraid to get his hands dirty. Whenever he noticed someone with car trouble, he asked me to pull over to offer help. He was such a sensitive, caring soul." She paused to draw in a deep breath. "It sucked he had to witness that fire on the farm where he worked."

Raven's eyes misted over, a white-knuckle grip on her phone. "His employer perished in the flames, along with two young farmhands he'd befriended. He was devastated, had recurring nightmares, and couldn't come to terms with it."

A single tear escaped from the corner of her eye, and she brushed it away with her sleeve. "The two guys who perished were the ones who nicknamed him Eagle."

Raven's story touched Emma deeply. "Do you know why they named him that?" she asked.

"Eagle was a birdwatcher, always observing the majestic

birds through his binoculars. You're just like them, they told him, referring to his journey across the country. You're an eagle in flight."

They sat in silence for a minute.

"It took us several days to reach Portland," Raven continued. "We camped along the way and found a spot where we could park overnight in the city's center. I didn't want to leave him, but for months, a brooding sadness held him in its grip. The wall around his heart so thick, that my love and support couldn't penetrate. To protect myself, I had to give up on our relationship and moved back in with my parents. Leaving him was the hardest decision I've ever made, and I don't know how he survived. Life on the street is sheer hell, the filth, cold, and constant empty stomach debilitating."

The last she'd heard was that Axel came to terms with his loss, quit drinking, and that he moved to Riversdale, a small town about two hours south of Portland. An older lady named Adelyn had offered him a job as a caretaker on her farm.

At the hotel, Emma informed the lady behind the reception desk she planned to check out the next morning. In her room, she sank down onto the bed, her cell phone gripped in her clammy hand.

Instead of finding Axel in the future, suddenly the moment could be as soon as tomorrow. She wasn't ready for her journey to end but couldn't hold out on an update. She owed it to Ruben and his father.

"Couldn't you ask for his phone number instead of wasting more time?" Ruben grumbled after he answered his phone. "Your four weeks are over."

She ignored him. "For about a year, Axel lived on the streets of Portland. During that time, he never owned a cell phone. Come on, Ruben. I'm so close. All I need is one more day."

The next morning, Emma drove farther south to Riversdale, a town of fifteen hundred people in the foothills of the Cascade Mountains. Dressed casually in a pair of khaki shorts, a light green blouse and her cowboy boots, she walked down Main Street, armed with a stack of flyers. With much more information at hand and the name Adelyn, she had success within minutes.

"I've seen Eagle around town many times," a middle-aged woman said after taking one of the flyers. "But I wouldn't have recognized him from this picture. What a cute and loveable boy he used to be!"

"By any chance, can you tell me where he lives?" Emma asked.

"I sure can," the woman replied. "Take route 323 out of town for at least four miles, past the country store and the nursery, until you reach Swift Road. The Gravenstein homestead is about two miles down Swift. Give my love to Adelyn when you see her, will you?"

Emma thanked her and headed back to her car. Her quest would soon be over, her mission coming to an end. Maybe as soon as tomorrow she would be back in Heemstead. Ruben had promised the divorce papers were almost ready. It was time to figure out her future.

The smell of fresh-baked bread drew her into the local diner. Over a turkey burger and a salad, the waitress confirmed the woman's directions. She'd known Adelyn Gravenstein,

Eagle's employer, most of her life. It was a small town indeed.

Emma made a phone call to Ruben, giving him the latest information, paid for lunch and walked back to her car. From about twenty feet away, she noticed a man leaning casually against her passenger door, his hands tucked in the pockets of his trousers, his ankles crossed. Her pulse raced with dread.

Jesse. As always dressed immaculately, his hair styled to perfection, and soft tan leather loafers on his feet.

How had he found her?

Frozen in place, she stared at him as he talked on the phone.

When he caught sight of her, he ended the conversation.

Although his eyes were hidden behind dark sunglasses, she sensed the sardonic smile in them and his scornful mood. When his lips moved, all she heard was the loud thudding of her own heart and the alarm bells in her ears.

"I said, give me the keys and get in the car," he repeated, his voice laced with impatience.

"What are you doing here?" she asked. Her voice sounded hoarse.

A powerful hand closed around her wrist. "You don't want to make a scene in the middle of the street, right? Give me the keys!"

She cowered, her fingers shaking as she retrieved the keys from her pocket and dropped them into his palm.

He unlocked the passenger door and shoved her inside. She practically fell across the seat.

"Lovely boots," he commented with disdain and pushed her legs inside before closing the door.

She stifled a sob of fear behind her hand as she watched him get in behind the wheel and start the car. Without bothering to look over his shoulder, he merged into traffic. A driver honked in protest.

They quickly left the city limits and headed east on route 323. Modest homes soon gave way to pastures, farmhouses, and barns. After they passed a country store and a nursery, he turned on the blinker to turn into Swift Road. It was the road to Adelyn Gravenstein's farm. Her nerves tightened with every passing mile. *How did he know?*

Jesse drove over the speed limit, and she nearly cried out when the car jounced over unexpected railroad tracks. He gave her a side glance. "You've been on quite the road trip, haven't you?" His fingers slid down her bare arm until they reached her hand, taking it in a firm grip. "It's so good to see you again, my lovely wife. I missed you." He patted her hand before letting go.

"How did you find me?" she asked, massaging the painful marks on her hand where his fingertips had dug deeply into her skin.

He smirked. "All this time, did you really think I had no idea where you were? You're so naïve." He laughed without mirth. "Ruben kept me informed every day, telling me about your travels and whereabouts, and he just called me to tell me where you were heading."

Stunned by his revelation, she stared straight ahead. The unfamiliar road narrowed as it wound its way farther up the Cascade Mountains, the farmlands giving way to tall pine trees, Douglas firs, and oaks. She hadn't seen another car for several miles.

"Can't we discuss this as sensible adults?" Increasingly anxious, Emma clutched her backpack against her chest, hanging on to it for dear life. "Preferably over dinner back in town. This road is going nowhere."

"You want me to turn around?" Jesse sneered. "Don't you want to find your precious Axel and fulfill your obligation to Ruben? I didn't know you became a quitter too, besides being a betrayer and a coward. Sneaking out of the house. In the middle of the night. Asking my best friend for help with a divorce. What did you think? That he would betray me, too?"

He slammed his fist on the steering wheel. The two right tires skidded off the pavement, the side of the car barely escaping the guardrail. Jesse hit the brakes and a few hundred feet farther, the car came to a halt in a gravel parking lot next to the road. With a decisive click, he shut off the engine, threw his sunglasses on the dashboard, and turned to face her.

She could finally see his eyes, the stony stare directed toward her alarming, his demeanor one of aggression and determination.

Emma wrung her hands, her right leg shaking uncontrollably. It hadn't done that in four weeks. Not even when she was up a lonely mountain road in Wyoming, staring down the barrel of a shotgun under the hostile gaze of a would-be Calamity Jane. From the smirk on Jesse's face, she knew her nervousness didn't go unnoticed. In the tense silence, they stared at each other with hostility.

"Listen, Emma." He took a deep breath. "When Ruben told me you were getting close to finding Axel, I decided it was time to pull the plug on your adventure. This morning I took an early flight, rented a car at the airport, and drove down here to pick you up and take you home, where you belong."

"Are you telling me Ruben only pretended to take care of my request for a divorce? That he sent me after his brother, while the two of you laughed behind my back?" Bitter tears threatened to fall, but she swallowed and pointed a condemning finger at him. "This isn't a joke for me, Jesse. You used me as a doormat, humiliated me, cheated on me, and hurt me more than anyone ever has! And the only reason I went to Ruben for help was for your sake, because I didn't want this to become public knowledge. God, I'm so stupid. I should have gone to a real divorce lawyer right away instead of worrying over your precious election."

Full of self-disgust, she opened the door and got out. With her hands fisted and her jaws clenched, she breathed in and out through her nose, willing herself not to lose control. She was such a fool to trust Ruben and feel sorry for what he went through with his father's illness. He'd probably lied about that, too, using her own mother's illness so she would be empathetic to his cause and inclined to help. While all he'd wanted to accomplish was to prevent her from speaking out.

And how about Axel? Was he really missing, or was he part of this as well? Had they never intended for her to find him?

A soft touch on her shoulder made her cringe.

"Listen," Jesse said close to her ear. He stood right behind her, taking both her shoulders in his hands. "I understand that you needed a break, a vacation. It's good to reflect on your life once in a while. But I want you to put that silly idea about a divorce out of your head. People are asking about you, and I need you at home." His voice sounded smooth and silky. When she didn't reply he turned her around, still keeping his hands on her shoulders. His eyes bored into hers. "You're my wife, Emma. Don't you remember your wedding vows? To have and to hold, for better or worse, in sickness and health, and till death do us part?"

"How about to love and to cherish, Jesse?" she spat at him.

"Be reasonable, Emma!" Jesse replied, giving her a heartless smile. "I gave you everything you wanted and all that bullshit about love is women's talk. I need you, and you need me, and that's all that matters."

"You used me!" she cried, shrugging out from under the hands gripping her shoulders.

"You're darn right," Jesse said harshly, painfully grabbing her arm. "I need a wife to help me win this election. Who'll stand by my side during my political career, and I'll never agree to a divorce." His grasp tightened, his fingers digging deeper into her flesh. "You had no business running to Ruben with your problems. What happens or doesn't happen in the bedroom is between a husband and his wife, and it should stay there. Do you hear me?"

Horrified, she stared at him as he revealed the duplicity of his true nature.

"I booked us a flight tonight. Now, get back in the car!" He dragged her with him. "We're going home."

"No, I'm not," she cried out, trying to hold her ground. His hand was a vice around her arm. "You're hurting me."

"Then stop being a stubborn cow and get in the car."

For a few seconds, they stared, challenging each other, barely contained rage in his eyes. Afraid of what he might do, she conceded and dropped her gaze. "All right, you win. I'll go with you."

He opened the passenger door and waited until she put on her seatbelt. "That's more like it," he grumbled and slammed the door shut.

The moment he turned his back, she slipped off the

seatbelt. When he climbed in on the driver's side, she flew out of the car, clambered over the guardrail and dashed into the underbrush. Branches scraped her arms and hit her face. Terrified, she glanced over her shoulder as Jesse climbed over the guardrail after her. He was dangerously close. A few seconds later, his hands closed around the fabric of her blouse and jerked her to a stop.

"You stupid bitch," he growled, staring down at her like a raging bull. He tried to pull her up, but one of his soft leather loafers slipped off. He cursed as he stepped on a sharp rock and lost his footing. To keep himself from sliding down the hill, he released his grip.

Arms flailing, Emma flew forward, barely able to stay on her feet. In total panic, she used the momentum to flee down the steep hillside. She stumbled over rocks and boulders covered with moss, through scrubs and bushes, the heels of her boots digging into the soil to keep her from sliding. Clinging to low-hanging branches to keep her balance, she made it farther down the sheer and unforgiving terrain until she reached a small stream. Heaving and choking back sobs, she glanced up the incline.

"Emma! You'll regret this for the rest of your life!" Jesse yelled from above.

Afraid he tried to find another way down, she jumped over the creek and scrambled up the incline on the other side. Her hands clawed in the dirt and clung to whatever she found. Jesse kept cursing and yelling, but his voice sounded farther and farther away. When she reached the top of the slope, she fought her way through the foliage of the dense forest until she was completely out of breath and the pain in her side from running forced her to stop. She leaned against a tree, the only sound her ragged breathing and the soft rustling of leaves in the wind. Her knees buckled, and she sank down onto the soft damp moss.

Only five months ago, she'd led a simple and content life, until Jesse walked into her life. She'd been star struck and flattered by his interest, especially when he'd asked her to help write his speeches. But what she'd thought was love had only been infatuation. At twenty-seven, she should have seen it for what it was. She could kick herself now, believing a man like Jesse had a serious interest in a gray mouse like her.

She touched her painful cheek, feeling several long scrapes. Her chafed knees hurt; her arms covered in scratches. She rubbed the painful red welts, noticing three broken fingernails and her dirty palms. Running away may not have been the smartest move.

It was cool underneath the thick canopy, the sun barely able to peak through the foliage. She shivered, the dampness from the forest's groundcover penetrating through the fabric of her shorts. Time to start moving. She got up and gasped when she noticed her torn blouse and two missing buttons. In an automatic prudish response, she glanced around and quickly covered the gap showing her bra and the swelling of her breasts. Of course, nobody was there to see her disgraceful state of undress.

To get a sense of direction, she looked around. If only she could find that stream, then all she had to do was climb up the steep slope to make it back to the road. Resolutely, she straightened her shoulders and headed in the direction from which she came. In case Jesse was still around, searching for her, she had to hide behind the thick vegetation, waiting for him to leave. Making as little noise as possible, she wandered around. It seemed the creek had mysteriously disappeared, every tree the same, every brush like the one before. The first finger of dread crept upon her when it dawned on her she might be lost. That couldn't be happening.

With fierce determination, she continued to push her way through the dense forest until she caught sight of muddy footprints in the dirt and several broken branches. It was the spot where she'd almost slid down the hill. She'd worked her way in a circle, not getting anywhere.

Despite the cool temperatures, nervous heat flushed her face. She sunk down onto a mat-forming deciduous ground cover, the leaves similar to poison oak. Could she have more bad luck? Careful not to rub against it, she moved away.

Based on the position of the sun, it had to be late afternoon, maybe even early evening. Her stomach stirred, and she was thirsty. That creek had to be close by, and she had to find it.

Her left heel screamed in protest as she scrambled deeper into the forest. It had to be caused by a blister, the leather from her new boots still stiff. How long could she keep on going before dark? She had no idea.

The sun set. A slight breeze carried the scent of the fir trees and the atmosphere was cool, announcing the end of a glorious day.

As night fell, and it became too dark to keep on ambling around, despair settled over her. She lay down on a pile of dry leaves, pushing thoughts of ants, bugs, spiders, and other creepy crawlers to the back of her mind. With her knees hugged to her chest, she closed her eyes. Stress and hopelessness had taken its toll on her endurance. Mercifully, she dozed off.

CHAPTER

26

AFTER A LONG and restless night filled with dread and nightmares, an unfamiliar sound awakened Emma. Her eyes flew open and terrified she sought protection against the closest tree. Everything around seemed peaceful and birds chirped somewhere close. Releasing a long breath of relief, she massaged her temples. She'd survived a long dismal night alone and the sound she'd heard was probably only from animals waking up and rummaging for food. She would be okay, as long as it wasn't a bear or mountain lion preying on her.

Back on her feet, she stretched to let the blood flow back into her stiff limbs and wiped the leaves and twigs from her clothes. It was chilly and her parched throat and the deep gnawing in her stomach were a reminder of her precarious state. With a sense of urgency, she tried to get her bearings. Route 323 they followed yesterday had taken them to the east. If she wanted to find her way to town, she needed to head in a westerly direction and keep the sun at her back.

Her progress was slow, but gradually the forest seemed less dense and the rocky wooded slope of the mountain gentler. Convinced it wouldn't be long before she found her way out, she struggled onward until she heard the faint sound of a dog barking in the distance. She stopped immediately in her tracks and listened carefully, hoping the dog would bark again. When it did, she almost burst into grateful tears. A dog meant people, and people meant water, food, and safety.

Soon, more sunlight filtered through the trees, the underbrush thinned out, and grass grew taller, mixed in with purple lupines, daisies, dandelions, and other wildflowers. Long blackberry vines loaded with purple berries caught her attention. She picked one after the other, the thorns from the bushes scratching her arms. It was worth it. The berries were so ripe; they dropped in her hands the moment she reached out to them.

After she couldn't take another bite, her fingertips purple from the juice, she continued west until she found herself at the edge of a swiftly running creek. The water, clear and cold, rushed over moss-covered boulders. She knelt to wash her fingers and sticky face. Her arms were scratched from the thorns and she rinsed them off. Over the noise of the water, she didn't hear the man approaching.

"Who do we have here?" he asked.

At the sound of his voice, her heart stopped beating. Then it raced at the sight of the stranger. He towered over her, his expression hidden behind a beard and mustache, his long hair unkempt. He looked downright menacing.

Her gaze followed his every movement, and she backed away when he moved closer. His shabby, short-sleeved shirt was completely unbuttoned, showing a bare chest and a knife in a leather sheath hanging on a cord from his neck. In his right hand, he held a foot-long machete with a wooden handle. One swing with that savage looking length and she would be dead.

When he approached her, she backed away. Arms flailing in the air, she fell backward into the creek. The strong current immediately swept her away. She shrieked in terror, struggling to find her footing as the rushing water dragged her downstream until whitewater closed over her head. When she resurfaced a moment later, she gulped for air and cried out in pain as her body slammed against a rock. Two powerful hands reached out and dragged her from the water before she could disappear beneath the tumult for the third time.

Soaked to the bone, Emma sat on a flat rock among the wildflowers. Water dripped down her face. Her blouse clung to her skin, outlining her bra, her shorts torn from the rocks. She was a heap of misery and terrified, she looked at the machete lying next to her in the tall grass.

"Do you think you can walk?" he asked, looking down at her with concern. "My home is just up the hill." He nodded to show the direction.

She narrowed her eyes suspiciously as her gaze shifted from the knife around his neck to the machete and back to him.

He didn't seem to notice her fear and extended his hand to help her up. When she cringed, he raised his eyebrow in question.

"Sorry, I'm a little dizzy and need a few seconds," she said quickly.

"We don't have to go far," he encouraged her, reaching out for the second time.

Not knowing what else to do, she took his hand and stood, still shaking.

When he seemed convinced that she wouldn't fall, he picked up his machete. "I took this to clear a path to the creek," he said. "This time of the year, the grass and weeds grow so tall."

"I see," she answered, staring up at the hill where she could see the trail he'd cleared.

He made a small circle with his thumb and index finger, put his fingers in his mouth, and whistled. At the high-pitched sound, a black Labrador came racing down the hill in their direction. When he reached them, he barked and weaved himself around the man's legs. Water dripped from his soaked carpenter-pants.

Her initial fear dwindled and changed into gratitude as she followed her rescuer up the hill. Her feet squished inside her boots, the blisters on her heels hurting like crazy. She sensed they were bleeding. Limping awkwardly, she trailed along until they made it to the top of the hillside and a two-story red barn came into sight. The two tall sliding doors stood open and several chickens clucked. They ignored the black dog running in circles and kept on pecking in the dirt as they looked for food.

In the shade of an open lean-to next to the barn stood two horses. They ate from a bag of hay, interrupting their meal to glance up as Emma and the man approached.

He guided her into the barn. The first things she noticed were several stacks of firewood against the wall and a huge, antique-looking white enamel stove. It stood on four legs, with two drawers on the left and an oven on the right. On top, it had a griddle and two burners. Images of the early settlers came to her mind.

She also noticed a huge shiny motorhome with several slide-outs, parked inside. It seemed at least forty feet long and stood in stark contrast to the rustic environment, the horse's tack, sawhorses, and multitude of garden, hand, and wood-working tools.

"You can take a shower inside," he told her.

At the bottom of the steps of the motorhome, Emma pulled off her boots and held them upside down. Water gushed, making a puddle on the concrete floor. She also peeled off her socks and wrung them out. "Are you sure it's okay to go inside? I'm soaked."

"Of course," he replied. "You need to warm up. There are plenty of clean towels in the closet in the bathroom. While you freshen up, I'll go to the house to find you something to wear. All your clothes are ripped."

If the man had wanted to harm her, he could have easily done so already. It was time to express her appreciation for rescuing her. "Thanks for plucking me from the river, Mr. . . . uh . . . ?"

"People call me Eagle," he answered, then turned around and left the barn.

Instead of feeling exhilarated she'd found Axel, she unraveled. Why couldn't it have been someone else who'd rescued her, saving her from drowning? She didn't want to be entwined in his life more than she already was. She slumped forward and stared at the concrete floor, clutching her arms so tightly that her fingertips began to feel numb.

A chicken made its way inside the barn and started pecking around her feet. Its feathers were light brown, and it had a funny pinkish crest on its head and dangling flaps of skin on either side of its beak. It wasn't afraid at all, not even when she rolled her shoulders to release some of her tension before she stood.

The inside of the motorhome was luxurious and spacious. It contained a regular dining table and four chairs, a full kitchen with marble countertops, a huge refrigerator and an island with a double sink. It even had an electric fireplace underneath a flat screen television, surrounded by an L-shaped couch and two recliners. Her feet almost disappeared in the plush carpet. She'd never been in a recreational vehicle before, and it wasn't at all like she'd imagined.

The sparkling clean bathroom at the other end of the RV was fit for a queen. It had a full-sized shower stall and two sinks.

In front of the tall six-foot mirror, she gaped at her reflection. Her skin was ghostly pale, and bruises discolored her face and arms. Why Axel had allowed her inside this expensive RV, she couldn't even fathom.

After stripping off her torn clothes, she opened the glass shower door and turned on the water. Steam filled the enclosure as she stepped inside. With hot water cascading down her body, she wanted to stay there forever, to forget about the world outside. She covered her face with her hands. It became too much, her legs barely able to keep her up. With her back against the shower's wall, she slid down until she sat on the floor of the stall and wept without restraint.

After her weeping subsided, the water became colder. She'd almost used up all the hot water. Time to pull yourself together and come up with a plan, she told herself. She stepped from the shower and dried off. With the towel wrapped around her body, she opened the door.

Axel sat at the dining room table. He gave her a warm smile and stood. "You can change in the bedroom," he said, handing her a small stack of clothes.

She avoided his eyes. "Thank you." Relieved to postpone a confrontation, she disappeared into the bedroom. She needed a little more time to process everything that had happened and to figure out how to proceed.

Everything in the bedroom looked soft and downy, and she wanted nothing more than to curl up between the sheets and push it all out of her mind. Would it be okay if she lay down for a few minutes?

The afternoon sun peeked through the window into the bedroom, waking her up. At first, she didn't realize where she was. Then she knew.

While she slept, someone had covered her with a thin blanket. Underneath, the towel around her body was still damp from the shower. Groggy, she sat up at the edge of the bed and rubbed the sleep from her eyes.

She hoped the clothes Axel had given her would fit, the first item a black cotton house dress with tiny ivory flowers. She pulled it over her head. It fell below her knees and was too wide, but after she knotted the matching belt around her middle, it didn't look too bad. One of the other items was an oversized pair of panties. She slipped them on. They came up to her belly button, and she giggled. They had to be from an older lady.

Still unprepared to face the world, she left the bedroom. She found the RV empty, and walked down the steps into the barn.

"I put your boots and socks outside in the sun to dry," Axel said. He stood in front of a workbench. Instead of a machete, he held a torque wrench in his hand.

It seemed he worked on a piece of equipment. Tools were scattered everywhere, his shirt and hands covered with greasy-looking stains.

"I stuck around in case you woke up," he said. "Are you hungry? It's dinnertime. I have a roast on the barbeque."

"Starving," she admitted. Other than the blackberries, she didn't have anything to eat in a long time.

"If you get the potato salad from the fridge, two plates and silverware, we can eat in about five minutes."

They watched the sun disappear behind the mountains while they ate at the picnic table, exchanging inconsequential sentences. About his dog Samson, the comfort of the motor-home, and the tenderness of the meat. Anything, except about herself, or what she'd done out there in the woods.

She had no idea what she should or shouldn't say. This was an awkward situation and she didn't want to ruin the peaceful moment. She felt grateful to just sit there.

When she looked up from her plate, she caught him staring

at her, his elbows on the table, his chin resting in his palms.

"I was lost," she volunteered.

He didn't flinch. "I know."

He knew? Taken aback, she frowned. "What else do you know?"

He thought for a moment, his brow furrowed in contemplation. "You ran away from a complicated situation and are trying to figure out what direction to take. Am I close?"

Behind his beard, she noticed a trace of a smile. Was he making fun of her?

"From your anxious look, the frown between your brows, and the tension in your shoulders, I can tell you're troubled," he continued, his eyes steady on her face.

What the . . . ? There was no way he could know all that just by looking at her, she decided. He had to know more than he let on and was probably part of the entire scheme. She eyed him with suspicion. "Did someone call you about me?"

He lifted an amused eyebrow. "I don't have a phone."

Sheep had told her he didn't have a phone, but she hadn't believed it. Nowadays, everyone had a cell phone. "So how do you stay in touch with the outside world?"

He pulled a small walkie-talkie from his pants pocket. "A twenty-five-mile, two-way radio is all we need."

Uneasily, she shifted on the wooden picnic bench, her misgivings growing into distrust.

"If you're uncomfortable around me, I can take you to the house," Eagle said, stroking his beard. When she didn't reply, he stood, picked up their dirty plates and disappeared into the barn. His dog immediately trailed after him.

Left alone, Emma sat with her shoulders slumped, staring at

the gaps between the boards of the table. With her fingertips, she traced one of them, deep in thought. If she could only stay here one night . . .

CHAPTER

27

EAGLE

EAGLE GOT UP from the rickety couch. Before Adelyn had bought the motorhome, he'd slept on it for several years, the barn his new home after living on the street for far too long. It all looked different now, with new wiring, insulation, and sheetrock, workbenches, a multitude of tools, and a concrete floor.

Samson looked at him, ready to go on their morning walk. He ruffled his coat. Yesterday, the smart back lab had alerted him someone was on the property. Finding a woman had been a huge surprise, her fall into the creek scary.

"Come, let's go," he said, slapping his thigh. The dog gave a happy bark. "No bark," he warned, thinking about the woman who slept in his bed, inside the motorhome.

Together, they headed up the gravel road leading away from

the barn until they reached a neatly paved circular driveway in front of an enormous log home. Terraced into the hillside, it featured heavy timber beams and columns, and an expansive plaza deck that overlooked the valley.

"Stay," he told the dog and jumped the few steps that led up to the front door.

As always, the heavy door was unlocked, and he entered. It was still early; the floor tiles echoing his footsteps in the stillness as he walked past the impressive log staircase toward the sunroom at the back of the house. It was Adelyn's favorite place to spend her mornings. She called it her sanctuary.

He noticed her in front of a window and knocked before entering. She beckoned him to join her among the orchids, hibiscus, and other tropical plants. Her stylish silver hair reflected the morning sun, her graceful figure barely reaching his shoulder.

"Do you see that green one with the red and orange, Eagle?" she whispered, observing the hummingbirds drinking from her feeder. "I've never seen it before. It's gorgeous."

They shared a passion for bird watching, both usually walking around with a pair of binoculars around their necks.

Eagle smiled down at her. "You don't have to whisper. You know they can't hear you."

She playfully poked him in the ribs. "Of course, I know that."

Eagle turned around and sank down onto one of the rattan chairs. With his elbows planted on his knees, he stared out in front of him. His fingers played restlessly with his mustache and beard. To find a gorgeous woman out in the meadow had been so unexpected. The property bordered miles and miles of forested wilderness. It was hard to comprehend how she'd ended up there by herself.

After a few minutes, Adelyn walked toward the cabinet that stood against the wall. "Care for some tea?" she asked. She poured two cups and placed them on the glass table, eyeing him with concern. "Are you all right? You seem awfully quiet this morning." She sat down in another chair.

"I need your advice," he chuckled. "Yesterday, I found a woman next to the creek. I brought her home and let her spend the night in the motorhome."

Adelyn raised her fine eyebrows. "It's about time. Don't you think?"

Shaking his head, he grinned. "It's nothing like that."

"That's too bad," she joked. "Because it would be wonderful to see you with a girlfriend."

She'd hinted at that several times before, and he always ignored the remark. He was perfectly content by himself, and she knew that. In a few minutes he explained the events from the day before, and that he'd given their unexpected visitor some old clothes Adelyn had bagged up for Goodwill. "You and Dora were gone the entire day. I thought you wouldn't mind."

"Why didn't you call 9-1-1?" Adelyn replied with concern. "She might have internal injuries or a concussion. Maybe we should call a doctor."

"I've kept a close eye on her the entire afternoon. She was agitated and famished, but other than a few scrapes and bruises, she seemed fine."

Adelyn shook her head in disagreement. "I feel we should contact Dr. Murphy. I'm sure he doesn't mind stopping by."

Eagle thought for a moment. "I'm not sure what's going on, Adelyn. She seems scared. And when I asked her name, she hesitated a few seconds too long before she told me it's Elsie. I got the feeling she wasn't telling the truth."

"Do you think she's in trouble with the police?" Adelyn asked, sipping her tea.

"No, I don't think so. Her skittish behavior reminds me more of the homeless women I met when I lived on the street. I detected distrust, stress, and fear. Probably from trauma, loss, or addiction. She asked if she could stay a day or two. I told her I had to check in with you first."

A silence fell between them while they pondered about their unexpected guest.

"Do you want me to talk to her?" Adelyn offered.

Emma had been awake for a while, gathering courage to face the day. When she finally left the bedroom, she found herself face to face with an elderly woman.

"I was just about to knock," she said, her finely wrinkled face breaking into a gracious smile. "My name is Adelyn."

Emma had assumed Adelyn was a much younger and robust matron, and nothing like the stylish and sophisticated lady in front of her. Her silver-gray hair was beautifully coiffured, her skin powdered, and her makeup flawless. She looked like she was ready to go to the country club instead of visiting a stranger in a barn.

"I heard you fell in the creek," Adelyn said. "That must have been so scary. How are you feeling?"

"I'm fine, thank you," Emma replied and extended her hand. "I'm . . . Elsie. Elsie Jones. Nice to meet you."

"Eagle made a pot of coffee, and I've brought croissants," Adelyn said. "I hoped the two of us could have breakfast together." She took two mugs from the cupboard, filled them with coffee, and sat down. The table was already set, the fragrance of fresh-baked pastry coming from a small wicker basket.

Emma sat down and took one of the warm crescent-shaped rolls. Following Adelyn's example, she cut it open, and topped it with blackberry jam.

"I also brought you a few toiletries," Adelyn said. "I live a little farther up on the hill, just behind those trees." She waved to a location beyond the barn. "I've lived there my entire married life. Unfortunately, Elliot left me seven years ago. Heart attack. Bless his soul. He was a wonderful husband. About five years ago, around the same time I met Eagle, my sister lost her husband, so she moved in with me. It's been nice to have the two of them around. I was awfully lonely here by myself."

"It must be difficult to maintain 320 acres of land," Emma commented, quoting what Axel had told her the night before, as she helped herself to a second croissant.

"My goodness, yes," Adelyn agreed. "Luckily, I found Eagle. Elliot and I weren't blessed with children and he's like a son to me. He's kind, honest, smart, and such a hard worker. I don't think there's anything he can't fix or do. He's restoring our old Volkswagen Campervan, and he takes care of the horses and chickens, the house, vegetable garden, orchard, and the rest of the property. He's even felling trees that provide too much shade for the vineyard he's putting in."

Within five minutes, Emma knew pretty much everything she'd wanted to know. It was obvious Adelyn loved to visit, and Axel was one of her favorite topics to discuss.

Adelyn placed her small veined hand atop Emma's. "Eagle

told me you want to stay here for a few days. I'm fine with that, but isn't there someone we should call for you? I'm sure somebody must be worried about you."

Emma dropped her gaze. She couldn't look into the kind eyes of her hostess and lie. "I'm on a trip across the country and they stole my car with all my belongings." She spoke barely above a whisper, sticking as close to the truth as possible. "I don't have any money or clothes." Her throat closed up at the thought of the hopeless situation.

Adelyn tucked a length of paper towel into her hand. "No reason to cry, dear. We can help. Why don't you come up to the house this afternoon? To see if we can find something more suitable for you to wear. This dress is dreadful."

Left alone, Emma blew her nose and dried her tears. Her best option would be to contact Ruben. She'd found Axel and that should account for something. But he had betrayed her, just like Jesse, who had probably returned her rental car and flown back home. The election was only a few days away. He had a tight schedule to keep with multiple public appearances and social events to reel in the last indecisive voters. She wondered how he would explain her absence. A much-needed vacation? A visit to relatives abroad? He was a great public speaker and knew how to lie. He would have no trouble finding a suitable answer and talk himself out of a precarious situation. Definitely a born politician.

Adelyn made her way back up the hill, the basket she'd used to bring the croissants now filled with fresh organic eggs.

As she rounded the house, she found Eagle in the vegetable garden and paused in front of the tall fence that kept the deer out.

Eagle looked up when she called out to him, his body almost completely hidden behind the giant stalks of green beans. She made her way in the direction of his voice.

"I've never seen the beans this high," she remarked. "It's unbelievable what a productive season we're having this year. What are we going to do with this abundance of fruit and vegetables?"

"I just picked a second bucket of beans and two buckets with cherry and heirloom tomatoes. We'll run out of canning jars soon. Do you want me to go into town and buy more trays?"

"That might be fine for all the peaches and tomatoes, but what about all those grapes? When you told me the property might be suitable for a winery, I believed I would prove you wrong because of the heavy rains and snow we get. But now I realize I was mistaken."

Eagle stopped in front of her, carrying the two full buckets of green beans. "Only the first rows of grapevines I planted are in their third year. Their trunks are thick, and the plants are mature enough to produce tasty grapes soon. Every day, I give them a taste for sweetness. I thought I'd try to make grape juice this afternoon. Might be a fun experiment."

"How about you try to make wine instead?" Adelyn winked. "A delicious, robust red, preferably."

"I could do that, too." They shared a smile.

"I also thought to get a head start on the apples this year,"

Eagle continued. "Your neighbor Darrel asked for two crates. I'm sure there are enough apples in the orchard ready to pick. But first I'll wash and can these beans."

"Sounds great," Adelyn answered. "I'm running late. My friends are waiting in town and before I leave, I'll ask Dora if she has any clothes for our new acquaintance. Why didn't you tell me she's so tall? Nothing that I have will fit."

Eagle shrugged. "I didn't notice."

She looked him over with her keen eyes. Elsie was a young and beautiful woman. That wouldn't go unnoticed by any man.

"I don't believe our visitor has addiction problems," Adelyn said. "She looks healthy. Her skin is clear. Her teeth are straight and white. Other than a few bruises and the scratches on her forehead and arms, she appears to be unscathed. She is, however, very jittery and claims they stole all her possessions. But she never mentioned wanting to call the police or anyone else. I'm inclined to believe she's hiding something important. I invited her to the house this afternoon, hoping to draw out more information."

Eagle put down the buckets with vegetables and placed his hands on Adelyn's shoulders, shaking her gently. "You can't put the troubles of the entire world on these two tiny shoulders."

"Don't worry about me," Adelyn replied with a warm smile. "I'm an excellent judge of character."

Eagle knew exactly what she meant. Without hesitation, she'd taken him in from the street after they'd only met once.

They headed to the house and entered the mudroom through the back door. Eagle stepped out of his muddy boots as Adelyn left in search of her sister Dora. On bare feet, he proceeded toward the scullery, the overflow kitchen where they did all the canning, and turned on the faucet. He emptied the buckets of beans into the deep stainless-steel sink and rinsed them thoroughly, recalling the day he'd met Adelyn for the first time.

On a gorgeous spring day, she'd visited Dora's husband at the hospital in Portland. Instead of going straight home, she parked her car and walked along the Willamette River. Two men began to follow her. Both skinny and dressed in grimy blue jeans and ragged shirts. They shared a bottle of whisky between them. "Hey lady, can you spare a couple of bucks?" one of them asked. When he grabbed her arm, Adelyn panicked, tried to jerk free, and fell.

Eagle didn't hesitate to chase off the two guys. He helped Adelyn back onto her feet. She wasn't hurt, aside from a sore wrist, a bruise on her hip, and dirty palms, but she was shaken up. He'd accompanied her back to her car, to make sure she was safe.

"The alcohol on their breaths was horrendous," she told him. "The stench coming off their clothes appalling. What horrible men!"

Her remarks hit home. After she left, her words kept spinning through his head. He hadn't taken a shower or changed clothes in several months himself; he slept in a makeshift bed on a cardboard box under bridges or in alleys. He was no better than those drunk vagrants.

Why she'd returned two weeks later to find him, he still couldn't grasp. To him, Adelyn was a saint. She was his savior, and he loved her dearly.

CHAPTER
28

LEFT BY HERSELF, Emma cleaned off the table and did the few dishes. In the bathroom, she opened the toiletry bag Adelyn had given her. A toothbrush, toothpaste, floss, deodorant, and shampoo. Exactly what she needed. After another shower, she rinsed her bra and panties and hung them up to dry. Her ripped blouse and shorts ended in the garbage.

Unsure of what to do next, she roamed around the motorhome and opened several kitchen cupboards. They didn't contain much besides the expected cups, plates, and glasses. In the pantry, she found peanut butter, rice, pasta, a bag of flour, and several boxes of granola cereal. All whole grain. Eagle ate healthy. In another cabinet, she found a stack of magazines and several books.

Hot VW's and *Four-wheel and off-road*. They gave her an insight into Axel's interests.

The books were field guides about survival, wildlife, plants, and birds. *Birds of the Pacific Northwest* and *Birds of Prey* seemed the most used.

Two pairs of binoculars in different sizes lay next to them, and what seemed like a spotting scope. She picked up the biggest pair and took them out of their protective black case. They weren't as heavy as she'd expected. Hearing a dog bark, she quickly put everything back where it belonged before heading outside. She didn't want Axel to find out she'd been snooping.

Owner and dog played fetch outside. She joined them, and Samson dropped the stick from his mouth in front of her. She patted his head, his shiny fur warm and coarse underneath her fingertips. She loved animals and hoped Carlton and the cleaning lady were taking care of her cat. Jesse hated Bert. He wouldn't care if he lived or died.

"He wants you to throw the stick," Eagle said.

"I'm game," she smiled, throwing it as far as she could. Samson immediately raced after it, leaving dust in his wake.

Eagle handed her a brown paper bag. "I picked strawberries, lettuce, green onions, and tomatoes from the garden. Perfect for lunch. Or would you rather have an omelet? The chickens are laying a lot of eggs."

"What time is it?" she asked.

He smiled. "No idea, but I'm hungry, so it must be lunchtime."

What a laid-back lifestyle, she thought, without a phone, computer, or internet.

Eagle followed her into the motorhome, telling her about Adelyn's abundant garden and the green beans he'd canned all morning.

Emma rinsed the salad and cut the tomatoes and onions,

and Eagle found mayonnaise, bread, and sliced ham. They ate at the picnic table outside.

"You seem to have recovered from your ordeal," Eagle said. "How're you feeling?"

She touched the scratches on her cheek. "I found antibiotic ointment in the bathroom cabinet and used several band aids for the blisters on my heels. Is that okay?"

"No problem," he replied. "But I also noticed those red bumps on your arm. Did you come in contact with poison oak?"

Emma looked at her left wrist where four bright red blisters had formed. "I think I did. They're very itchy."

"Try not to scratch them," he said. "It could cause the rash to spread or result in infection. If it gets too itchy, Adelyn has a huge medicine cabinet. I'm sure she has plenty of calamine lotion, hydrocortisone cream, and antihistamine pills."

Emma let out a nervous laugh. She didn't want to be a bigger bother than she already was. "I think I'll survive," she said.

The walkie-talkie in Eagle's pocket crackled and Emma welcomed the interruption. His inquisitive gaze noticed far too much.

"I'm back at the house," Adelyn said, her voice coming through loud and clear. "Tell Elsie she can come over whenever she'd like,"

"We hear you," Eagle replied. "She'll be on her way soon."

A few hours later, Emma returned from the house, a pair of flip-flops on her feet. They were too small, but better than having to go barefoot, the blisters on her heels raw and painful.

"I'm not sure if we own anything that might fit you," Adelyn said, concern written in the lines of her face.

"Don't worry, Adelyn," Emma assured her. "Those two dresses Eagle brought yesterday are fine."

Light footsteps came from the kitchen and another elderly lady appeared.

"You were right, Adelyn. She's far too pretty to wear something so dreadful," she said.

"Dora!" Adelyn corrected her older sister. "You can't be so rude to a guest."

The sisters could be twins, with the same hairstyle and taste in clothes, both at least six inches or more shorter than her.

"I'm so sorry you lost all your belongings," Dora said, taking Emma's hand in a welcoming grip. "Let's see if we can find you something more suitable to wear."

The three of them rummaged through their closets.

"What do you think of this, Elsie?" Dora said, holding up a purple jumpsuit. "I haven't worn this in years."

"Absolutely not, Dora," Adelyn frowned. "You always looked ridiculous in that ugly thing."

It had been fun to listen to the sisters engage in friendly banter and offer advice. But instead of coming clean, as she should have done, she'd dug herself into an even deeper hole by adding additional lies to the ones she'd already told. Shame welled up inside her. The sweet ladies didn't deserve to be lied to. With each step, she became angrier about her deceitful behavior and her brain whirred as she tried to come up with a solution.

The smart thing to do would be to ask for a ride to the airport and demand Ruben pay for her flight back home. The idea alone gave her the shivers. She wasn't ready to face the conniving men who'd hurt her deeply. She needed a few days, to lick her wounds and gather enough courage to confront her past.

But what if they showed up out of the blue? They knew exactly where Eagle lived, and only yesterday Jesse had been within a few miles' distance of the farm.

Halfway down the trail, she stopped to look over the valley, bathing in the golden light of the late afternoon sun. The red barn, with the doors wide open, looked picturesque in the middle of the fields of yellowed grass. The grapevines planted in straight rows up the slope, full of promise. What a beautiful and peaceful place to live.

Inside the barn, Axel still worked on the engine. At the sound of her footsteps, he turned around and wiped his grease-covered hands with a blue shop towel.

"You're empty handed?" he said.

"The ladies are so petite." Emma shrugged. "I don't see any other option than to raid your clothing closet, Eagle."

"Be my guest," he said, looking at his stained shirt. "But it won't be flattering."

They shared a smile, lifting her somber mood. "Adelyn said she doesn't mind if I stayed for several days. Are you okay with that?"

For a moment, he fell silent, his long stare unsettling. Then, his eyes cleared, as if he came out of a daydream. "I knew Adelyn wouldn't mind. She has a big heart, and the habit of taking in strays."

"But she doesn't know anything about me," Emma said, still struggling with Adelyn's kindness and for opening her home. "I might be a drug addict or a thief."

"When Adelyn took me in, she knew absolutely nothing about me, either. Five years later, I'm still here." He crumbled the soiled hand towel in a ball and tossed it in the garbage can.

"Five years?" She laughed. "I wasn't thinking about anything that long."

Axel's brown eyes sparkled with humor. "Then let's start with five days."

That would be pushing it, she knew. "Only if I can make myself useful," she said, swallowing her uncertainty. "I'm not used to doing nothing."

"Do you know anything about cars?" Eagle asked. "This engine is from a Volkswagen Syncro. It used to be Adelyn and Elliot's. They used it for many trips before upgrading to that huge motorhome. Unfortunately, they regretted the switch and only took that monster out twice before Elliot passed away. I told Adelyn to sell it, but she doesn't want to, so in the meantime I use it as my house."

The luxurious motorhome in the barn, surrounded by power tools, car engines, lawnmowers, and other unfamiliar contraptions was the strangest setup and way to live she'd ever seen. "What's a Syncro?"

He guided her through the backdoor into a second part of the barn. Inside were several quads and a red Volkswagen bus.

"It's a 1987 water-cooled Westfalia campervan with a pop top roof," Eagle explained. "I'm trying to bring the van back to its former glory." He opened the sliding door and Emma peeked inside. It had a cute little kitchen, swivel seats, a rear bed, and an upper bunk. Everything was in excellent condition, the recent improvements evident, with the exception of the curtains. They were faded and showed major wear and tear. "I know my way around a sewing machine and can help with new curtains," she offered.

Eagle didn't answer right away, giving her a hesitant glance. "Are you sure?"

Although Axel's appearance had changed drastically over the years, watching him brought back forgotten memories of what he'd looked like as a young boy. Painfully shy, even more so than her, always avoiding interaction, his brown eyes guarded. She noticed that same restraint now and hoped she hadn't overstepped her bounds. She had no desire to offend him.

"Of course," she replied. "I would love to help."

His brown eyes lit up. "Well, if it's not too much to ask. Dora has a sewing machine at the house, and we could drive to the department store in town. They have a fabric section."

Emma took the curtains down to take measurements. She also noticed the mattress pads of the beds needed reupholstering and offered to do that as well.

While they worked side by side, questions whirled in her mind. About Axel's childhood, his relationship with his father and Ruben, his trip across the United States, and why he'd left. There was so much she wanted to know. But asking questions would only bring up the past and much more than she was willing to share.

With ease, he lifted one of the van's tires on the hub and reached for another tool. Under the appearance of a pot-smoking hippie, he had the build of a man who did a lot of physical labor. Mesmerized by the play of muscles under his shirt and his bulging biceps as he torqued the lug nuts with a wrench, she had trouble concentrating on her own work.

Eagle. What an impressive nickname. It reminded her of a bright blue sky, snow-capped mountains, and endless forests, where the powerful bird spread its wings and soared high above, toward the horizon.

Had it been like that for Axel after he left home? Had he felt that he flew over unknown territories, leaving the world and all its problems far below?

CHAPTER

29

EAGLE

THE NEXT DAY, Eagle drove Emma to the fabric store in town. She sat next to him on the front seat of his pickup truck, quiet and stiff-limbed.

"How's your poison oak?" he asked.

Yesterday, she'd tensed with every question and he wanted her to relax, to feel more at ease with him.

She looked at her wrist. "Much better. Thanks."

"Have you been in Riversdale before?"

"Only once."

"It's a cute town, don't you think?"

She nodded. "Yes, it is."

He watched her fumble with the hem of her dress, her gaze anywhere but on him. Guarding his privacy had always been important to him, his solitary life on the farm exactly what he preferred. So he understood her reluctance to talk and knew he shouldn't pry, but his curiosity got the better of him. She'd worked her way under his skin in a few short days, and he wanted to find out everything about her.

Instead of bombarding her with questions, he decided to take a different approach and tell her something about himself.

"Before I moved to Oregon, I worked on a ranch. They taught me how to operate a tractor, a backhoe, and other farm equipment," he began. "But I never drove a car."

She stayed quiet.

"Hard to believe, right?"

"Yes, it is."

"My father never owned a car, and school was close by, so I either walked or biked. After I graduated high school, I either lived where I worked, or had no money to spare. One of the first things Adelyn made me do was to get my driver's license."

"Living so remotely, you definitely need a car," she replied.

Eagle always tried to avoid thinking about the North Fork Cattle Ranch in Wyoming, the memories still painful. He clenched his hands tightly around the steering wheel, when he thought about the owner. He'd run his own whisky distillery, making moonshine with the highest alcohol content one could imagine. Most of his fellow farmworkers were hardcore alcoholics. They drank themselves into oblivion every night, and soon, he became one of them, the two guys closest to his age were his best pals. They worked together, bunked together, ate together, and drank together. Life on the farm was tough. It had been an exciting, but life-altering time. A time in which he never ate so much meat, eggs, and potatoes. He also learned to play poker and joined the guys at the strip club. Since they were often out in the fields for days, to repair fences and check the cattle, cleanliness was on the back burner. It's when he'd let his hair and beard grow.

He'd also learned to ride a horse. There was nothing that gave him the feeling of freedom like the powerful muscles of the horse underneath him, the hooves pounding the fields, kicking up dirt while galloping over the endless acreage of ranch land.

"There was a fire on the ranch where I worked," he said. "The barn burned down to the ground, taking the owner, several ranch hands, and all the horses with it." He swallowed the lump in his throat down as he recalled how the flames consumed it all, the memory of the sounds and smell so vivid that it made his stomach squeeze.

"It was traumatic. A nightmare."

He fell into a gloomy silence as he thought about his ensuing breakdown and excessive drinking.

People who tried to support him in those days claimed he suffered from PTSD and needed help. He didn't agree. He had looked it up at the library. He didn't experience flashbacks, nightmares, or severe anxiety. All he felt was an inexplicable brooding sadness that resulted in negative thoughts and a sour mood. If only they hadn't been so tanked-up, his friends would still be alive.

For months, he'd continued to drink. To drown out his misplaced feelings of guilt. To avoid reminiscing about his miserable life, and what he'd become. A homeless bum. A fucking loser, with nothing to his name but the clothes on his back.

It wasn't until Sheep handed him a wriggling black bundle

of hair and fur that his life changed. His friend had found the pup in an abandoned warehouse, chained to a metal bar. How or why someone could be so cruel, he couldn't fathom. Anyone would have loved the little black lab. For him, it had been the watershed moment he'd needed to begin his recovery from depression. Samson had literally saved his life.

"I'm so sorry you lost your friends," Emma whispered.

CHAPTER

30

ON THE WAY HOME, with a bag of fabric at her feet, Emma stared out the window. They drove through Riversdale's main street, past quaint shops and restaurants, and the diner where she'd had a sandwich, just before Jesse had shown up. Riversdale, City of the Falls, it said on a sign. Another road sign indicated to take a right to a state park.

Her eyes quivered, the constant tension exhausting. She was in this gorgeous place, but everything was too messed up and complicated to enjoy it.

She shifted in her seat and carefully glanced at Eagle. He'd barely spoken since he talked about the ranch in Wyoming, and kept his eyes on the road, his hands tight around the steering wheel.

Since her arrival, she'd tried to be careful, pondering over each word, thinking everything through. But the instant she let her guard down and allowed her emotions to come into play, she'd messed up. She couldn't have known the coworkers that had passed away had been his friends. From his quick side-glance and furrowed brow, she knew he'd definitely noticed. Instead of asking why she would say something like that, he'd retreated in silence. Or was she making too big of a deal out of this, and was his somber mood caused by his own memories?

"I noticed a farm stand along the way, selling lots of fruit and produce. With the vegetable garden, you probably never have to buy anything from them," she said, breaking the silence.

"They also sell local honey, oranges, and lots of preserves, and we stop there occasionally," Eagle replied.

"My mom and I used to go the farmer's market all the time. It must be amazing to eat what you grow yourself."

He nodded, increasing speed when they left town. "The three of us eat dinner together several days a week. I do most of the cooking. But today Adelyn is making lasagna. We have so many tomatoes, bell peppers, and onions. It wouldn't surprise me if she makes enough for several days."

"Where did you learn how to cook?" she asked.

"I worked in a deli for several years. It was fun. But I've told you enough about me. Where are you from, Elsie?"

"Guess," she said playfully.

"My best guess is the East Coast," Eagle replied.

"Correct. What state?"

He thought for a moment. "I'm originally from Massachusetts and believe you are, too."

Her heart skipped a beat. "Why do you think that?"

"From the way you lose some of your Rs." He grinned. "But also, because there's something familiar about you." He drummed his fingers against the rim of the steering wheel. "I know it sounds weird, but I have the feeling we've met before. Is that possible?"

With increased suspicion, her gaze skimmed over him. It wasn't the first time, she believed he knew more than he let on. That he was trying to lure her out. She laughed nervously, tension back in the air. "Of course not."

She turned away from him, to look at the landscape. They just passed the country store. In half a mile, Eagle would take a left onto Swift Road, the highway busier than usual.

"It always is on Friday," Eagle said, slowing down for a shiny red SUV that pulled out in front of them. It was the same make and model as her rental car. Her imagination kicked into overdrive, and she took a shaky breath, fidgeting like a nervous patient waiting to see the doctor. What if it was Ruben or Jesse in that car, exposing her for the liar she was, dragging her back home? For a long moment she sat frozen in fear, holding her hand to her face.

"Are you okay?" Eagle asked.

She heard the concern in his voice, adding to her distress.

"I'm fine," she blurted out, crossing her arms in a defensive gesture.

They didn't speak for the rest of the trip.

~~~~~

When she stepped out of bed the next morning, Axel had already left. She'd heard him outside with Samson at least a half an hour ago. Probably best. Since their trip to town, he'd been quiet and standoffish. She couldn't blame him. He wasn't a fool, her evasive behavior bordering on rude. She'd overstayed her welcome and it was time to leave after she'd finished the curtains and mattress pads for the campervan.

At the house, she found Dora watering the flowerpots and the colorful baskets hanging from the porch. A hummingbird with bright iridescent feathers watched from a slight distance, perched on a branch of a nearby shrub.

"They can flap their wings about eighty times per second while their legs are so small and feeble, they can't walk," Dora told her. The impatient little bird hummed by so fast, they immediately lost sight of it.

"Can I help with the flowers? Those watering cans look very heavy."

"Thanks for offering," Dora replied. "But I believe your agenda for today is full enough as it is. Who taught you how to sew?"

"My mother," Emma said. "She was amazing."

"So was mine," Dora smiled. "Let me know if you need help."

Yesterday, Eagle had carried the sewing machine into the office. They made room on the table by stacking up all the publications about winemaking, Home and Garden, and Birds and Plants magazines. A computer and printer stood on the desk near the window, with stacks of notes scattered all over. Someone apparently used it often.

Emma immediately got to work. First, she wanted to alter the shorts Dora had found. There was a seam in the back waistband, making it easy to adjust them to a smaller size. She concentrated on the task for an hour until an indistinct clamor caught her attention. She listened for a moment. When it stayed quiet, she went back to work until she heard another faint noise. It came from outside. She opened the screen door and walked out onto the deck. "Dora? Are you there?"

A soft whimper came from the direction of the circular driveway. Emma flew down the front steps and spotted Adelyn's sister sprawled on the black pavement. Her age-marked hands clutched her chest, her breathing shallow and fast.

Dora's having a heart attack, Emma thought. She flew inside to use the phone in the kitchen.

"Someone is having a heart attack," she told the 9-1-1 dispatcher. "The Gravenstein residence off Swift Road in Riversdale. Hurry, please!"

With the phone to her ear, she rushed back outside.

"Adelyn?" Dora moaned with a tortured expression on her face.

"I don't know where she is," Emma replied, trying to stay calm. "I'm talking to 9-1-1. Since we're so far away from the nearest hospital, they tell me to get you in the car, if possible, to better the chance of your survival. Do you have any aspirin in the medicine cabinet?"

Dora nodded.

"In the bathroom?"

Dora nodded again.

"I'll be right back," she promised, springing into action. A minute later, she knelt at the elderly woman's side and put two low dose aspirin into her mouth. "Chew and swallow if you can," she instructed. "Don't move. I'm getting the car."

Adelyn had told her they owned an all-wheel-drive minivan. She rushed into the garage and opened the car door. No keys. Think, Emma, she ordered herself. Did you see any keys? Where? The kitchen? She rushed through the house, looking around. "Adelyn! Eagle! Where are you?"

On the counter next to the cooktop sat an ashtray. It held matches, double-A batteries, and a set of keys. Yes!

She rushed back and pressed the button of the automatic garage door opener as she stepped into the car. The engine started right away, and she put the transmission in reverse, her movements frantic, her fingers trembling.

With screeching tires, she backed out of the garage. In case of a heart attack, every minute counted. Holding her breath, she placed herself behind the distressed woman, slid her arms under her body and clasped her hands in front of her chest. With everything she had, she lifted her up. Dora was in her mid-eighties, her body thin and frail, but she felt like dead meat. "Sorry, Dora," she said, almost hurling the old lady inside the vehicle, "but I know you'll forgive me."

"Thank you," Dora managed to say. Behind her glasses, her pale blue eyes brimmed with tears. Her thin gray hair was disheveled, and her finely wrinkled skin had a bluish tint.

Emma lifted Dora's feet into the car and pushed her farther into the seat so she could close the door. Before she took off, she grabbed the phone still lying in the driveway. The dispatcher was still there. "I got her in the car," she said, with the phone between her chin and shoulder. "This is a home phone, so I won't be able to talk to you much longer. I'm heading down to Swift Road and will take 323 into town. I know where the department store in Riversdale is. Can you tell the ambulance to meet us there? It should take me less than fifteen minutes."

The connection crackled after her last words and she tossed the phone on the floor mat. Dora sat slouched against the door and panic rushed through Emma's veins. Was she still alive?

"Hang in there, Dora," she shouted. "Hang in there, sweetie. I'm taking you to the ambulance."

As she sped away, Emma broke into a cold sweat, her breathing shallow. She was one step away from a panic attack. White-knuckled, she drove down the winding road, eyes focused straight ahead, her forehead furrowed in concentration. She'd forgotten to strap Dora in. God forbid she had to make an emergency stop. "Please, please, please, don't die, Dora. Please, please, please," she begged.

From afar, Emma noticed the bright blue lights from the ambulance. Her tires squealed their protest as she made a sharp turn into the parking lot, narrowly avoiding an oncoming car. The driver lay on the horn and gave her the finger. She ignored him.

The paramedics spotted her right away. As soon as she stopped the car, they opened the passenger door, catching Dora as she fell out. Within seconds, they had her in the back of the ambulance.

"We're taking her to Providence," the paramedic told her. "Thank you for meeting us halfway."

In the middle of the parking lot, Emma watched the ambulance speed off, sirens blaring. She shivered, all the adrenaline that had powered her depleted. She'd done all she could, and Dora was in professional hands. If they could save her, they would.

Emma stopped the minivan in front of Dora and Adelyn's home and turned off the ignition.

Immediately, a frantic-looking Adelyn flew out of the house, followed by Eagle. "Elsie. Where have you been? And where's Dora?" she cried.

Emma could easily imagine what had gone through her head, finding the doors wide open, the car and her sister gone.

"I took her to Riversdale, where an ambulance waited to take her to the hospital. I believe she had a heart-attack."

At the news, Eagle wrapped his arms around the shaking Adelyn.

"She's in good hands. They'll save her," Emma said, her words sounding hollow.

Adelyn freed herself from Eagle's embrace. "You have to take me to the hospital, immediately."

"I'll grab your purse," he said.

Emma helped the shaken Adelyn into the car and retrieved the home phone from the floor mat where she'd tossed it. "Sorry about taking the phone with me. I was talking to 9-1-1."

"Don't worry about a thing, my dear. You may have saved my sister's life."

Instead of going back to her sewing, Emma wandered around the rest of the day, restless thoughts running around inside her head. Had she done enough for Dora? Would she need to undergo surgery?

Samson kept following her around, the dog agitated without his owner.

Around six, she prepared a salad inside the RV, praying that Dora was still alive.

"Here, Samson," she said, filling his bowl with dog food after refreshing his water. "Eagle will be back. I promise."

Another hour went by, Samson's exciting bark announcing his owner's return. He raced outside to greet him.

Nervous, Emma wet her lips, and waited.

"She's alive," Eagle said, easing her concern the moment he walked in, his face drawn, his expression tense. "An angiogram revealed severe blockage, and they inserted a stent into the artery to restore blood flow to her heart. They hope this will be sufficient but warned she may need to undergo bypass surgery after her heart has time to recover from the attack. They'll keep her in the hospital for at least a week."

With a deep sigh of relief, Emma released the tension that had tightened her jaws and neck muscles. "I've been praying all day for this." She smiled through unshed tears, and Eagle pulled her in a comforting embrace.

"You saved her," he breathed in her hair. "Thank you."

The faint antiseptic smell of the hospital and the fragrance of fresh flowers hovered around him. In an automatic response, she clasped her arms around his waist and held him tightly, taking comfort from his presence and physical strength.

With his chin on top of her head and her face against his soft luxuriant beard, they stood in silence for a few minutes until he drew away. "Adelyn and I were with the horses. I still can't believe how lucky we are that you were with Dora when it happened." He sighed, rubbing his fists across his eyes.

Emma nodded. "I panicked but am glad I kept it together."

"Did you eat?" he asked, reaching for her hand.

She nodded.

"Then let's sit outside and talk for a while."

Next to the picnic table stood two white Adirondack chairs around a fire pit. They both sat down and looked out over the valley, the constant chirping of the crickets filling the quiet evening air.

"My mother died when I was a toddler, and I never knew my grandparents." Eagle spoke just above a whisper. "I was practically raised by our nanny. She was the only mother figure I had until I met Adelyn and Dora. Having them in my life helped me in so many ways. I would be devastated if I lost one of them."

He placed his hands loosely on his knees and stared in front of him, the vulnerability and pain in his eyes a contrast with his rugged mountain-man appearance.

Emma observed his profile. His dark brown hair hung past his brawny shoulders. His nose straight and perfect, his long dark eyelashes touching each other as he squinted against the setting sun. She couldn't imagine being afraid of him any longer.

Not wanting him to catch her staring, she forced her gaze away.

CHAPTER
31

"ADELYN STAYED at the hospital overnight," Eagle told Emma the next morning. "I promised to pick her up around eleven. Do you want to go with me?"

"Yes, for sure," Emma replied. She looked forward to seeing Dora.

"After what happened yesterday, I regret not having a cell phone," Eagle said as they drove to the city. "I want to stop at the store to buy one."

They bought a phone, picked up Adelyn, and brought her home. Her creased face was pale and drawn, and she looked fatigued. Suppressing a yawn, she went straight to bed.

At the kitchen table, Eagle familiarized himself with the new device.

"I used a cell phone when I lived in Iowa and worked at the deli," he said. "Afterwards I kept it. Edwina and Henry wanted me to stay in touch. I was in their family plan, so it didn't cost me anything. Unfortunately, the phone burned in the fire at the ranch, along with all my other possessions."

Every time Eagle talked about his past, she felt like a traitor. Out of the corner of her eyes, she noticed his inquisitive stare. He expected some kind of response, a story of her own, the silence she'd forced upon herself inexcusable.

"That's too bad," she mumbled, knowing it wasn't enough. Not by a long shot.

In the minutes that ticked by, neither broke the silence. Each aware that she left too much unsaid, the tension ratcheted up. How much longer could she keep it in? What could she say?

"I still didn't fix that fence," Eagle said. He slapped his hands on his knees and stood. "Do you want to stay here and keep an eye on Adelyn?"

"I'd be happy to."

With pain in her heart, she watched him leave. The truth wanted to come out, doubt and misgivings apparent in Eagle's eyes. But she wasn't ready. Relieved to postpone the moment of truth a little longer, she finished the alteration of her shorts and started sewing the curtains, passing the thread through the needle almost impossible without her reading glasses. When her eyes got too tired, she brought in tomatoes, basil, and two sweet onions from the garden to make spaghetti. Bundles of oregano hung to dry in a scullery cabinet.

The rustic, roomy kitchen of the house had a solid hardwood floor, red and white checked ruffled curtains at the windows, and a china cabinet filled with matching dishes, cups, bowls, and platters. Emma loved everything about it.

At the end of the afternoon, Eagle walked in, his hair dripping, his shirt hanging casually over his right shoulder. The essence of the fresh outdoors clung to him. It tickled her nostrils and she tore her eyes away from his trim body and bare chest.

"I was covered in dust and took a quick jump in the creek to freshen up," he explained and reached for a kitchen towel.

Her eyes were drawn to him as he dried his back and chest and then rubbed the wet from his hair. After he slipped his arms into his shirt and started setting the table, her pulse returned to normal. She grabbed two potholders and poured the boiling spaghetti noodles into a colander to drain.

"Those shorts look great on you," Eagle commented. He stood right behind her.

When their eyes met, there was no mistaking the appreciative gleam in his gaze. The corners of his mouth pulled up in a smile, and he reached out to touch her face. His warm brown eyes cast an enchanting spell, drawing her in. It felt like the temperature in the kitchen rose twenty degrees. Heat rose in her cheeks and she held her breath as he moved in closer until inches separated them. He exuded a sensual energy to which her body unconsciously responded. All her senses focused on him, and she was aware of everything about him.

Adelyn's sudden appearance made them both take a step back.

In the quiet days that followed, Emma took it upon herself to do the cooking, the watering of the flowers, and the work in the vegetable garden. With Dora gone and Adelyn spending most of her time in and out of the hospital, she thought it was the least she could do. During that time, she didn't see much of Eagle. He stayed busy with the orchard and construction of the new horse stable after taking the old one down to make room for the expansion of the vineyard.

The hours by herself gave Emma time to reflect on her life, her future, and her developing feelings for Eagle. Every time she thought about him, a jolt of attraction tightened her stomach. Whenever she caught sight of him, her heartbeat quickened. It had never been like this with Jesse, and that made it even more disturbing. She feared she was falling in love with him.

She realized she'd placed Jesse on a pedestal and had mistaken admiration for love. She'd fallen for a fantasy concocted in her own brain, believing some of his charm and allure might rub off on her. That he might lift her up and change her into the confident, sparkling woman she'd always wanted to be. How could she have been so narrow-minded and stupid? To believe she could be happy as the wife of an ambitious businessman and an up-and-coming politician. With a man who was never home, chasing his dreams elsewhere.

Her foolish ambitions had brought her to this spectacular property, where she lied constantly by evading the truth about her past, her marital status, and everything else. She couldn't fool herself any longer. Eagle had no idea who she was, and neither did Adelyn. They were warm and generous people, who had kindly taken her in. And every day that went by without her telling the truth only made it harder.

The damage to Dora's heart wasn't as severe as the doctors had feared. They considered the stents sufficient to prevent another heart attack and told her she could go home. Before picking her up from the hospital, Eagle and Adelyn wanted to stop at a garage sale advertised in the newspaper.

"I've never been to a garage sale," Emma said from the backseat of the minivan, excited at the prospect.

"It's the best place to find treasures." Eagle laughed. "I mainly hunt for tools and whatever else we can use on the property. Fence posts, building materials, watering hoses, garden tools, you name it."

"Don't they have garage sales on the East coast?" Adelyn asked.

"I'm sure they do," Emma replied. "But not in the neighborhood where I lived with my mother. It wasn't the best part of town."

Adelyn looked at Emma over her shoulder. "Elsie, you have to contact your mother. I'm sure she must be worried about you."

"I lost her about three months ago," Emma replied. Every time she thought about her mother, she choked up. "Thank you both so much for giving me a place to stay. I needed time to recover and decide on my future. You made that possible, and I appreciate it so much."

"Losing a loved one is difficult, and it takes time to heal," Adelyn said. She opened her purse, pulled out a package of tissues, and handed it to Emma. "I still miss Elliot every day."

This was the moment to share more about her past. "It's one of the reasons I went on a cross-country trip," Emma said, drying her eyes.

"What was the other reason, Elsie?" Eagle asked. He turned onto route 323, the garage sale just outside Riversdale along the way.

"Someone hired me to find a missing person," she replied.

Adelyn turned around in her seat, her eyes sparkling with excitement. "Like Magnum, that adorable private investigator? He always wore those colorful Hawaiian shirts. Do you remember? Or was that show before your time?"

"No, it's nothing like that, but I sure had fun pretending to be one," Emma laughed.

"Then what do you do for a living, Elsie?" Adelyn wanted to know.

"Before my mother passed away, I worked as a caregiver and library-aide, until I became involved in politics."

"Politics?" Adelyn blurted out. "How terribly boring."

Jesse would be shocked if he'd heard Adelyn's honest opinion, and Emma couldn't help but grin. "I can't agree more."

CHAPTER

32

EMMA WALKED DOWN the hill with two bags. At the garage sale she'd found a pair of reading glasses, blue jeans, several cute tops, and two summer dresses that fit perfectly. Adelyn insisted on paying for the purchases.

"Compared to what you did for Dora and your help around the house, this is the least I can do," she said.

A happy Samson raced in her direction and she petted him. Whacking his tail, he ran in circles until they reached the barn. Eagle had moved the two horses to their new enclosure. He had told her they were twenty-five years old and happily retired, although on a rare occasion Adelyn still rode them. How the eighty-two-year-old could still climb into the saddle, she had no clue.

After a shower, she changed into the red button-up fitted sundress with shoulder straps. It fell just above her knees. Eagle whistled his appreciation when he saw her.

She gave him a half-smile. Since Dora was home and doing well, the time had come to say goodbye.

Eagle's eyes searched her face. "Are you okay?"

"Of course. Why wouldn't I be?"

He regarded her closely, not quite sure if he believed her. "I'd like to think I've come to know you fairly well and can tell something is bothering you." He touched her chin, gently lifting her face. "Is it about Adelyn's offer? She told me she wants to hire you. There's so much to do on the farm and in the house. They can really use your help."

He stood so close, she felt his body heat. "I told her I'd think about it," she replied and tried to free her chin. He wouldn't let her. Instead, he moved even closer.

"For what it's worth, I'd like you to consider it." He cupped her face in the palms of his hands. "I enjoy having you here."

The weeks with him had been the best of her life, the thought of leaving it all behind depressing. She brought a hand to his face and touched his silken brown beard. So soft. Much softer than she'd expected. "Eagle," she whispered.

He lowered his face to within inches and nibbled on her lips before capturing them in a deep, warm kiss. His mustache tickled her nose. She'd never kissed a man with facial hair before and longed to find out how it felt. With a life of their own, her hands slid up his chest, savoring his hard muscles, before her arms crept up around his neck.

Their kiss was tentative at first, lips and tongues exploring, but it deepened and their breathing quickened. Wrapped in each other's arms, they made their way to the couch, touching and kissing every step of the way.

When they reached it, Eagle sat down and pulled her onto

his lap, one arm around her waist, the other one tracing the contours of her face.

Admiration and yearning radiated from his eyes, his desire evident beneath her bottom. She burrowed against him, her lips parted in invitation.

That was all the assurance he needed. He groaned deep in his throat as they melted together, her mouth closing seductively around his circling, darting, and thrusting tongue. There was nothing tentative about their attraction any longer.

He caressed her back and moved lower until he cradled one of her buttocks, massaging it. The fingers of his other hand drove deep into her shoulder-length hair as he pulled her head back to give him access to her neck.

She moaned from the surge of lust that raged through her as his lips scorched a path down the velvet skin of her throat. Her nipples tightened, and the deep throbbing between her legs increased as inexplicable desires rocked her. Soft, yearning gasps escaped her throat. It had never been like this in the arms of a man. With James it had been clumsy and awkward. And when Jesse had kissed her, it hadn't been about sex or lust. It had been about comfort, assurance, and support, until he became condescending and ruthless. Unable to keep the disturbing memories of Jesse at bay, she stiffened in Eagle's arms.

Eagle paused between kisses as she distanced herself. "What is it, Elsie? Am I moving too fast?"

She reluctantly loosened herself from his embrace, slid off his lap, and stood. She couldn't do this to him. She was still married, and he deserved better than deceit. Much better. Her hair fell forward as she looked down at him with regret, and she pushed it back behind her ears. "Sorry, I just can't." She straightened her dress and turned away from his inquisitive stare, aware of her flushed face and swollen lips.

Eagle reached for her hand, and she took another step back, making sure she remained beyond his grasp.

Samson appeared, sensing his owner's distress. He jumped up, trying to lick his face. Eagle ruffled his coat. "Ready for a walk?" he said with a gruff voice. "I have to cool off."

Watching him leave broke her heart. Eagle had done so much for her self-esteem, showing her with every glance, smile, and touch he found her attractive and desirable. She should go after him, to tell him there was nothing more she wanted than to be in his arms.

An hour later Eagle returned, his long hair tied back with a strip of leather, his wide shoulders stretching a bright yellow T-shirt. He looked incredibly attractive.

"I noticed you built a campfire. Do you mind if I join you?" he asked.

Emma sat in one of the Adirondack chairs, sipping a glass of grape juice. It had gotten chillier as the sun started its descent behind the rugged mountains in the distance. Eagle had lit a campfire several evenings in a row with old newspapers and kindling. She'd tried it herself with success.

"Please, sit down. I hoped we could talk," she replied.

He nodded and lowered himself in a chair. "I haven't told you yet how sorry I am you lost your mother." He stretched his long legs in front of him and took a handful of mixed nuts from the jar between their seats. "I hope you didn't have to face it alone. Do you have any siblings?"

Watching the smoldering fire, she gave a sad smile. "I remember begging my parents for a brother or a sister, but it wasn't meant to be."

"My brother and I were complete opposites, and I often wished I was an only child," Eagle said. He added another log to the fire, to bring it back to life. "After my mother passed, my father lost interest in life. He became depressed and started drinking, leaving my brother and me to fend for ourselves. But Ruben was a pest. Stealing or destroying my toys, kicking and beating me for no apparent reason, blaming me for the things he did. As we got older, his obnoxious behavior got worse. Shoplifting, starting fires, picking fights. He even rebelled against our nanny Martha until the point that she couldn't take his abuse anymore. I was devastated when she resigned."

Ruben had told her Martha passed away last year. She doubted if Eagle knew.

"Ruben had no respect for anything or anyone. He did whatever he pleased, and for some reason, he detested me." Eagle continued. "The atmosphere in the house was bitter. My father made several futile attempts to control him. In the end, he gave up."

Shocked by the description of Ruben's character and his awful conduct toward his family, she placed her hand on Eagle's forearm. "I had no idea."

He covered her hand with his own and held it there. "For years, I stayed out of his way as much as I could. Until my graduation day. That day my brother hurt me so much, I couldn't take it any longer. I went to my father for support, but the moment I laid eyes on him I knew better than to try. He was lying on the floor, next to his bed, with an empty bottle of whisky clutched in his hand, too wasted to care. I threw some stuff into a backpack, emptied my father's wallet, and used the money for a train ticket. I haven't been back home or talked to them since."

Raven had told her Eagle had left home on his graduation day after finding his brother in bed with his girlfriend, both of them stark naked. It had been the last straw for young Axel. Her heart broke for him, and she longed to crawl into his lap to console him.

"I'm so sorry," she said, choking up.

"Don't be." He shrugged, then squeezed her hand in reassurance. "I got over it a long time ago."

Despite the heat from the fire, she shivered. "Eagle, there's something I need to tell you."

CHAPTER

33

EAGLE

PURPLISH-BLUE AND RED tinged the evening sky above the valley. The day ended on a glorious note, and Eagle couldn't be more content. With their conversations becoming more personal, Elsie finally warmed up to his advances and let her carefully protected guard down.

Someone must have hurt her terribly, he thought, longing to hold her in his arms and protect her. Something he'd wanted to do since the first moment he'd laid eyes on her. He reflected on when he'd scared her so much, she'd fallen backward into the fast-flowing creek. Talk about a frightening moment. She could have easily been swept away.

Maybe he would tell her tonight how she touched his heart. She wanted to talk, and that might just be the opportunity he waited for. He felt nervous and excited about the idea at the same time. She looked so beautiful in her red dress. The lyrics from the song Lady in Red trickled into his brain.

Although it wasn't cold, he noticed her shiver. "Let me get something warm to wrap around your shoulders." He pushed up from his chair.

"Don't worry. I'll get it," she said.

They got up at the same time and found each other only inches apart. She stood so close, he could feel her breath tickling his beard in short little puffs. It took every ounce of willpower to keep his hands to himself. His mouth, suddenly dry as dust, could barely form a sentence. "I, uh," he stammered.

Her gaze roamed over his face. As she leaned in toward him, her lips parted slightly. The temptation to kiss her became almost unbearable. Before he turned away, she placed her hands on his chest and slowly slid them up to his shoulders. She stepped even closer, wrapping her arms around his neck and drawing his head down.

Their mouths met, hers sweet and seductive. Sizzling electricity jolted through him, and his body hardened as the tip of her tongue probed tenderly against his mouth. Groaning deeply, he drew her against him. Her mouth was open and ready, their desire matching. This time, he sensed she wouldn't withdraw.

Free from restraint, they kissed endlessly, touching and stroking, until he cupped her behind in both hands and lifted her up. With her legs wrapped around his middle, he carried her into the RV. Between urgent, hot kisses, they hastily shed their clothes, leaving the scattered pieces in a trail on their way into the bedroom. Following her down onto the bed, his hands closed over her breasts, stroking, petting, and plucking their crests. She sighed with pleasure as his mouth molded with hers, arching into him, skin to skin. His fingertips circled the generous swell of her breast and trailed down over her flat belly. "You're so gorgeous," he sighed against her mouth. "Oh, Elsie, I love you."

When it was over, he could have lain there forever, snuggled up together in a state of euphoria. Their lovemaking had been sensuous and intense, so amazing, so right. He brushed a few loose strands of hair off her forehead, his need to touch her overwhelming.

Her deep-blue eyes held his for several long moments, before she rolled over to her side.

Immediate concern washed over him. "Did I hurt you?"

"Not at all," she replied and snuggled with her back against his chest, her bottom against his crotch. "It was perfect."

He sensed she was crying and draped his arm around her, pulling her closer. "I love you," he whispered in her ear. "Did I tell you that already?"

She didn't answer, and he touched her face, only to discover that her cheeks were wet. "Sweetheart, don't cry. I've never experienced anything like this, and I'm so grateful you walked into my life. You're my dream girl, my everything."

The distant sound of his cell phone interrupted them. The only one who had his number was Adelyn. Not wanting to let go of Elsie, he ignored the sound, until his concern took over. He pushed himself up on one elbow. "I'm sorry, but that has to be Adelyn."

She turned around in his arms. "Please, get it. Something

might be wrong with Dora."

He kissed her wet cheeks and drew away. Leaving her was the last thing he wanted to do. He gathered his clothes and found his cell phone the moment it rang for the third time.

"Hello, Adelyn?"

Back inside the RV, Eagle found Elsie waiting for him, toes buried in the carpet, the bedsheet wrapped around her naked body. He noticed the whisker burns around her lips from his fervent kisses, and had never seen anyone more gorgeous. He loved her. God, he really loved her.

"Is everything all right?" she asked.

He gave her a reassuring smile. "Adelyn told me a man came to the house, looking for me. When I didn't answer, she sent him down this way to find me."

Emma's blue eyes flickered with shock and worry. Her shoulders sagged. "After your visitor leaves, we really need to talk." She let out a shuddering breath. "If it's not too late."

He frowned but saved his questions. They would talk as soon as he returned.

CHAPTER

34

EAGLE

BUTTONING UP HIS SHIRT, Eagle watched a car drive down the dirt road and park next to his truck. An unfamiliar man stepped out. Gray hair, suit, and tie. That didn't bode well. Distinguished-looking men like him usually only came to sell you something or deliver unwelcome news.

When the man stopped in front of him, he looked Eagle over several times before a smile appeared on his clean-shaven face. "Axel, is that you?" He extended his arm and grabbed his hand in a firm grip. "I barely recognize you with all that hair."

Then he was drawn into a manly half-hug and slapped on the back.

"It's been far too long, Axel. Far too long."

Frozen on the spot, he tolerated the stranger's hug. He hadn't heard his real name in years. It sounded almost alien to him.

When the stranger released him, he raked his hand through his neatly trimmed black hair, gilded with gray, and grinned.

"It's so good to see you. How have you been?"

The man looked very familiar, and Eagle finally sensed who stood in front of him. "Uncle Travis? Is that you?"

"Yes, it's me! Don't tell me I aged so much in ten years that you don't recognize me?"

After his initial surprise, resentment washed over him. Travis was his father's brother. There had been no love lost between the two, their relationship very similar to the one he had with his own brother, Ruben. "What are you doing here?"

"I'm here for you."

Eagle had left his past behind. To find his uncle show up unexpectedly, invading his newly built life on the worst moment possible, wasn't something he appreciated. An expression of grim determination settled on his face. "Why didn't you just call, instead of coming out here?"

"Please, don't be like that, Axel," his uncle protested. "I've come a long way."

While talking to Elsie about his past, old pain had resurfaced. Pain he'd much rather kept buried under the new memories he'd created. With his uncle's sudden appearance, he realized that wouldn't happen. Travis would only show up for something important, and that was more than likely bad news. *Did someone pass away? Was it his father?*

Dressed in a pair of blue jeans and a shirt, Emma appeared in the barn's entrance. Her face lost all color when she noticed Travis.

Travis nodded in her direction. "Hi Emma, I heard you

found him." He raised an amused eyebrow. "It seems you and Axel are getting along. That's great."

Emma's eyes flitted back and forth between the two of them. She seemed frozen in place and Eagle could tell something was wrong.

"Who's Emma?" Eagle asked.

Irritated with the situation, he walked toward Elsie. All he wanted to do was take her in his arms and make love for the second time. He reached out to touch her face. "Are you all right?"

Travis followed and hitched a leather western style backpack from his shoulders. "Jesse gave me your backpack, Emma," he said, handing it to her. "Everything is still in it, including your cell phone, wallet, and debit card. Ruben said you can use it to pay for a return flight home."

The expression on her lovely face reflected the most profound sadness. "I'm so sorry, Eagle." Choking back a sob, she accepted the backpack. After giving Eagle another sad and apologetic glance, she whispered, "I'll leave the two of you alone." Then she turned and hurried off, leaving Eagle gaping after her.

Travis mumbled something under his breath. "Come, Axel. A conversation is long overdue. Let's sit and talk." He extended a comforting hand and patted Eagle on the shoulder. "Those two Adirondack chairs next to that fire look very inviting."

That wasn't what Eagle had in mind. He wanted to go after Elsie, to sort out this whole misunderstanding.

"I can tell you want to go after her," Travis said. "But let her go for now. There's something very important I need to talk to you about." He grabbed a piece of wood and added it to the dying fire before lowering himself in a chair.

Watching his uncle get comfortable, Eagle felt cornered. He knew he wouldn't leave before they'd talked, and it was better to get it over with. "Elsie told me her car with all her belongings got stolen. How did you end up with her backpack?" he asked.

Travis shook his head. "It seems your new girlfriend hasn't been honest with you. That's unfortunate."

Eagle planted his fists on his hips, tension knotting the muscles at his neck. "What do you mean?"

After an apologetic gaze, Travis cleared his throat. "She didn't show up here by chance, Axel. Ruben hired her to find you. She's been on the road for weeks, following your trail all the way across the United States."

Axel struggled to absorb the words his brain refused to comprehend. "That's impossible. She would have told me." He sank down into the chair next to his uncle and sighed.

"I don't know if you want to hear more about the details of her trip," Travis said. "About an old lady in Iowa who used to have a deli, a farm in Wyoming that burned down to the ground, and a girl called Raven who pointed her in your direction." Travis shrugged. "I don't understand why Emma wouldn't tell you anything about that."

Eagle gazed into nothingness, a cold weight of disappointment entombing his heart. Every time his brother was involved, he got hurt, and for that reason, he'd left. But he wasn't that young, insecure teenager anymore. He was a man who'd found himself. This time he needed to get down to the meat of the matter, fight for his happiness, and discover the truth.

"Why didn't Ruben come himself if it's so important?"

Travis scratched his head, evading his eyes. "It's your father.

He's gravely ill and is asking for you. You should pack a bag. I'm here to take you home."

Bitterness darkened his eyes. "You're telling me Ruben hired a woman to find me because my father is sick, and when she did, she kept that from me?" He got up from his chair and kicked a burning log, sending sparks flying. With his mouth set in a straight line, he glared down at his uncle. "Anything else?"

"Just a message for Emma. That Jesse agrees to sign the divorce papers."

The words hit him hard. She was married, and she had kept that information from him, too? He shut his eyes and swallowed a sob, her betrayal hurting like hell. "How soon can we leave?"

"My return flight leaves at ten-thirty tonight. If we leave now, there will be time to have dinner at the airport before our departure."

He nodded. "Considering my state of mind, I think we better leave right away."

Eagle walked into the barn and immediately noticed Emma. She sat on the steps of the motorhome; her face pale, blue eyes wide-open and filled with dread. She jumped to her feet the moment she saw him. "I was going to tell you everything. Tonight."

He gave her an ice-cold stare. "You should have told me the moment you walked into my life." He pushed her aside and entered the RV.

She rushed in after him. "Please, Eagle, let me explain. Please."

He opened a cabinet, pulled out a duffel bag, and stuffed

clothes into it.

With tears streaming down her face, she tried to stop him. "In the beginning I was afraid you knew who I was. Jesse and I had a fight, and he knew where you lived. I thought he'd stopped by to talk to you, or that Ruben had called, and that you were playing dumb to keep me here."

Ignoring her, Eagle disappeared into the bathroom. When he came out, she placed her hands against his chest. "I know. I was stupid. I should have known better. But I didn't."

He shrugged, freed himself, and headed outside. Not giving up, she chased after him. "And then I was afraid of how you would react if I told the truth."

When he stopped in his tracks, she slammed into him.

He grabbed her shoulders to steady her. "Do you have any idea how much you hurt me?" he growled. "The pretense, the deceit, the lies." With a look of disgust, he released her and turned away, trying to bolster himself against the hurt raging through his entire being.

With both hands, she got hold of his arm. "Can't you give me a few minutes?"

He tried to free himself, but she held him tightly, still not willing to let go. "I don't want you to leave without an explanation. Please, I'm begging you."

With gentle force, he broke away. "Take care of Samson, the chickens, and the horses."

In the fading light of what had been a gorgeous day, Eagle stepped into Travis' car and gave her a last accusing glare over his shoulder before they drove off.

CHAPTER

35

ON THE WAY to the airport, Eagle watched the mountains disappear behind them, making way for farmlands. The moist climate of the valley ideal for many different field crops, such as wheat, oats, hops, and hay. Soon they drove in heavy traffic on the interstate.

He stared out the window, not in the mood to talk. Besides a few comments about the diversity of the landscape and the smell of cow manure, Travis didn't say much either. Eagle realized he barely knew his uncle. His father had never wanted his brother to be a part of their life. As a child he hadn't questioned him, taking it for what it was. Now, he wondered about the reason, and if they'd reconciled their differences. He knew the Templetons were often stubborn, believing everything was either black or white, himself included.

But he had softened over the years. Time and distance had done wonders, his disappointment and anger gradually dissipating until it wasn't important any longer. Not even the fact that Ruben had slept with his girlfriend, while he'd never even touched her breast. If it was so easy to cheat, their budding relationship had been doomed from the start. Ruben might have only done him a favor by revealing who she really was.

"Over the last few years, I often wanted to reach out to my father," he said. "Last Christmas, I even called him, but the phone was disconnected."

"August has a cell phone and disconnected the landline several years ago."

Another long silence fell. At the car rental, they took a shuttle to the terminal. Eagle had never flown, the hustle and bustle at the airport a new experience.

In one of the restaurants, they ordered steak and fries with an I.P.A., and soon after, they headed to the gate.

A flight attendant showed them their seats in business class. Eagle stared at his worn-out jeans and work boots, feeling uncomfortable between the businessmen in suits and the women in slacks and suit jackets.

"You still haven't told me what's wrong with Dad," Eagle asked, fastening his seatbelt.

"It's his heart." Travis yawned. "Sorry, on East Coast time it's past midnight, and I'm exhausted."

The plane backed away from the gate, and Eagle listened to the flight attendant's safety announcement. In the air, with the fasten-your-seatbelt sign turned off, Travis reclined his chair and covered himself with a blanket.

"There will be plenty of time to talk later," he said, propping a pillow under his head.

The flight attendant came by, handing out menus. They both declined. "Just a bottle of water would be great," Eagle said.

Left to his own thoughts, images of Emma floated through his mind. How she'd smelled of warmth and fresh flowers when he buried his face in her neck. The feel of her breast in his palm. How her fingertips dug into his back as she'd arched up to meet him.

The corners of his mouth raised up in a warm smile. She was the stuff of his dreams. His other half he'd always known was out there. Until the image of her naked body in the arms of another man splintered his thoughts.

He turned toward his uncle. "What can you tell me about Jesse?"

Travis opened one eye. "The Kimballs have been my neighbors for thirty years, and I've known Jesse since he was a toddler. He's Senator Jesse Kimball II only son, a well-respected, prominent businessman, an aspiring politician, and Ruben's best friend."

Eagle gazed out the window at the dark sky, processing the information. He'd preferred that Jesse turned out to be a three-time-loser. But no such luck. Emma's husband came from an influential family and was successful in life. He wondered why she'd left him.

"Care for a cup of coffee, Mr. Templeton?" the flight attendant whispered behind her hand, interrupting his reverie. She nodded her head toward Travis, who snored softly.

"No, thank you," he whispered back.

Closing his eyes, he tried to follow Travis' example.

Sleep evaded him during the six-hour flight. Every time he closed his eyes, he saw Emma's tear-streaked face and heard her cries, the hurt in her eyes unmistakable. He regretted leaving without hearing her out. There had to be more to the story, and he should have listened, giving her a chance to explain. Instead he'd let pain dictate the moment. He wasn't proud that he'd let history repeat itself, with him running away with his tail between his legs the moment his feelings got hurt.

With just their carry-ons, they left the airport shortly after disembarking the plane. In the parking garage, Travis opened the trunk of a four-door Mercedes and they put their bags inside.

"I bought this beauty earlier this year," he said with pride in his voice. "As an early retirement gift to myself. It's a Mercedes-Benz AMG S 63 Sedan." He opened the door and stepped in.

"When do you plan to retire?" Eagle asked. He lowered himself into the soft leather passenger seat. Not for the first time, he wondered what he'd missed since he left.

"Ruben has worked for me since he graduated from Yale. I planned to leave the reins in his hands by the end of this year." He cleared his throat and backed out of the parking spot. "Unfortunately, life often throws you a curveball and nothing is going according to plan. It's been a stressful time."

His uncle's voice sounded strangled, his brow furrowed, as though something saddened him deeply.

Eagle assumed it had to do with his father's illness. "I'm glad I'm here," he mumbled.

Travis paid the parking fee, went through the gate, and drove onto the freeway.

"You may be happy to hear that your father remarried," Travis said, the short distraction seemingly enough to pull himself together. "I'm sure you'll meet Mary while you're here. She's an exceptional lady who takes excellent care of him. You should try her lemon-scones one day. They're the best."

While Travis spoke, Eagle took in the familiar landscape, noticing the differences. New buildings, another off ramp, a commuter rail, and heavy early morning traffic. Had it always been this busy? He didn't think so.

"After your father stopped drinking, he made amends with everybody, including me, and he's been sober for nine years or more. Mary has been his rock. They met in AA, so you won't see a drop of alcohol at their house."

Eagle had quit drinking from one day to the next, and was able to enjoy a good glass of wine or beer so now and then without any problems. But he knew what a difficult and long process overcoming an addiction could be.

They passed the exit to Dunedam and he noticed the tower from the Catholic church from afar. Next to it was the grade school, and not much farther down the pharmacy, where they had the biggest selection of candy. Long forgotten memories popped up in his mind, and for the first time in ten years, he allowed himself to reminisce about the past. About the ocean and the dunes. The lady that had lived next door and baked cookies every day, and the friendly elderly couple from across the street, paying him generously for taking care of their tiny yard. His high school math teacher, telling him he had a knack for geometry and algebra, and that he should apply for a scholarship.

Buried emotions welled up inside him. Growing up in

Dunedam hadn't been all bad, and regret for turning his back on everyone, without ever looking back, constricted his throat.

"I'm glad to hear that about my father," he said. "Having someone special in your life can be so important. How about you, Travis? Are you married?"

Travis grinned. "Believe me, I had my fair share of relationships throughout the years, and finally met someone I feel fantastic about. His name is Gustavo. He's from Brazil, and we married three years ago."

Eagle hadn't known about his uncle's interest in men, and for a moment, he didn't know what to say. "Gustavo?"

"Don't worry, Axel," Travis chuckled. "Being same-sex attracted is as natural as being opposite-sex attracted, and I'm very comfortable being gay."

"I don't have a problem with that," he answered, fully aware that someone's sexual orientation wasn't a choice and couldn't be changed. But he also knew that some gay people were cast out by their families. He wondered if that had been the reason for the rift between his uncle and his brother.

Travis took his eyes off the road when they stopped for a red light and looked him over. "My interest in men has caused a lot of problems in our family," he said, as if he'd just read his mind. "Our parents didn't understand. Their strict religious beliefs condemned me, and they never realized how much their rejection hurt. It's no wonder I lashed out at them and left home when I was sixteen. But that's all resolved. Our parents are long gone, and your father completely understands and accepts me now."

It seemed much had improved since his departure, and that was great news. It would also make coming home much easier, especially if Ruben's attitude had changed for the better as well.

"That's wonderful to hear," he said. "And congratulations on your marriage. I look forward to meeting him."

"Unfortunately, he's gone for work. He travels a lot, but he should be home in several days."

The Mercedes entered a gated community. The road meandered gradually up the hill with mind-boggling villas on either side. Travis pointed at a gigantic mansion behind a tall fence. "That's the Kimball's residence," he said. "Our backyards are connected. Years ago, Ruben and Jesse made a hole in the fence so they could walk back and forth. They still use it all the time."

"Is Ruben married?" Axel asked.

Travis pressed a button on the remote and one of the four garage doors at his house opened. "No, he's like me," he replied and stepped out of the car, leaving Axel to stare after him in disbelief.

Ruben was like him? Did he mean that Ruben was gay too? No, he must have misunderstood. Girls had always surrounded his brother, vying for his attention. And if he'd been interested in boys, he wouldn't have crawled into bed with Judy, his old girlfriend.

They grabbed their bags from the trunk and walked from the garage into the kitchen. The grandeur of the mansion was awe-inspiring, the kitchen huge and sparkling clean.

"I asked Carlton to make a bed in the spare bedroom upstairs. You're welcome to stay as long as you want."

"Carlton?"

"The Kimballs and I share butlers," Travis replied. "I hope you don't mind, but I have some catching up to do. If you need me, I'll be in my office, right down the hall."

"Weren't you planning to take me to see Dad right away?" Axel asked.

"General visiting hours are from one to eight-thirty p.m. so that gives you at least five hours to sleep. You look tired. Go to bed and take a nap."

Axel walked up the stairs. The first door in the hallway led to an office with a massive desk, a computer, and bay windows overlooking the yard. The second door opened into a bedroom. Looking at the row of shoes, this had to be Ruben's. Axel understood why Ruben enjoyed living in his uncle's house. Obsessed with his looks, the right clothes, money, and status, it fit his brother's flamboyant lifestyle to a T.

At the end of the hall was another bedroom. He walked in. All the closets were empty, the king-sized bed impeccably made with a dazzling gold and red bedspread and eight matching pillows. Worn-out, he dropped his duffel bag on the floor, and headed to the window overlooking the driveway. Going to sleep at eight in the morning seemed strange. Instead, he'd rather leave to visit his father.

What would his father say to him when he walked in? he wondered. Would he be angry? Or would he welcome him as the long-lost son?

With nothing else to do until visitor hours, he stacked the pillows in a heap on the floor and pulled the comforter back. The sheets felt invitingly smooth and crisp. He sat down on the mattress, removed his shoes, and stretched out on the bed.

After dozing a few hours, Eagle headed downstairs. The smell of broiling meat came from the kitchen. At the counter, a man was busy peeling potatoes.

"Good morning, Mr. Axel," he said. "My name is Carlton. Can I get you anything? Coffee, tea, breakfast, lunch? I'm here to help."

"Nice to meet you, Carlton," Axel answered. "A cup of coffee would be great, but I'm sure I can figure out how to make one."

Carlton immediately got busy. "Mr. Travis has this multi-function appliance that lets you brew one cup at a time. It even makes lattes if you prefer."

"A regular cup is fine for me, Carlton," he replied, watching the machine produce a steaming cup within seconds.

"Travis just left. If you need to talk to him, he's right next door," Carlton informed him. He squatted down in front of the oven to check the meat. "He told me to let you know we're having guests for dinner tonight and that you're free to use his old Mercedes in case you want to go somewhere. It's in the garage." He walked to one of the kitchen cabinets, opened the top drawer, and handed him a set of keys.

"Thanks," Axel answered. "That's exactly what I'd hoped for."

CHAPTER

36

Axel took the familiar roads out of the city. It didn't take long before he entered Dunedam, the small coastal town where he grew up. Along the Dune Road, he steered onto a parking lot. It overlooked the ocean and he rolled down the window to breathe in the aromatic sea air. In the distance, a fog bank crept up from the water into the dunes. He knew it would soon cover the entire town before dissipating as the sun grew stronger and the day warmed up.

The cawing of seagulls and the distant roar of the waves brought back memories of sand between his toes and dried up salt on his skin. The distance from the dunes to his childhood house was less than a mile. He'd loved living so close to the ocean. It was one of the few things he missed living in the mountains.

Reminiscing about the old days, he drove through town until he entered the familiar trailer park. Across the street from his childhood home, he stopped to take it all in. The owners had painted the picket fence. There were several flowerpots in the yard, and a cat slept on top of a pillow in a lawn chair. He also noticed new round steppingstones replaced the old broken up pavers, and the front door had an unfamiliar deep maroon color. Other than that, not much had changed.

Angry knocks on the windshield made him look up. A full head of gray hair above a very familiar face glared at him. He pressed the button to lower the window.

"What are you doing in my brother's car, scumbag?"

Axel's eyes widened. "What?"

The man tried to open the door, but when he found it was locked, he clenched his fist. "Get out, you son of a bitch, or I'll call the police!"

Axel unfolded his lean, long body as he stepped out.

Unafraid, the angry old timer immediately approached him. In the middle of the quiet street, they sized each other up.

"Don't you recognize me?" Axel asked after a tense minute.

"I recognize a piece of lowlife scum the moment I lay my eyes on one," the man raged on. The small white dog he had on a leash barked at him.

Axel smiled. "For a man who's supposed to be in the hospital, you're in good shape." Tears sprang into his eyes. "It's me, Dad. Your son, Axel. Didn't Travis tell you I was coming?"

The expression on his father's face turned from anger to shock. Then his face turned ashen.

"Let's get out of the street," Axel said when a car approached. He guided his father toward the house, opened the gate and let him go through first, followed by the dog.

Shaking his head back and forth, his father turned around to look at him, his brown eyes full of disbelief. "I hope this isn't some kind of joke?"

The front door opened and an older woman in white capris and a purple top stepped outside. "Is everything all right, August?" she asked, taking a protective stance with her feet apart. "Who are you? And what are you doing here?"

"He says he's my son, Mary," August replied. For a moment he closed his eyes.

"You're Axel?" Mary asked, looking at him with suspicion. "But you're so tall! And ... hairy."

Fighting tears, Axel nodded. "Ruben hired someone to find me, and when she did, Travis came to bring me home. He said you're gravely ill, and that you asked for me."

Understanding appeared in his father's gaze. He reached out with both arms and drew him into an encompassing embrace. "We can talk later, but now all I want to do is hold you, Son. This is the miracle I've been praying for since the day you left."

They held each other in silence for several minutes, each trying to control his emotions, until Mary came in between.

"Time for coffee, don't you think?"

New furniture brightened up the living room, the touch of a caring woman evident in a vase with fresh flowers on the table and the smell of apple pie. An ironing board stood in a corner, with a stack of shirts hanging across, waiting to be ironed.

Axel sat down on the couch, his father in a recliner. "A lot has changed here," he commented. "Congratulations on your marriage. I can tell it's doing you good."

His father glanced in the direction of the kitchen. "I love

her," he stated in a way that showed his sincerity.

Axel leaned back in his seat, his arm across the back, taking everything in. It was good to be home and see his father sober and clear minded. He seemed a different man.

"There's so much I want to talk about," his father said, changing position in his chair, "But let's first clear something up." He attempted a smile, but failed. "Besides arthritis in my knees and high blood pressure, there's nothing wrong with me. But I understand why Travis lied. He must have believed you wouldn't have come home if you'd known it was Ruben who's deathly ill."

Axel's mouth dropped open. "Ruben? What's wrong with him?"

August nodded with a pained expression on his face. "He suffered from migraines and unpredictable mood swings for months before he finally went to the doctor. It turned out a tumor deeply embedded in his brain caused all his symptoms. The doctors told him it was inoperable, and they gave him half a year to live, at the most."

Axel gazed at the ceiling, letting his father's words sink in. His brother couldn't be dying? He was far too young. Astonished at the severity of his grief, he shuddered. He cared more about his brother than he'd realized. With difficulty, he swallowed back the lump in his throat. "I wasn't pleased to see Travis show up on my doorstep, but now I'm grateful he did, so I can be here for you during this stressful, trying time. How are you coping, Dad?"

Using the sleeve of his shirt, his father dabbed his eyes. "A father should never have to bury his son."

The grief in his eyes almost brought Eagle to tears.

"Ruben is in the hospital. He had another horrible seizure last week. The doctors want to alleviate the pressure but warned he might not survive the surgery, because of the location of his tumor. That's when he must have decided to send Travis to get you. He wants to make amends."

Mary walked in from the kitchen with a tray and served them coffee and apple fritters. "Milk and sugar, Axel?" she asked.

The normalcy of drinking coffee gave both men the chance to compose themselves.

"I shouldn't have stayed away so long," Axel said. "I hope you can forgive me, Dad."

"Don't start apologizing," his father replied. He leaned forward to squeeze his son's knee. "If someone has to do that, it should be me. I was never there for you, and it's all my fault. Including Ruben's horrible behavior. I should have listened to both of you and paid closer attention to what was going on in your lives."

"You shouldn't be so hard on yourself, Dad," Eagle replied. "I know how much you loved Mom, and you had to work your way through your pain. I understand that now."

August Templeton sat slumped in his chair and stared at the floor, shaking his head. "Maybe, but I should have realized much sooner that you can't find solace at the bottom of a whiskey bottle. I was selfish and failed the two of you in so many ways. There's no excuse, and all I can do is try to make amends."

Mary touched his shoulder and he looked up, pain in his soulful brown eyes.

"You should be happy, sweetheart," she said, and bent over to kiss the top of his head. "You're reunited with your son.

This is a day to celebrate."

August rubbed his eyes, expelling a deep breath. "How long are you staying, Son?"

"For as long as I'm needed," he replied.

CHAPTER

37

STRUGGLING WITH everything he'd learned, Axel returned to Uncle Travis' mansion. He found his uncle in the kitchen, preparing a sandwich.

"Axel, I'm glad you're back," he said. "Do you want something to eat before we go to the hospital? I'm having a roast beef sandwich."

"No, thanks, I just had two homemade apple fritters at my father's house. I have to say, he's doing remarkably well for a man who's supposed to be in the hospital."

Travis' hands fell silent in midair. "So, you know the truth." He sighed. "Sorry I lied, Axel, but Ruben believed you wouldn't have come with me otherwise."

"Don't worry about it," Axel said. "I understand and am glad to be here. It's time to reconcile and forget about the past, especially in the light of what Ruben is facing."

"I can't tell you how relieved I am to hear you say that,"

Travis said. His Adam's apple bobbed as he tried to hide his emotions. "Ruben is anxious to see you before going into surgery on Monday."

Axel closed his eyes for a moment, massaging his forehead. "I can't imagine what he's going through."

Travis drew in a lengthy breath before letting it out in a deep, sad sigh. "There's nothing more important than our health. As I age, I'm becoming more and more aware of that."

An hour later, Eagle followed Travis down the long, white corridor to Ruben's hospital room. He walked with a measured stride. The heels of his boots echoed against the walls. He hoped his nervousness didn't show.

They found Ruben in a wheelchair, wrapped up in a silk robe with black lapels. A man Eagle had never seen before lay on top of the crisp, white sheets on the bed, his arms folded behind his head. As soon as they walked into the room, he stood and extended his hand. "Nice to meet you, Axel. I'm Jesse Kimball."

Emma's husband, Eagle realized. Pushing aside every thought of Emma, he said, "Likewise," before turning his attention to his brother.

"I hardly recognize you," Ruben said, giving him a critical once-over. "Thank you so much for coming, brother."

Eagle took his brother's hand in a warm grip, his skin warm and scaly, the bones fragile. "Good to see you, Ruben."

They stared at each other, testing the waters.

"There's not much left of me, is there?" Ruben smirked, his eyes unnaturally bright and restless.

Axel let go of his hand and sat down in one of the plastic chairs Jesse had set out. "At least your spirit is still the same."

Ruben pulled a handkerchief from his sleeve and blew his nose, his face pale and drawn, the shoulders under his robe scrawny.

"We should give the brothers some privacy, so they can talk," Travis said to Jesse. "Let's get a cup of coffee in the cafeteria."

Jesse nodded. "We'll be back in an hour, Ruben. Is there anything you want me to bring back up?"

"I'm good," Ruben replied.

A heavy silence fell after the two men left. There was so much to say, but neither knew how to start.

"You don't have to apologize or worry about anything that happened between us in the past, Ruben. Sending Emma and Travis proves you care. That means a lot to me."

Ruben leaned back in his chair, his hands steepled under his chin. "You know what your problem is?" he said. "You're too darn agreeable. Too kind." He shook his head. "Man, if I'd found you in my bed, fucking my girlfriend, I would've killed you. But no, you had to run away."

"There was nothing kind or agreeable about that," Axel replied. He stood up and moved around the room, his hands clasped behind his back. "All I did was take the coward's way out."

"There you go again." Ruben sighed. "Taking the blame for something you didn't do, instead of lashing out. It's no wonder everybody always favored you."

His words sounded strangled. Axel turned to face him. "What do you mean by that?"

In the harsh fluorescent lights of the hospital room, he saw the deep shadows under his brother's eyes and the worry lines around his mouth. Ruben looked dead tired, but his eyes threw daggers.

"All I ever heard was, Ruben, why can't you be more like Axel? He's so sweet, so gentle, so nice. He never causes problems. Why can't you be polite? Say a friendly word? You can learn a lot from your little brother." His voice changed from a complaint to accusation and fury. "I resented and hated you for it."

Completely taken aback by the venom in his brother's voice, Eagle froze. "Don't tell me you were jealous of me! It was the other way around," he rebuked. "Darn it, Ruben. People always told me how handsome and smart you were, with all the girls from the neighborhood parading after you. While all they had for me was contempt because I didn't match up. How do you think that felt?"

The atmosphere was charged with hostility as they flung accusations at each other, forgotten pain flaring up. ""Why did you need to destroy everything that was mine?" Eagle hissed, trying to control his temper.

Drops of perspiration appeared on Ruben's forehead and he shriveled in his chair. It was as if life was getting sucked out of him. "At least we have that out of the way," he sighed. He used his handkerchief to dry his forehead before a satisfied grin appeared on his face. "Feels good, doesn't it, to fight back and clear the air? You should try it more often."

Axel had to admit it was liberating to speak up against his brother, instead of letting him bully him in submission as he'd always done. He sat down in the chair; a heavy weight lifted off his chest. "It sure did," he smiled.

Ruben smiled back. "Man, it's so good to see you, although all that hair looks terrible. How long has it been since you had a haircut?"

"If you're going to insult me, I'm out of here," Axel replied. They were teasing each other now, all the tension between them gone.

Ruben reached for his glass of water, and Axel handed it to him.

"Before Travis and Jesse return, I want to tell you about my upcoming surgery," he said, taking a few sips. "Did they tell you it will be an intricate and life-threatening surgery? That fucking tumor is eating away at my brain. I don't want to sound morbid, but I've been preparing for the end for quite a while. Making peace with you was an important part. That's why I sent Emma to find you, and I'm very grateful you're here."

"I appreciate that you did," Axel replied. "A visit was long overdue, and I apologize for that. We're family and I never understood how important that is until now."

Ruben almost disappeared in his chair. He seemed exhausted, fighting to stay alert.

"I'll let you rest and will be back tomorrow," he promised. He squeezed his brother's frail shoulder and walked out.

Back at Travis' house, Eagle walked into Ruben's office upstairs. All their childhood problems seemed so trivial in retrospect to his brother's illness. At thirty-one, at the top of his career, he could die while undergoing brain surgery. The idea frightened him to the core, and he couldn't imagine what his brother had to go through.

A computer stood silent on top of a mahogany desk. He sat down on the leather swivel chair, picked up the day planner that lay there and leafed through the empty pages. No appointments. No future. Filled with grief, he put his hands over his face. The events of the last twenty-four hours were taking its toll, and he longed to crawl into bed. Unfortunately, he couldn't. His father and his wife Mary would be here for dinner soon.

Looking for a distraction, and curious to find out more about Jesse Kimball, he booted up the computer and opened a search engine.

After typing in Jesse's name, thousands of pages popped up. Quickly he realized that most of them were about his father and grandfather, Jesse Kimball I and II. Both of them had been senators for the Republican Party. He thought about Emma, clad in Dora's ill-fitting dress and the second-hand shorts and shirts she'd bought at the garage sale. Somehow, he couldn't picture her in Jesse's world, where looks were just as important as character and demeanor.

Something else bothered him. Travis had told him Jesse spent each spare moment with Ruben. He even stayed overnight. Why did he do that? And why had he ordered Carlton to help take care of Ruben? Were they such close friends? Or was there something else going on?

To sift out most pages, he added III behind Jesse's name and read: Jesse Kimball III loses the race for Heemstead's Mayor. In the post below it said: Andrew Voss Declares Victory in Heemstead.

Just as he wanted to click on one of the other articles,

someone called his name. He recognized his father's voice and headed downstairs.

They first had coffee on the terrace. Not much later, Jesse walked up through the backyard and joined them.

"Jesse, I'm sure you'd rather be at the hospital with Ruben, but I'm glad you decided to join us," Travis said. "Carlton made meatloaf. He told me it's one of your favorite meals."

Jesse nodded. "I promised Ruben to bring leftovers. A man can only take so much mushy, overcooked hospital food."

"He's too thin," Mary said. "If he loves meat, I have a wonderful recipe for a farmer's casserole and can bring some by tomorrow."

Carlton appeared in the doorway. "Dinner is ready," he said.

"That was fantastic," Jesse said at the end of dinner. He disappeared into the kitchen and returned a few minutes later with a plastic container. "I'll take this to Ruben," he said, and left through the backdoor.

"I'm so thankful that Jesse is constantly staying at Ruben's side," August Templeton said.

"Of course," Travis replied, gathering the dishes. "He loves him." With his hands full, he left the dining room, followed by Mary.

Left alone, August looked at Axel. "If it's still warm enough, let's sit outside so we can talk."

Eagle stood immediately. Since he'd seen Jesse in the hospital, and again here at the dinner table, talking like he was part of the family, a tension headache had started to develop from the back of his neck. He needed some fresh air.

It was a little chilly on the veranda, with summer making way for fall. Instead of sitting down, they walked around, breathing in the fragrance of the well-kept garden.

"You must have figured out by now that Ruben and Jesse are lovers," August said, confirming what he'd already expected.

He opened his mouth to say something, but then clamped his lips together and swallowed several times. Although it made sense, he still struggled to wrap his mind around it.

Noticing his confusion, his father grinned. "I already knew he was homosexual before Ruben even realized it himself. He was the spitting image of Travis. In every way." For a few moments he was quiet, gathering his thoughts. "You have to understand, Axel. When I grew up, people weren't tolerant like they are now. It horrified my parents when they found out about Travis. I believed if I did things different with Ruben, he could change." He snorted. "Little did I know. A man can't change how he's born."

"Were Ruben and Jesse openly gay?" Eagle asked, although he already knew the answer. Emma would have never married him if she'd known.

"No, Jesse's parents would never accept it. They expected their son to become a senator and drilled his entire life into him that people would never vote for him if they found skeletons in his closet. So, they kept their relationship secret, and even dated girls to keep up the charade. I warned Ruben they made a mistake, and that I didn't approve. These days, there's no need to hide your sexuality. Travis tried to tell him that, too. But Ruben never listened to anyone. He ignored us, saying what he did was best for him and Jesse. And that how they lived their life was none of our business."

"But why did Jesse take it so far by getting married?" Eagle demanded. "That's ridiculous."

"I had a hard time believing it, trust me," his father replied. "When I attended the wedding, I wondered if she knew, if they'd paid her to play a part, or if she was kept in the dark. She seemed so sweet."

The first hint of anger shot into Eagle's eyes. He didn't believe for one second that Emma had known. She wasn't that kind of person. Those calculating assholes. They'd taken advantage of her, weaving her into their scheme. No wonder she hadn't talked about her marriage. "Didn't you question them?" he said, massaging the back of his neck to relieve the mounting tension.

August grimaced. "What good could that have done? By then, Ruben was already sick and more unreasonable than ever. On top of that, he was often irrational, with fits of unconuncommtrollable anger and despair. Mary used to be a nurse. She told me the change in his personality could be caused by the location of the tumor." For several moments he stared at Axel, his eyes begging for understanding. "When Ruben found out the tumor was inoperable, it became even worse. He became obsessed about securing Jesse's political future and decided he should marry. He went on the hunt for the right woman and found that cute librarian."

Eagle had heard enough and closed his eyes as regret for leaving Emma throbbed through his mind. The moment he'd met her, she'd crashed through his defenses and stolen his heart. All he wanted to do was fly back home, to tell her he understood.

"It's easy to blame it on a tumor," he said, his tone harsh.

"But that still doesn't explain why Jesse went along. With his background, he could have easily succeeded without using Emma as a pawn."

His father raised his left eyebrow in surprise. "Do you know her?"

"I sure do," he replied.

CHAPTER

38

EAGLE HURRIED down the pebbled walkway, through the hole in the fence, and into the Kimball's backyard. It was time to ask Jesse a few questions.

When he rounded the house, one of the garage doors opened. A gleaming black Mercedes backed out. Jesse spotted him immediately and rolled down his window. "Hey, Axel, what's up?"

"Glad I caught you before you left," he said. "I was hoping we could talk."

A glint of impatience flickered in Jesse's blue eyes. "About Emma, I presume?" Then he shrugged his wide shoulders. "Sure, hop in. We can talk on the way to the hospital." He unlocked the passenger door.

Eagle climbed in. What's up with all these shiny, brand-new Mercedes-Benzes and leather seats? he wondered. Was that the required vehicle if you lived here? His thoughts went to his own four-wheel-drive pickup truck on the ranch, and he grinned. This Mercedes wouldn't stand a chance out there.

"I heard you're in the winemaking business," Jesse said as they drove off. "One of my friends recently took a wine country vacation in the Pacific Northwest. Villa-hopping, helicopter rides, hot spring visits, nature walks, all included. He said his favorite wine comes from your Willamette Valley. It's nice out there, I have to admit."

Eagle told him in a few sentences about the practice lot he started several years ago, his dream of producing Pinot Noir becoming a reality.

"Excellent," Jesse said, giving him a quick side glance. "But I know you don't want to talk about wine."

"That's right," Eagle said. "I'm here to talk about Emma."

Jesse stopped for a red light and turned to look at him. "Did you fall in love with her?"

Eagle met his curious gaze. "I did," he admitted without hesitation. "She's the most beautiful woman I've ever met. She deserves nothing but goodness and happiness. Why did you marry her? Was it just to help you work your way into politics?"

Jesse's hands tightened around the steering wheel. "Listen. I did what your brother asked. He wanted to see me with a wife. I obliged. What else could I do? He's dying, and all I wanted to do was make him happy. I love him." He swallowed hard, the corners of his mouth bent down into a sad smile.

The traffic light turned green. Instead of continuing, Jesse pulled over to the side of the road, hanging his head and shaking it back and forth. "Sorry, I need a minute," he said, his voice cracking.

Eagle released a deep sigh, feeling his pain mirrored in his own heart.

They sat in silence for a few minutes, both deep in thought, until Jesse composed himself and merged back into traffic. He inhaled deeply. "I acknowledge the situation with Emma was messed up, and it may look like I used her, but I gave her a lot in return. Just ask her yourself. She won't deny it."

Eagle didn't answer. He had yet to talk to Emma about her relationship with Jesse.

"Like you said, Axel. Emma's a sweet and smart girl and I came to appreciate her. I don't know what she told you, but I never wanted to hurt her, and when she fled into the forest, I was horrified. My father had contacts in Portland. Within three days, I knew she was safe and stayed on the Gravenstein Homestead, with *you*."

"You knew for weeks?"

"I did. But I had the election, and then Ruben fell ill. Listen, man, since my relationship with Ruben is out in the open, I'll sign the papers for an annulment. I'm sure Emma will be happy with that."

Hearing Jesse mention an annulment instead of a divorce surprised him.

"An annulment declares the marriage invalid," Jesse explained. "Over time, the public will forget about it, and it'll be like it never happened." He released another deep sigh. "At least that's what I hope for."

"Thanks for talking about the situation so frankly," Eagle said. "I'm sure it must have been tough. Keeping your relation-ship with Ruben a secret for so long, and then seeing him fighting for his life. But somehow your words sound hollow, and it'll take a long while before I can forgive you for using Emma so cruelly."

Jesse slowed down to turn into the parking lot of the hospital. He retrieved a ticket, and the automated barricade opened. "If you knew my parents and grandparents, you would understand why." He found an empty parking spot, shut down the engine and looked Eagle straight in the eyes. "American politics are defined by the values and priorities of older generations. Believe it or not, it took an article in Time Magazine several weeks ago to open my eyes. It was an article about the coming millennial wave." He scoffed. "It won't be long until these old-fashioned baby boomers are replaced by millennials, like me. We will bring different political views to the table. Views that will appeal to young voters, like health care for all, free college tuition, legalization of marijuana, gay marriages, equal rights, and attention to climate change. Who knows, being gay might prove to be an advantage. At least nobody will ever accuse me of sexually harassing a sexy blonde, redhead, or brunette, like they so easily do nowadays with every righteous politician."

Jesse raised his fist to emphasize his words, as if he talked to a crowd instead of just him. "Mark my words. Politics will change dramatically in this country, and I'll be at the forefront."

CHAPTER

39

EMMA'S RUNNING FOOTSTEPS sounded hollow in the fine dust on the trail. When she reached the barn, she bent forward to stretch her legs.

Samson barked. "You miss him, too, don't you?" she said, taking his head in her hands and shaking him affectionately. "I don't know what I would have done without your company."

She choked up. The day after Eagle left, she'd gathered enough courage to tell Adelyn and Dora everything, and this could be her last morning on the ranch.

"You're in love with him, aren't you?" Adelyn had asked. "Don't worry about anything. He'll be back soon, and then you can sort it all out."

Adelyn was right. But what would he say? He'd been so angry.

"Yes, I love him," she'd replied. "But waiting for him to return won't solve my problems. I need to go home, to face my past and deal with the consequences, as unpleasant and scary as they may be. If it's not too much to ask, can you give me a ride to the airport and take care of the animals?"

Sue Stremler waited for her at the airport in Heemstead. The two women embraced.

"I was so worried about you," Sue said, holding Emma at arm's length to inspect her. "But I don't think I needed to. You look different, more confident and determined. And those shorts and cowboy boots look great on you."

"I changed a lot," Emma agreed. "More than I ever thought possible."

"Where's your luggage?" Sue asked.

Emma showed her the backpack. "This is it."

They headed to the parking garage and stepped into Sue's car. "There's so much I want to tell you," Emma said, on the way to Sue's apartment. She could barely keep her eyes open. For her it was the middle of the night. For Sue, it was already morning. "About Jesse, my trip across the country, and all the wonderful people I met along the way. Bernard, Edwina, Sheep, Raven, Adelyn and Dora. It was an incredible experience."

"And you said over the phone you met someone on a farm in Oregon?"

Emma clutched her hands around the seatbelt, her nerves wired, her emotions in chaotic disarray when she thought of Eagle. It still seemed impossible how fast and hopelessly irretrievable she'd fallen in love with him. At the thought she might have lost him, she almost wept.

"I did," she replied, trying to get a handle on her fear.

"That's why I came back. I need to confront Jesse and ask for a divorce, otherwise I don't have a chance for happiness or a future."

"I don't think Jesse will cause trouble," Sue said. She gave her arm a quick encouraging squeeze before pulling into the parking lot of the apartment complex where she lived. "You must have heard he lost the election, right?"

At the news, Emma bit the inside of her cheek, realizing Jesse would blame his loss on her disappearance, and that he might retaliate. Distraught, she followed Sue inside, and up the stairs to her apartment on the third floor. "I didn't know he lost," she said, squelching the dejection at the back of her throat. Then she straightened her shoulders. "You know what? I don't care. All I want is his signature on the divorce papers, and I'll be out of his life."

"I can't wait to show you something," Sue grinned, elation written all over her face. "Come in." She closed the door behind them and hurried over to her desk. "I saved several articles for you." She riffled through a stack of papers until she found what she was looking for. With a triumphant smile, she handed Emma two clippings. "Read these."

"What's this about?" Emma asked, feeling some of Sue's excitement rubbing off on her. She pulled her reading glasses from her backpack and sat down at the dining table. The headline said, Jesse Kimball's Downfall. That couldn't be good.

With the compromising photo of Attorney Ruben Templeton and Jesse Kimball III gone public, Andrew Voss won the mayoral election with a landslide.

The consensus is that Mr. Kimball didn't lose the election because of his sexual orientation, but because of his marriage to Emma Bowen. The sweet young librarian an innocent victim on his way up the political ladder.

Next to the article was a photo of two men in an intimate embrace, their lips locked in a passionate kiss.

"I don't understand," Emma said, the words not making any sense. She was so tired; she could hardly think. "Who are these men?"

"I can tell you're exhausted, but before you go to bed, let me explain," Sue said, sitting down next to her. "Just before the election, Ruben was rushed to the hospital after a violent seizure left him immobilized inside his car. When Jesse heard about it, he hurried to the hospital. A journalist took that picture of the two of them in an intimate embrace."

Emma blinked several times. "I still don't understand. Are you trying to tell me that those two men kissing each other are Ruben and Jesse?"

"Yes, they are," Sue grinned.

"But why would they do that?" Emma said, her foggy brain still uncomprehending. "They're not gay, are they?"

"I understand this must be difficult, but it was all over the news and I can assure you they are."

Emma exhaled a sharp breath of doubt. "I can't believe it." She clutched her elbows with her hands, her thoughts a muddle of disbelief. "They always had girlfriends. Jesse married me."

Sue placed a comforting hand on her shoulder. "Most people believe that Jesse expected to gain the confidence of the voters if he was married, that they would never vote for him if he was gay. I don't understand why. Perception has changed so much in the last decade."

"This is too bizarre," Emma said, her brain refusing to take it all in. "I need to sleep."

CHAPTER

40

AFTER FIVE HOURS of uninterrupted sleep, Emma stared at the ceiling, the fog in her brain lifted. The newspaper articles about Jesse and Ruben lay next to her on the bed. She'd read every word over and over until it all made sense.

A gurgle of laughter bubbled up in her throat as the cold weight of disillusionment, self-doubt, and failure that had encompassed her heart for months loosened its grip. Lonely months, in which she'd assumed that Jesse's indifference was her fault. That it was because of her lack of sexual desirability, inexperience, or wrongdoing. Now it turned out that hadn't been the case at all. She'd only been a member of the wrong gender.

Filled with energy, she pushed the blanket away and got up.

Emma found Sue in the living room, behind the computer.

"I feel relieved and so much lighter," she told her.

"Jesse didn't deserve you, Emma," Sue said. "You're my friend, and his behavior was ruthless and despicable. I doubt he'll ever make it into politics. He'll never get my vote, that's for darn sure."

All Emma could do was smile. "I don't care what his reason was to marry me. All I want is to put this behind me, so I'm free to love somebody else."

"And that someone is Eagle, right?" Sue asked.

Emma's entire face lit up. "He's here in Heemstead, staying at his uncle's house. I can't wait to see him. There's a lot we need to talk about."

"He better hear you out," Sue said. "You've been through enough."

With renewed confidence, Emma called Jesse. He answered immediately.

"Hi, Emma. I was expecting to hear from you one of these days. Are you still in Oregon, or did you make it back?" He sounded remarkably cheerful.

"I flew in yesterday and am staying at Sue's apartment," she replied. "Is it possible to meet somewhere? I want to talk."

"Of course," he answered. "Where are you, so I can pick you up?"

That didn't seem like a good idea. "No, rather not."

In the silence that followed, she heard voices in the background. People laughed and said their goodbyes.

"Hang on a minute, Emma," Jesse said. "Give me one second." She heard a car door close before he came back on the line. "I just picked Ruben up from the hospital and am driving him home. Sue lives along the way and I can pick you up."

Dumbfounded, she agreed and waited at the window. At least with Ruben there, she wouldn't be alone with Jesse and that suited her just fine.

Ten minutes later, his familiar Mercedes convertible stopped in front of the apartment building and she hurried downstairs.

Jesse had parked along the sidewalk, the door open so she could slide in right away.

"I hope you're ready to go," Jesse said, taking off before she had the time to fasten her seatbelt. "Ruben needs to get home as soon as possible."

This wasn't going the way she'd expected at all.

Ruben didn't say anything. He sat slumped in his seat, his head wrapped up with bandages.

Jesse looked at her through the rearview mirror. "For a man who just underwent brain surgery, Ruben looks remarkable, don't you agree? All he needs is more color on his cheeks and more flesh on those bones, and he'll be as good as new."

From what she could see, Ruben looked like a shadow from the man he used to be. At a loss for words, she stayed quiet.

"Ruben had a brain tumor removed. The doctors told us it's benign and I get to take him home," Jesse continued with glee. "Since we still have your mother's hospital bed in the guesthouse, he can recover there."

Painful memories of her mother's last weeks squeezed Emma's heart. She caught Jesse's eyes as he studied her, his brows knitted in concern. "I'm sorry I brought it up."

What had brought on this transformation in Jesse, she wondered. Nothing about the situation seemed real.

At the next red light, Jesse turned around in his seat. "Prepare yourself. There's a small group of people at the house to welcome Ruben home."

She understood he referred to the Kimballs' inner circle, and she had no desire to see any of them.

"I changed my mind, Jesse," she said, digging her fingers into the leather of the seat. "Please take me back to Sue's apartment."

Jesse shook his head. "I had a long talk with Axel the other day. He's staying at Travis' house and will more than likely be there too. Does that change your mind?"

Her heart started thumping loudly in her chest. It certainly did.

Ten minutes later, they pulled into the garage of the Kimballs' mansion. Jesse's parents stood waiting for them with a wheelchair. With careful regard, they helped Ruben from the car into the chair and wheeled him into the house.

Jesse held out his hand to help her climb out. "I believe my parents didn't notice you," he apologized.

For a moment, they stood so close to each other that she could see the pores on his nose, the spot he'd missed shaving this morning, and the tiny beads of perspiration on his forehead. How she'd ever found him attractive, she couldn't even fathom anymore.

A cat meowed and rubbed against her ankle. "Bert," Emma cried out. She scooped him up and squeezed him, kissing the top of his head. It felt so good to hold him again.

With the cat purring in her arms, she followed Jesse inside. In the kitchen, she noticed Jesse's mother. She talked to two men, one of them Travis Templeton.

"Emma?" her mother-in-law said when she caught sight of

her. She opened her arms and drew her in for a warm hug. "My dear. It's so good to see you. We've been so troubled since Jesse told us everything. If we'd only known." Careful not to ruin her make-up, she dabbed her wet eyes with her manicured fingers, her nails a shade of deep purple.

Jesse's parents had always been kind to her, and Emma didn't have any hard feelings. "Don't worry. I'm fine," she assured her.

"What an unexpected surprise to see you here, Emma," the second man said. He extended his hand and gave her an enthusiastic shake. Warm energy emanated from him, and she was immediately drawn to his kind brown eyes.

"I'm August," he introduced himself. "Ruben and Axel's father."

"It's wonderful to finally meet you, Mr. Templeton," she replied, nervously wetting her dry lips.

"Please, call me August," he smiled.

"I would like that," Emma replied.

His attention got pulled away from Emma when Jesse walked by, pushing Ruben in his wheelchair from the kitchen into the living room. Ruben's right eye drooped a little. He looked pale and weak, with dark circles bruising the skin beneath his eyes.

"It was touch and go for the first several hours after his surgery, but Ruben pulled through, and we're so grateful for that," August Templeton said, his voice filled with emotion. "Axel told me he would be here, too, to welcome his brother home. I heard you're the one who found him?"

"Yes, I did," she replied, smiling as she recalled the incident at the creek.

"Thank you so much, Emma," August continued, his eyes misting over. "I have both my sons back and couldn't be happier."

Travis interrupted their conversation. "If you want to talk to Axel, just head out through the backyard. You know there's a path, right?"

"I sure do," she replied.

She nodded her goodbyes, then left the room.

CHAPTER

41

EMMA WALKED THROUGH the hall and opened the door to the back patio. She'd never used the walkway to Travis' home before but knew where it was. Bert trailed behind her, and she shooed him back. She didn't want him to follow. When she crossed into Travis' backyard, the flagstone changed into pebbles, stone edging keeping them in line. Bert remained on her heels, winding around her ankles and purring for attention.

"Go home, Bert," she told him, and pushed him for the second time in the house's direction.

The sudden appearance of a shadow next to hers made her quickly turn around. Before she could take another breath, a pair of brawny arms embraced her.

"Eagle!" She flung her arms around his neck.

Eagle lifted her off the ground, almost crushing her, his deep laughter resonating against her breasts. When he set her back on her feet, he lowered his face. Their breaths mingled before he captured her lips in a long, deep kiss.

"I can't believe you're here," he said, smiling down at her. "I was just thinking about you."

Before she could answer, he claimed her mouth with another scorching kiss. She kissed him in return without hesitation. Her body and soul cried out for him, and she held nothing back. She knew exactly what she wanted. She wanted him, and no one else.

"I missed you so much," Eagle whispered in between kisses. Love radiated from his eyes, and she melted like warm butter under his gaze.

"I was afraid you would still be angry with me," she confessed. "I'm so sorry for misleading you about my identity. I should have told you right away."

"It doesn't matter," he assured her. "I lived under the nickname Eagle and hadn't been honest about my identity in years. So how could I blame you?"

She knew it wasn't the same, but she loved him even more for trying to make her feel better.

"Yes, it matters." She smiled through her tears, her eyes fixed on his face. She longed to touch him everywhere, to make sure he was real. With her fingers, she tucked his long hair behind his ear, savoring every moment.

"I was on my way to see Ruben," Eagle said, "but he can wait. Let's go, so we can talk."

With their arms wrapped tightly around each other, they followed the pebbled walkway through the yard, back to Travis' house. Reaching the veranda, they sat down next to each other, shoulder to shoulder. Everything around them inspired relaxation and enjoyment. Wrapped in emotions, they didn't even notice.

Eagle took one of her hands in his lap. "I heard all the details about Ruben and Jesse's deception," he said. "I'm so sorry they manipulated you so cruelly."

Her throat seized up with embarrassment, and she looked down at her shoes to avoid his eyes.

"Please, Emma, don't look away."

Her real name sounded strange coming from his lips. A single tear slid down her cheek. Yes, they'd misled her, but whatever mess she'd created on the farm was her own doing, and she took full responsibility. "I should have told you right from the start who I was, and I'm so sorry I lied," she said, wiping away another tear.

"You don't have to keep apologizing," he replied. His brown eyes only reflected understanding and love. He was so warm and alive next to her, his thigh pressing against hers. All she wanted to do was crawl into his lap and bask in his innate tolerance and acceptance.

His mouth curved into a smile. "If it wasn't for Ruben, I would never have met you, and I wouldn't have reconciled with my father. It might be a hard pill to swallow, but we should try to look at it with a smile. It brought us together, and I'll always be grateful he sent you to find me."

She realized it wouldn't be easy to move past her failed marriage, and to forget about all that had happened, but she had to agree. She'd never felt safer than when she was in his arms. Meeting Eagle was the best thing that could have happened to her. Filled with love, she leaned into him.

"I had a lengthy conversation with Jesse, and later with Ruben," he said.

Instant fear exploded inside her. In a few short months, she'd seen so many sides of Jesse, his behavior unpredictable, his actions contradicting what he stood for. She had no clue who he was, what went on inside him, and what kind of stories he could have told Eagle to justify his abhorrent, shameful behavior.

"It pains me more than I can say that my brother was the instigator behind the entire charade."

"No way. He had no reason to do that." she protested, pulling away.

"Listen," Eagle said, his expression serious. "Besides headaches, Ruben also suffered from fatigue, pins and needles, and blurred vision. He hid his symptoms well, and most people had no idea what was going on with him. Except the change in his personality. That didn't go unnoticed."

It was true. Nobody had mentioned Ruben's illness, although she recalled noticing his weight loss and slightly grayish skin tone the last time she saw him in his office.

"Ruben became frantic and obsessed about finding a suitable wife for Jesse," Eagle continued. "Jesse told me he played along. To ease Ruben's mind, he invited you to his birthday party, believing it wouldn't harm anyone if he dated you for a while. It backfired. After seeing the two of you together, Ruben became determined you both made the perfect couple, and that you were exactly the wife he needed to win the election."

"Do you have to drag all this up?" Emma protested, the memory about how those jerks had taken advantage of her vulnerability during her mother's illness still too painful to talk about.

"I also heard your mother was ill for a long time and that

you were her primary caregiver," Axel said. "I'm sure you miss her a lot."

She searched for his hand in need of support. "My mother was a wonderful woman. Strong, determined, and all those years not a single complaint came from her lips. At the end, her only concern was for me, and I knew she wanted to see me married. But I won't lie. Jesse charmed me, and I was flattered he chose an ugly duckling like me over so many gorgeous women vying for his attention." She bit her lip to stop it from quivering.

"Don't talk about yourself like that!" Eagle insisted in disbelief. When she tried to look away, he slid his hands into her hair and held her head still, so she couldn't hide her expression. "You're the most beautiful woman I've ever met."

Knowing very well she wasn't a knock-out and that her looks would never stop traffic, she gave him a wry smile. "I've always been a bookworm and a loner and never troubled myself too much with makeup. Why Jesse chose me, I didn't understand at the time. Now I do. He wanted a complacent, undemanding wife, and assumed he'd found it in me."

"Maybe in the beginning," Axel agreed, "But Jesse told me that after he got to know you, he appreciated your intellect and sweet personality, and he valued your input to his campaign."

Emma scoffed. It was obvious Jesse portrayed himself to Eagle as Mister Innocent in the entire scenario, hiding behind Ruben's illness, blaming him for his own selfish conduct. She didn't buy it. But the usual mixture of anxiety and sadness when she thought of Jesse wasn't there any longer. It seemed all the insecurities and doubts he'd instilled in her mind had calmed and were replaced by a newfound confidence. She inhaled a reassuring breath through her mouth.

With all the insight she'd gained, she felt liberated and no longer susceptible to Jesse's influence. He couldn't hurt her any longer. He had his own struggles, with Ruben's recovery, his parents, and the people who had trusted and supported him, climbing the political ladder. It wouldn't be easy to overcome.

"Jesse told me your annulment could be finalized in a few weeks. That's all I care about." Axel beamed, moving in a little closer. "You know I'm madly in love with you, right?" His eyes searched hers. "There's nothing more I want than to share my life with you. Here, or wherever you want. I don't care, as long as we're together."

His words made her deliriously happy. In her eyes, he was the most handsome man who ever walked the surface of the earth. She'd found the love of her life and would follow him everywhere, even to Mars or the North Pole.

"I love you, too. With everything inside me," she vowed. "And I can't wait to go back home and start our future together."

Out of nowhere, Bert showed up on the porch. He gave her a leg rub and purred. She picked him up and put him in her lap. "This is my cat, Bert. Do you think Samson and Bert will get along?"

He looked down into the deep blue of her beautiful eyes. "I'm sure they will."

CHAPTER

42

"THE CONTRACTOR TOLD me they'll finish the kitchen and bathroom by the end of the week," Eagle said, entering the scullery.

Emma looked up and smiled.

"That's excellent news. I can't wait to move into our own house."

His arms circled her growing waist and he lovingly nuzzled the side of her neck.

"I promise it'll be ready before the baby comes."

She turned around to look at her husband.

"Only two more months," she warned and placed her palms on his chest, his muscles strong under his shirt, his heart thudding under her hand. Gazing deep into his eyes, her own heart rate soared. "Are you excited?"

"You know I am. I can't wait to meet him," he replied. He

took her hand and kissed each finger before he noticed the huge mountain of potato peels on the counter. "That's a lot of potatoes. What are you making?"

"Potato salad." She felt a flush rise into her cheeks. She'd been daydreaming about their baby and the nursery in their newly built home, peeling one after the other. "Do you think it's too many?"

"Not if you want to feed the entire work crew," he grinned. "Can I help?"

They heard the garage door open and the slamming of car doors.

"That must be Dora and Adelyn coming home from town," Emma said, giving him a quick kiss. "You better help them carry in whatever they bought."

As soon as the sisters found out they were expecting, their favorite place to shop became the Baby Boutique, each time bringing something else home.

Eagle winked. "Maybe another mobile?" He headed to the door, but the sisters already walked in.

Dora held three helium balloons by their strings and Adelyn carried a bouquet of early spring flowers.

"Happy first anniversary," they smiled.

A few months after Emma and Eagle returned to Oregon, the annulment of Emma's marriage was declared. Soon after, they married on the farm. August and Sarah, Travis and Gustavo, and Jesse and Ruben had all flown out to be present. Ruben was recovering well. His only physical problem was weakness in his right leg, and he walked with the aid of a cane.

Eagle spread his arms and took both ladies in a bearhug, almost crushing the flowers.

Emma quickly walked over to rescue the bouquet. "They're beautiful, thank you."

After exchanging well wishes and unloading the car, they sat around the kitchen table, drinking tea and enjoying the delicious chocolate cake the ladies had brought in.

"It's been the best year of my entire life," Eagle said, his rich voice resonating with gratitude. "We sold all the grapes, we're building our home, we have a baby on the way, and I'm surrounded by love." He looked at the three women, his eyes misting over. "I'm so thankful for everything."

"You deserve nothing but the best," Adelyn said. Her bottom lip trembled as she struggled to hold back her tears.

Emma tried to control her own emotions as she thought about the wonderful home she'd found in the mountains, about Eagle who showered her with unabated love each day, and the two sisters who held her so dear.

She reached across the table and laid her hand on Eagle's forearm.

"You 're my home, my heart, my everything," she said.

"Now, don't start crying, all of you," Dora interrupted, trying to lighten the mood. "This is a day to celebrate."

"Oh, before I forget," Adelyn said, pulling out the mail from her purse. "There's a letter for you, Eagle. It looks like an invitation."

Eagle looked at the envelope, the return address in Heemstead. He tore it open and pulled out a card.

"You're right, it's an invitation. Ruben and Jesse are getting married this summer. That's fantastic. We have to go."

Emma stared at him, her heart overflowing with love and adoration.

Happiness is being like the eagle in flight that soars above the troubles of the world, relishing the present and letting go of the difficulties in the past.

"You're my eagle," she whispered.